THE COLOR OF A LIE

THE COLOR OF A LIE

KIM JOHNSON

Random House  New York

Text copyright © 2024 by Kim Johnson
Jacket art copyright © 2024 by Chuck Styles
Map art copyright © 2024 by Mike Hall

Visit us on the Web! GetUnderlined.com

Educators and librarians, for a variety of teaching tools, visit us at
RHTeachersLibrarians.com

Library of Congress Cataloging-in-Publication Data
Names: Johnson, Kim, author.
Title: The color of a lie / Kim Johnson.
Description: First edition. | New York: Random House, 2024. | Audience: Ages 12 and up. | Summary: In 1955, a Black family relocates to the suburbs, where they must pass for white, but dark secrets about the town and its inhabitants threaten their new home.
Identifiers: LCCN 2023042366 (print) | LCCN 2023042367 (ebook) | ISBN 978-0-593-11880-1 (trade) | ISBN 978-0-593-11881-8 (lib. bdg.) | ISBN 978-0-593-11882-5 (ebook)
Subjects: CYAC: Passing (Identity)—Fiction. | Race relations—Fiction. | Secrets—Fiction. | African Americans—Fiction. | Family life—Fiction.
Classification: LCC PZ7.1.J623 Co 2024 (print) | LCC PZ7.1.J623 (ebook) | DDC [Fic]—dc23

The text of this book is set in 11.3-point Warnock Pro Light.
Interior design by Cathy Bobak

Printed in the United States of America
10 9 8 7 6 5 4 3 2 1
First Edition

Random House Children's Books supports the First Amendment
and celebrates the right to read.

To Westley and Joelle

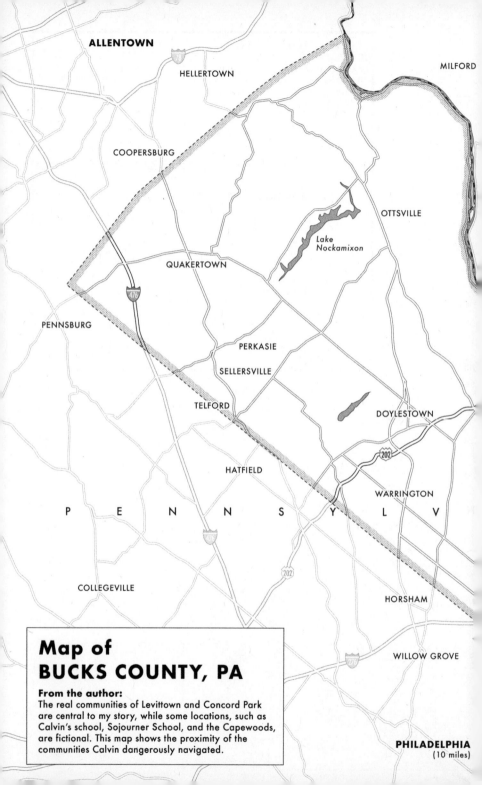

ALLENTOWN

MILFORD

HELLERTOWN

COOPERSBURG

OTTSVILLE

Lake
Nockamixon

QUAKERTOWN

PENNSBURG

PERKASIE

SELLERSVILLE

TELFORD

DOYLESTOWN

202

HATFIELD

WARRINGTON

P   E   N   N   S   Y   L   V

COLLEGEVILLE

HORSHAM

202

WILLOW GROVE

Map of
BUCKS COUNTY, PA

From the author:
The real communities of Levittown and Concord Park
are central to my story, while some locations, such as
Calvin's school, Sojourner School, and the Capewoods,
are fictional. This map shows the proximity of the
communities Calvin dangerously navigated.

PHILADELPHIA
(10 miles)

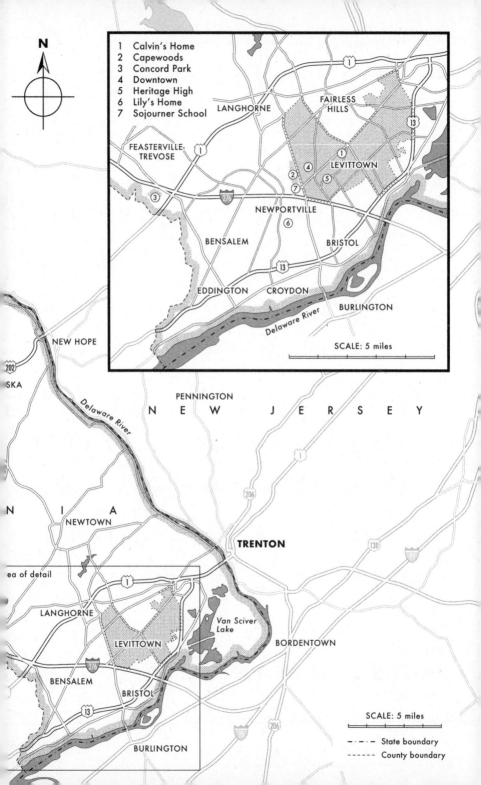

N

1 Calvin's Home
2 Capewoods
3 Concord Park
4 Downtown
5 Heritage High
6 Lily's Home
7 Sojourner School

LANGHORNE

FAIRLESS HILLS

FEASTERVILLE-TREVOSE

LEVITTOWN

NEWPORTVILLE

BENSALEM

BRISTOL

EDDINGTON   CROYDON

BURLINGTON

Delaware River

SCALE: 5 miles

NEW HOPE

SKA

PENNINGTON

NEW JERSEY

Delaware River

NIA

NEWTOWN

TRENTON

ea of detail

LANGHORNE

LEVITTOWN

Van Sciver Lake

BORDENTOWN

BENSALEM

BRISTOL

BURLINGTON

SCALE: 5 miles

– · – · – State boundary
------ County boundary

PROLOGUE

WHEN YOU HIDE PIECES OF YOURSELF, OR IN MY CASE ALL OF YOURSELF, it's hard to put those fragments back together. It started with harmless little white lies. The ones you drop to make things just a bit easier. Then, one day, the lies get so big you're drowning in them—unable to distinguish the truth.

Whatever happened in the years between, well, I take the blame. But if you want to understand what led me here, you must go back to the beginning. I will tell you every recollection of my early life. Then you decide for yourself.

This is my truth.

CHAPTER 1

NERVES DRONED INSIDE ME LIKE A SWARM OF ANGRY BEES. I HATED how my dad driving through Pennsylvania's rolling hills and endless farmland left me feeling exposed. I wanted to go back to Chicago, where I could feel insignificant and important all at once, standing downtown amid the chaos of five o'clock. Not even riding in my dad's new turquoise Chevrolet Bel Air hardtop could purge the mounting sense of dread. Because I couldn't fool myself: this wasn't just a road trip—it was a final destination. A promise of a brand-new life I never wanted.

"Ray'll be looking for me." I broke my silent protest when the Bucks County sign came into view.

Mom leaned across the back seat to touch my knee. "You can call him when we're settled."

"What if he asks when I'll be home?"

"Calvin," Dad said.

"He's my best friend."

"You can write letters," Mom said. "Aunt Vera will get them to him."

I swallowed hard. An in-between messenger like my nosy Aunt Vera could never be a replacement for friendship, for missing my junior year.

"Can he visit?" I gritted my teeth because I knew the answer. I just wanted to make my dad say it.

"You know that's not possible." Dad adjusted the rearview mirror so his whiskey-colored eyes could bore into mine. They were always striking against my father's pale skin, which turned a fawn color under the sun.

"What about Robert?" I said my older brother's name.

"Robert's made his choices."

"You'll like Levittown," Mom said. "The neighborhood's beautiful. You'll have your own yard. Maybe Dad will finally let you get a dog."

"Two dogs." Dad flicked the words, gripping the steering wheel. "There'll be room."

I'd only accepted moving to Levittown, Pennsylvania, because Robert was out in a township just eleven miles away. It was only after I said yes that Dad revealed his grand plan. Robert couldn't come with us, because Robert was a Red. And Charlotte was gone forever. It was as if my twin siblings had never existed, as if I, too, had ceased to exist. Only to emerge to a new life built on a white lie.

4

We turned off the highway, zigzagging through routes carefully laid out on the map. I tugged at my clothes, itchy from being new, wondering if the real estate agent would see through this charade. Mom in her Sunday best, a flower-print dress, white gloves, a designer scarf on her head, and cat-eye sunglasses. Dad's pressed white shirt with black slacks and a tan fedora.

The street was sickly quiet. I already missed the noises of city life. The girls in my neighborhood. Nancy. Especially Nancy.

"Which one's ours?" I took a hard gulp.

"That one." Dad puffed out his chest and pointed to a home close to the end of the block with a FOR SALE sign lying flat on the ground. He pulled up to the driveway and shut off the engine.

"It's everything the pictures promised." Mom laced her fingers together.

"What'd I tell you!" Dad jumped out of the car, flinging his arms wildly.

The neighborhood was just like the Levitt & Sons ads: affordable assembly-line-made homes that, from above, looked like perfectly carved-out squares for blocks. To people in Levittown, this was *the* American dream. But to *me,* this was a delusion. I knew that one day this place would pop.

I stepped out, shoving my hands in my pockets, looking left to right. Row after row of Cape Cod–style homes for as far as I could see, with identical-sized backyards. No fences to mark their territory, just invisible lines of trust to live by.

Mom got out last. She touched the scarf on her head, tightened the bottom, and then tucked in her flax-colored hair. As their hands met, Dad and Mom exchanged a meaningful smile. I kept my mouth tightly shut. Not a chance I'd give them any satisfaction. I hated it. And at that moment I hated them.

"There he is." Dad pointed to the real estate agent who'd brokered the deal. He was tall and slender with light, sandy-colored hair. The tip of his nose was red, like he easily burned.

"Welcome." Mr. Vernon met my dad halfway down the driveway and shook his hand. "You're gonna love it here."

"It's so quiet." Mom tentatively stepped forward.

"Nothing like Chicago, I bet," Mr. Vernon said. "Heard it went to hell after people moved in like cockroaches. Homes out here are the good life for *nice* families like you. Real safe."

Mom clutched her scarf and looked away.

"Quiet is good." Dad kept a smile.

"You must be Ann," Mr. Vernon said.

My eyes went wide. She was always quick to correct someone because Agnes was a family name. But as I swept my gaze over my parents, I realized this was another white lie they'd keep up.

"Yes." Mom tugged her glove tight before shaking his hand. "Nice to meet you."

"Calvin." Mr. Vernon slapped his hand on my back. My shoulders relaxed with relief—my name would stay the same. "I hear you might be looking for work. I need someone part-time. Turn in an application, and we'll see what we can do."

"Thank you, sir." I shook his hand limply. I hadn't even unpacked yet, and my dad was already planning my future.

Mr. Vernon led us on a tour of the expansive three-bedroom, two-bathroom home. Compared to our modest two-bedroom apartment in Chicago—where the couch had been my bed for so many years—this place was massive. The ads in the paper had made it seem too good to be true, like propaganda from World War II. But it was real: dishwasher, fridge, stove. And what caught my mother's eye: the brand-new washing machine. No more hand-washing clothes.

"Always snags the attention of the missus." Mr. Vernon chuckled. "Nice setup for a housewife, isn't it?"

Mom coughed and gave Dad an uncomfortable gaze.

When men had left for the war and jobs had opened up for women, that's when Mom got work downtown. She'd kept working when Dad came home. I let out a satisfied smile because I wasn't the only one caught by surprise at things changing.

Cold white walls greeted us along the halls. From all the ads, they were meant to stay that way. I wanted to see if Mom was thinking the same thing, but she was already looking at her new bedroom.

As I passed the first room, I thought of Robert. How he would have claimed the farthest room from my parents'. Even though Robert was disowned, I chose the other bedroom, sight unseen.

"It's beautiful." Mom floated through the house. "This is all updated. William, look." The Southern drawl she'd picked up as a girl in Alabama snuck out. Dad gave Mom a quick glance. She patted her dress down and attempted to calm her excitement.

"It's nice, Mom." I forced an obligatory smile.

I opened the back door, irritated that I could feel my heart flutter at having a yard for the first time.

"You'll be happy here. Just give it time." Mom squeezed my shoulders from behind.

Mr. Vernon pointed at the row of houses all connected to perfectly manicured grass. I approached the yard between our house and the neighbor's. Sprouts of grass grew in oddly shaped patches.

"What happened here?" I kicked at the ground with my shoe.

"Fire." Something flitted between Mr. Vernon and my dad.

"What about the neighbors? Friendly?" Mom's voice quavered. Her lifelong friends and her sister, Vera, now lived hundreds of miles away. Mom might be trying to bury her feelings, but I could hear the sadness there.

"Very. Lots of high schoolers on this block as well. The Freemens are solid." Mr. Vernon pointed to our back neighbor, who shared our mishmash spots of new grass. "You have to keep up your lawn. I've got some names you can use. Colored help is fine as long as they leave town before sundown."

"I won't need—" Mom stopped as Dad steered Mr. Vernon to the side of the house.

We both knew Mom was about to say she wouldn't need *help.* And the last thing we wanted to hear about was sundown laws. I gritted my teeth because Dad had forgotten to mention that, too.

When the agent finally left, Mom unwrapped her scarf from her head, peeled her gloves off, and slapped them together. I'd been praying she'd wake up and eventually put her foot down, but all I saw was relief running across her face. We'd finished the first test.

"We can't possibly stay here." I stepped closer to my mom.

"Maybe this wasn't a good idea." Mom looked to Dad.

"We gonna fit in just fine, Calvin," Dad said. Two white boys rode their bikes down the street. "You'll make friends—see, they're probably your age."

Mom recovered. "He's right. They probably go to Heritage High."

"What if someone finds out you lied? The bank could easily look into your GI records."

"Enough," Dad said. "They won't find out."

Shame crept through my body—he was willing to risk our lives, again.

"We don't know how to be like them. Ain't gonna fit in here." I dug my foot into the grass, kicking up dirt.

"Watch your tongue. They hear you talking like that, you'll have more to worry about than just the bank."

Another white neighbor passed the house, walking their dog and waving. I gritted my teeth as we flashed simultaneous fake smiles.

"I thought you said I could be me," I whispered, my eyes beginning to sting. "That as long as I didn't say anything, it wasn't a lie."

"You can be you," Dad said. "Just watch how you talk and who you friendly with."

I almost unraveled right then, knowing he meant no Black friends. I flung a betrayed look to Mom. This fresh start wouldn't just be about starting a new life. It'd be about *playing white*.

CHAPTER 2

THE MORNING HEAT HUNG OVER US, SUFFOCATING AND RELENTLESS. Mom moved through the house with a frantic energy, her eyes flickering from one corner to another, as if searching for something she couldn't name.

"The church is only blocks away. We could walk." Dad gave Mom a smile she matched, but her eyes didn't light up.

"Have some more." Mom offered me another heaping spoonful of eggs. She'd made enough to feed a family of five that no longer existed.

As we ate, the silence was heavy in the air, punctuated only by the sounds of forks scraping against our plates. Mom's hands trembled as she sipped her coffee, awaiting our first trip out of the neighborhood.

I wanted to speak. To ask if she was staring at the cold, empty walls that should be covered with Charlotte's artwork. To see if she'd noticed that the absence of color was the absence of Charlotte. But she was stoic, her eyes distant. I already knew the answer. My throat ached, and I could feel my head going dizzy as the memories crept in.

There was the before, and there was the after. We were forced to lock away our memories of Charlotte, hidden from the outside.

We should've learned our lesson from Trumbull Park and the damage that living there had done to our family, but Dad refused. Instead he tore out ads in the *New York Times* and the *Tribune* with flashy marketing language about the Levitt & Sons mass-produced homes for veterans. He pinned them to the fridge, where they taunted us every time we walked in the kitchen. Dad was done with the *war* at home. He had a new plan: blending in—passing. He said he wanted peace, and the price was selling our souls and leaving behind a now-untraceable past.

We walked toward the church, my blue suit snug and proper. Mom had pinned her hat to her hair, a purse clutched in one hand and a Bible in the other. I swept my gaze to the matching homes and robotic people. Nothing felt right about this. Nothing at all.

Mom smoothed her pastel dress, reserved for special occasions, but it looked wilted against the backdrop of the church's stone walls. She gripped Dad's hand as we entered. Inhaling deeply, I held my head high, the rhythmic thumping of my heart echoing through me.

We followed Dad's lead, nodding and repeating, "Good morning. God bless you."

Mom stayed silent as her eyes skittered around the altar and instruments, a hint of longing on her face when she saw the choir.

We scooted into a pew in the back half of the church. The sanctuary was filled with the sound of the organ echoing to the ceiling. Paranoia swirled in my head like a tornado. As I pushed the thoughts aside as far as I could, my focus went to Dad's gentle touch on Mom's rigid back.

I bristled when a hand brushed past me to tap my mom's shoulder. Mom's head jerked abruptly, her eyes like a deer caught in the glare of headlights.

"You must be Ann," a woman whispered. "I'm your backyard neighbor, Dolores Freemen."

Mom stayed frozen for a second too long.

"Mrs. Freemen." Dad shook her hand. "We've been meaning to say hello."

"Nice to meet you." Mom's formality made me do a double take. She was usually chatty, making us the last to leave church as she took in compliments for her singing and organ playing. Until that moment, passing to her had been all theory and make-believe.

"We know how it is, getting the house together. So much to do," Mrs. Freemen said. "This is Ed, and our daughter, Mary; she's a junior at Heritage."

Keeping my eyes forward, I pretended I wasn't listening to the chatter. I smoothed down my hair and hoped the Brylcreem would hold.

When the sermon began, my mom's grip on my hand tightened. I glanced up at her, witnessing her closed eyes and silently moving lips, focused in prayer. I wondered, was she praying for acceptance? For safety? For Charlotte? Or was she simply praying for the strength to endure? I closed my eyes and prayed for the same.

Church whizzed by; we fumbled through it. The music was disorienting, and while the sermon preached righteous good acts, it felt flat to my soul. I knew we weren't included. Not when the congregation would turn into a mob if they knew *our* truth. It simply didn't take with me. And as I looked at my mom, I knew it didn't take with her, either. She clasped her purse and was out of her seat the second church ended.

I paced the grass, scoping the neighborhood. Pretending I didn't know Mom had locked herself in the bathroom crying behind the sound of the water running.

"Show you around," a soft voice called from behind. Even still, I bristled. It was Mary from church.

"Sure." I forced the pensive look off my face. "Anything exciting?"

"Not really." She flipped her hair over her shoulder. "Where you from?"

"Illinois," I said. "What happened here?" I pointed at the spots of browned grass up across our shared yard.

"Probably needs water." Something flickered across her face and then disappeared.

I opened my mouth to press, but Mary had already begun walking across the grass. I reluctantly followed as we took to the sidewalk.

"Those are the Scotts. The Joneses. The Jamesons." Mary pointed out neighbors. Who was kind. Who you could borrow sugar from. When milk deliveries came, and how to get on the list for Monday cupcakes to be dropped off at your doorstep. Everything sounded like golly gee, sugar, and lollipops.

"Play sports?"

I shook my head.

"What do you do for fun?"

"I don't know." My mind went blank. "Regular stuff, I guess. What about you?"

"Sewing. Cooking. Music."

I knew better than to get caught up in a music conversation, so I stopped short of asking what kind.

"So where exactly did you say you're from again?"

"Are you writing a book?" I slipped out a joke Ray would have appreciated. I forced a smile to brush off the defensive armor that was riding up my stiff neck.

I wasn't prepared to answer so many questions all at once. It was too hard to remember the details. What I could answer truthfully. What had to be lies.

She fired more questions. I kept my answers brief as she practically floated around the neighborhood. I imagined her starry blue eyes widening as she watched the first ad from Levitt & Sons. And then I was certain: either everything about her was exactly as she presented—or Mary Freemen was trouble.

"That's Ben." She pointed to a tall, heavyset white kid riding toward us.

I caught gold and bronze flashes of light glinting off his bike each time the sun hit it.

"You the new kid in the neighborhood?" he asked when he reached us.

I wanted to say, *Who's asking?* Instead, I nodded.

Normally I'd have avoided eye contact for fear of an altercation or the inevitable *What the hell are you looking at?* response. But I was supposed to be white, so I looked him in the eye.

"Calvin Greene."

"Ben Smith." Ben stuck his hand out. I kept my hands in my pockets for a second too long as I contemplated my next move. "What year?"

"He's a junior, like us," Mary said.

"Tough starting a new school, but you'll get along fine—just stick with me." He grinned.

I nodded again before stealing a glance at his intricately designed bike.

"Nice, right?" Ben slicked back his sandy-brown hair and gave me another grin. This time I matched it.

His bike was custom designed, with handlebars made from pieces from old musical instruments that were welded to the bike frame. The detailing was immaculate.

"This a Schwinn Phantom?"

"What else would it be?" Ben grinned.

Ads for the Schwinn Phantom had been popping up with

a tagline *America's most beautiful bicycle.* But this was one of a kind.

"You do this yourself?"

"Who else?" Ben kept asking me questions instead of answering mine. A trick I'd have to master.

"Can I?" I pointed to the handlebars and stepped closer.

Ben hopped off and kicked the stand down.

"Now, don't go flipping your lid. I'm not selling." Ben gave a hearty laugh I sort of liked.

I was careful not to leave smudges while tracing my fingers along the spokes of the wheels that were spray-painted a brass color. Parts of saxophones and trumpets lined the frame and matched the wheels' shade. As I examined the valves and brass pipes that jutted out, all melded with the bike's frame, I was lost in admiration. I must've taken too long, because Ben bounced back and forth on his feet.

"Sorry," I said. "I play the trumpet."

"You do?" I could see Mary mentally adding to her list of information she'd gathered.

"Yeah." I swallowed hard. "I used to, anyway."

"Haven't seen you ride that around, Ben." Mary inserted herself again, and I found myself irritated that she was there. I forced a smile and her eyes lit up. I immediately regretted it.

"Been working on it for a while."

"What do you play?" I tried not to sound too eager, hoping I'd find someone who was into jazz and rock and roll by Black artists.

"I'm not that good. I picked up a few things here and there."

"Oh." My shoulders dropped a bit.

"But I like music for sure. And dabbling in bike work. I could show you."

I perked up at the thought of riding my own custom bike. Ray would be so jealous.

"But if my dad sees another instrument in our house, I might need to move in with you."

I chuckled, imagining the shock from my dad if that happened. It'd serve him right.

We joked around a lot more. This time I made sure to include Mary.

"I gotta get back. Cutting the grass today," Ben said. "I live down that way if you ever wanna swing by."

"Sure. Yeah." I smiled.

I walked back with Mary, now talking freely about school until we stopped awkwardly at my front door. Mary lingered like she wanted to be asked in. I did my best to avoid her questions, then faked like I had to go. She started to walk away, then stopped and called out to me in a singsong voice.

"Welcome to the neighborhood. It's a great community. Your very own American dream." She smiled, then skipped off.

It was the Levitt & Sons jingle I despised. Because for us it was a dream deferred.

I gave her a contorted smile as she cut through the yard.

CHAPTER 3

DAD HAD A WATCHFUL EYE AS I KEPT THE PHONE BY MY EAR EVEN AFTER the line went dead. Ray wasn't home yet. And even though his parents had said he was still visiting family down South, I didn't believe they'd relay my message. Not by the look Dad gave me.

I hated the way I'd left things with Ray, telling him I was only going on vacation to New York City. Ray had made it all too easy to lie. I didn't want it to be easy. I wanted him to grip my shoulders and ask me why I couldn't look him in the eye. Instead he'd been too occupied planning for his own summer trip to Mississippi with his cousin Bobo—without their parents. And now that I was gone, I feared Ray would forget about me. That once I crossed over, we could never return.

"You'll talk to him soon enough," Mom said.

I nodded, fighting back the burning that welled up in the back of my throat.

Dad closed his newspaper like he was satisfied he'd fulfilled our agreement and there would be no more talk about Ray.

As I got up, there was a knock at the door. I swear my stomach flip-flopped as a small part of me imagined Ray, somehow transported to our house, with a wide smile like we were back in Trumbull Park. I flung the door open.

But it wasn't Ray.

"Hey, Calvin! Mr. and Mrs. Greene." Mary waved. "I don't have your number. Wanted to see if you were up for the junior gathering."

I raised an eyebrow.

"It's a tradition."

"Tradition?" Dad said behind me.

"Well, maybe not a tradition, since we're the first junior class." Mary blushed, pressing closer to me until I had no choice but to let her inside. "We're having a football rally before the start of school. And, well . . . since Calvin doesn't know anyone, I thought he'd want to join."

I had no interest in a rally. But as I looked over at my dad's firm scowl, I smiled and said, "Sure."

I didn't wait for his approval. I was going to show my parents exactly what blending in required.

When we got in Mary's car, she gave me a mischievous grin. "Ready?"

"Yeah, where's the rally?"

"No rally. It's Saturday night before the first day of school, and we're blowing off steam." Mary stopped a few blocks over to pick up Ben. I stepped outside, prepared to meet him at the door and make up some story, but Ben was already rushing out. He jumped into the car, yelling, "Go. Go. Go!"

Ben's dad flung open the front door. He wore a white under-shirt and held a can of beer in one hand. "Where the hell do you think you're going?"

I blinked hard, unable to compute the breaking of the Levit-town image. At the sight of Mary and me, Ben's dad hid his beer behind his back and scanned the neighborhood before slamming the door.

Mary peeled off.

"Should we go back there?" I said.

"For what?" Ben laughed. "He'll beat my ass for something anyway. Might as well give him a reason."

I bristled at the thought.

They were full of chatter, radio blasting, but I kept silent. My eyes were on the road as we passed through neighbor-hoods, headed downtown. I sat up when I noticed the first Black family I'd seen since moving to Levittown.

"What's this?"

"Levittown Shopping Center. I'll show you."

There were mostly white patrons, but there was still a mix of Black patrons on the street. I was most interested in the diner and the record store. An overwhelming surge of curios-ity overtook me as I pulled out my wallet for Mr. Vernon's busi-ness card.

Vernon Realty
Exclusive homes sold for Levitt & Sons
Suite 121, Levittown Shopping Center

"Do you mind if we stop by Vernon Realty?" I said.

"You buying houses now?" Ben chuckled. "We got some partying to do."

Mary ignored Ben, parking in the nearest spot.

"It'll just take a minute."

The gold placard signs of Vernon Realty caught my eye. I'd expected a small office, but instead it was a large office suite. A sign read FHA LOANS FOR VETERANS, with pictures of new developments for sale and plots ready for breaking ground.

I stepped to the display window to look at the homes that I had learned were on the edges of Levittown, closer to where Robert lived. The image had illustrations of happy Black families. The prices in Levittown were ten thousand dollars, while the prices for the designated homes for Black families were at least fourteen thousand. No VA loan guaranteed. The rows of houses were replicas of my neighborhood, except closer together. I stepped inside.

"How can I help you, son?" A woman greeted me.

"I'm C-C-Calvin Greene, ma'am." I stuck my hand out. It was a forced move; I'd never do that to a white woman in Chicago. "Mr. Vernon said I could fill out a job application. I just moved into town."

"William Greene's son! Too bad your father's working for the competition. But they can't beat what our properties offer. True safety." She winked. "I'm Sharon. Let me go get that application."

My father hadn't told me he was a competitor. I'd only known he was in a similar industry. I took the application with shaky hands and walked out.

Mary and Ben leaned against her car.

"Want to walk around?" Mary said. "Things won't get going until after dark."

I nodded, eager to check out downtown. I'd passed before, but only in brief moments of convenience. In Chicago, it was a game to me and my friends. Rule number one of playing white was to never be seen alone. I'd enter all-white diners, not hiding out in the back hoping to be ignored, but sitting right next to a person at a counter. This way I could blend in with the customers. Then I would gather up multiple food orders and meet my boys in an alley. But here, passing wasn't playing. It was permanent.

We walked through stores, taking up the sidewalk, and I always found a way to stay in the middle. We stopped in front of a record store but didn't go in. Then Mary took me past the high school, showing me routes to take if I was to get a job and work after school. Eventually dusk came, so we made our way to the parkway, then parked our car on the side of Bailey Road.

Above us was a large billboard ad for a drive-in theater that read *REBEL WITHOUT A CAUSE* COMING OCTOBER.

"He's so dreamy," Mary said at the image of James Dean wearing a leather jacket, propped in front of a car.

"Open your eyes, Mary." Ben flung his arm around me. "Two dreamy guys right in front of you."

"Right." Mary rolled her eyes, but she kept a glance at me a beat too long.

"Where are we going?" I diverted my gaze to the grassy area that led to the woods.

"Where our parents won't be looking," Ben said.

As we walked along the road, I noted that most of the drivers passing us now were Black, in what must be a mass exodus from town before sundown. The only thing that gave me comfort was that I was headed in the same direction.

"Come on, let's go. Just a little farther down," Ben said.

I watched the trees sway as we stepped over the grass toward a wooded area. A few steps in, I knew what they meant: unseen from the road were clusters of teens. Their laughter and playful banter filled the air as they slammed down beer and threw wood in firepits made from metal garbage cans.

"Know many people here?" I whispered to Ben, scanning the long shadows.

"A few," Ben said. "The school's pretty new, so we've got people coming in all the time. Last year was my first year."

I played like it was no big deal. But I was ready to split.

They mingled while I leaned against the trunk of a tree, standoffish.

"Who's this?" A blond guy about my age spoke next to Ben.

"This is Calvin."

"Another new kid?"

I nodded.

"I'm Darren." He tossed an empty beer can through the trees. I looked around at the piling trash of wrappers, food, and cans launched out into the dark corner of the woods away from the fire.

"It's cool." Ben nudged. "Nobody goes in those woods anyway."

I bit my lip, my facial expression betraying my disgust.

"Dare you to go further in," Darren said to Ben. "Give you a quarter and another beer."

"I'm not going in there again."

"What, you chicken?"

"Nah. Just don't trust you to pay me. Come on, let's keep walking."

Ben looked back at me, and I reluctantly trailed.

After an hour I'd started to settle into conversations. Glad the darkness shrouded me like protection. I knew it was safer to begin school with friends.

As the fire dwindled, Mary returned. "We should go soon," she said. "Police usually scan Saturday night."

My chest went tight, and I watched to see if this would alarm anyone else.

"Yeah, I'm out of here too," Darren said. "Got football."

I glanced at Mary. I wanted out right away. Her keys were clutched in her hand. A group of guys put out the fire and carried a bag over to the large sign that read CAPEWOODS. They hunched in front, marking it up with white paint, sloppily covering up old markings.

"What is this place?" I asked Mary.

"No place, really. Open land."

"And the sign?"

"The Capewoods?"

"Why's everyone so edgy about that place?" I said with a lift in my voice.

Mary shifted her weight nervously. "It's haunted."

"No way." I belted out a laugh, but Mary didn't join.

"No one goes in there."

"Why?"

Mary shrugged. "It's always been like that, I guess. Think people died or something. And *everybody* says it's haunted."

I furrowed my brow.

"That's just ghost stories," Ben said. "I heard it's because they got tired of it being a place where kids got drunk. It's an old wives' tale to get us to stay off this side of town."

"No, it's true," Darren said, stepping closer to us. "Been like that forever. Some people go in and they don't come out. That's why they don't develop that land over there. They leave it to the colored."

I swallowed hard, ready to leave.

"But Ben and I've been through there."

"And that was the last time," Ben said.

"You got something out of it last time. You sure you don't want to join me for some beers again?" Darren gave an easy smile, but he betrayed a hint of something unsettling.

"Let's go," Ben said.

I followed quickly as he and Mary walked back to the car, leaving behind a small group of people. Their voices carried from afar, echoing under the quiet night. I heard the sound of crickets, which were usually silenced by the city sounds I'd known so much of my life.

"What was that about?" I asked.

"Darren found some spot to hang out. I didn't like how it turned out last time. Not going back."

I walked slowly, looking between Ben and the Capewoods. "You come out here a lot, Mary?" I wanted to know more about the secrets Ben was holding in.

"This is actually my first time."

"Why'd you wanna come?"

"Something to do, I guess. To show you around, make friends."

I bumped my shoulder into hers. "Thanks. It's not really my scene. I'm not much of a 'rebel without a cause.'" I looked out toward the woods one more time, a shiver running down my spine. "Let's hurry."

As we drove off, a flash of light pulsed ahead, followed by the familiar wail of a police siren. Relief washed over me as we headed in the opposite direction.

CHAPTER 4

AT THE TABLE, MY DAD ASSUMED THE ROLE OF A GENERAL STRATEGIZ-ing for a battle deep behind enemy lines, but in this war he was leading a command of one.

"This won't be like your old school," Dad said. "You need to observe, blend in like I did overseas."

"Yes, sir."

"You been watching *Ozzie and Harriet*?"

"Yes, sir."

"Making those friends in the neighborhood should help." Dad paused. "But don't get comfortable."

I nodded because there was no arguing to be had. I'd lost all the battles before we arrived.

"Good." He clapped my back. "They ask you about food, music, television, you stick with what we talked about."

He'd been drilling this in me for weeks. He made sure I focused on things that I didn't hate and were race neutral. Those became my answers—they weren't deceptions, he'd said. But anything Black I had to swallow. Even Black artists who were played on mainstream white radio stations weren't allowed. *It will open Pandora's box,* he'd said.

"What about when you don't have an answer?" Mom's voice was raspy and dry. She ran her fingers through the subtle waves in my hair but withdrew them abruptly when I noticed that her hands were shaking.

"I'll do what's worked with Mary and Ben." I rubbed my forehead. "Ask them what theirs are before responding. Shrug my shoulders. Give open-ended answers without locking myself in."

"He's got it." Dad gripped my shoulder gently as he reached for Mom's hand. "He'll be fine."

Mom averted her gaze, unwilling to witness the dread on my face.

"Remember what I said." Dad parked in front of the school. He had a wild look in his eyes. "This is for the best. A chance at a good life."

"I won't let you down, sir."

I hated that I still wanted to please him.

Hated how I noticed that his grip on the steering wheel settled.

Hated how his body, reverberating with thunderous energy, silenced my protests.

As I walked the hallway, my eyes were drawn to the way my white classmates effortlessly occupied space in a hall of sweater vests, polo shirts, checkered patterns, knee-length skirts, and dresses. My throat tightened and I pulled at my collar, trying to catch more air as their laughter escaped, as they jostled and bumped into each other with no worry. I felt my schedule slip from my fingers like sand. Being aware of my *space* was impossible to erase. All my life I'd learned how to stay out of a white person's way. I crossed the street if I had to. Never made eye contact unless they said, "Look at me, boy." Now I had to swallow each shudder coming from almost saying *pardon* or *excuse me* anytime my skin touched someone. And as I walked through the sea of white faces, I wondered who would be the first to turn against me.

"Calvin Greene! Calvin Greene!" My name rang out from behind me.

I shrank when it wouldn't stop.

"You were supposed to check in at the office." Ben practically grabbed my shoulder, halting me in my tracks.

The heads of my classmates turned toward me, and I could feel heat rising in my cheeks.

"I'm your buddy," Ben said.

I groaned inwardly at the thought of having a *buddy.* Buddies meant Goody Two-shoes asking too many questions.

"I was running late." I eyed him suspiciously. He'd never mentioned being my buddy before.

"It's not what you're thinking," Ben said.

"What am I thinking?"

"I'm some brownnoser. Hallway monitor. Teacher's pet."

I relaxed my shoulders, then bit my lip in disappointment that I gave away my thoughts so easily. If I wanted to play white, I'd have to be better at hiding my feelings.

"So, what are *buddies,* and how'd I get so *lucky*?"

"Detention."

"Detention?" I raised an eyebrow.

"They thought I'd be a better student if I took some pride in the school. Introduced a new kid to the lavish life of Levittown's finest." Ben stretched his thick arms wide. "So . . . what do you think?"

"You're not my type."

"Funny one, eh. What do you think of the school?"

Growing up in Chicago, I was used to large crowds that I could easily blend into. And while new schools were popping up all the time in the city, they weren't for Black kids. As I'd walked through the hallways here, I'd noted several empty classrooms ready for increased enrollment.

"No response?" Ben let out a long whistle. "Don't care where you are coming from, I bet you've never been to a brand-new school."

"I haven't," I said, my voice icy.

"How about I show you around and you put in a good word with the principal?"

"Drop this buddy stuff and it's done."

"Done." We shook hands, but Ben didn't leave.

"Am I missing something?" I said. "We made a deal, right?"

"We're in all the same classes."

"Is this your punishment or mine?" I chuckled, loosening up.

"Ha!" Ben bellowed a laugh, and heads turned.

"Calvin!" Mary ran toward me with two friends flanking her. "This is Allison and Sarah."

Allison was short with a toothy smile and freckles over her nose. Sarah stepped in front of me, studying me up and down. Out of the corner of my eye I swear I saw Mary wince.

Sarah's hair bounced at her shoulders. "Nice to meet you."

"I drive to school," Mary cut in. "If you don't want to ride with your dad."

I gave her a puzzled look, until I realized she'd watched me leave.

"I'll let you know."

I nudged Ben to get moving; he was starry-eyed over Mary's friends. I, on the other hand, couldn't get out of that situation fast enough.

Ben led me to room 25 for our English class. On top of my assigned seat were stacks of books. *Of Mice and Men, Catcher in the Rye, The Adventures of Huckleberry Finn,* but what caught my attention was *Lord of the Flies.* Back in my old school, our books were used copies discarded by white schools. Pages would be ripped out, notes scribbled in the margins, things already underlined. I locked my hands over my new prized possession, then picked up a book I hadn't heard of before: George Orwell's *1984.* I flipped to the back and smirked. This was the kind of book my brother would push me to read. Fill my head with how it's about the future if we don't watch out.

I found it ironic that the English teacher didn't recognize that the Big Brother society this very book was talking about probably started in places like Levittown.

I swallowed hard at the absence of works by Black writers like Countee Cullen, Claude McKay, Zora Neale Hurston's *Their Eyes Were Watching God*. It made me immediately thankful I'd hidden James Weldon Johnson's *The Autobiography of an Ex-Colored Man* away in my dresser. It was a book I was hoping would help make sense of what living a life passing would be like.

The final bell rang, and a young blond woman with short hair stood up. She was the first woman I'd seen wear pants in Levittown.

"Class, we have a new student," she said, gesturing toward me.

My cheeks flushed as I felt the weight of everyone's eyes boring into me, making me dizzy. However, Ben's encouraging smile settled me.

She introduced herself as she walked toward me. "I'm Miss Brower. Why don't you share a bit about yourself?"

"Calvin Greene." I cleared my throat as I stood. "I'm a junior. From Illinois . . ." I trailed off, then took a seat. Ben beamed proudly like we were already best friends.

The class started and I tried to keep up. I wasn't used to the teacher having to wait patiently for people to raise their hands. At my old school everyone automatically raised their hand, because if you didn't, you were guaranteed to be called on.

"Do we have any volunteers to stand up and read this passage?"

Darren from the Capewoods kicked Ben's chair, rocking him forward.

"Come on, Ben, do us a favor and volunteer," he whispered.

Ben flashed a smile, nudging the other students next to him as he raised his hand. My stomach sank. I'd been buddied up with the class clown.

"Anyone other than Ben?" Miss Brower scanned the classroom.

With Ben volunteering, no one lifted a hand. I gulped, fighting every urge to raise mine.

"Darren, how about you?" Miss Brower stood next to him, giving him an eye that read, *Watch yourself.*

Darren sank his head low. "Come on, Miss Brower. Ben wants to do it."

"You can show us how it's done."

I held back a smile and waited as Darren stood up. When he was finished, he sat back down, sulking like Miss Brower was the only teacher who didn't fall for his tactics.

At the next request, Ben's hand flung up on its own, and Miss Brower let him read.

When class was over, before I could even get up, Ben was by my side. Right next to him was a short, small, dark-haired boy who had been sitting quietly in the back of the room.

"Meet my buddy Calvin." Ben slapped the back of the boy.

Before the boy could speak, Ben was doing the talking for them.

"This is my best friend, Alex."

I shook Alex's hand, but he didn't meet my eyes, which I liked.

"Well, don't just stand there," Ben said. "Say something."

"Nice to meet you," Alex said. "I live near you, off Gordon Lane."

"Th-that's me," I stuttered out, more focused on Alex's olive skin and nose peppered with freckles. My mind raced in desperate excitement, searching for a hint that there was someone like me at school, even someone Greek or Italian. I shook my head to stop the hopeless thought.

Second period was shop class, which Ben was surprisingly bad at; I mean, he was clearly good with his hands, having welded his bike together. Third period was homeroom. I smiled at the sight of a reel-to-reel projector. An easy cruise into class. But as the film played and its narrator explained the rules for good American boys and girls, my mouth hung open. I looked around to see how others were reacting to the propaganda, but it was too dark to tell.

> *This production is brought to you by Social Guidance Films, an educational initiative.*
>
> *Our America has been through a lot since the generation before yours. Ten years of economic depression, six years of war, crime, and hard times marked city life.*

The film was emphasizing the harsh reality of poverty with visuals of hungry children in schools, men forced to sleep on benches, and people packed together in cramped city environments. Then an image showed a bus stopping, and its doors opening to reveal a group of eager passengers ready to join the city in droves. Black people. I felt a wave of discomfort wash over me; my shirt dampened with sweat as I twisted uncomfortably.

As the voice-over continued, I listened, perched at the edge of my seat.

> *The cities are now overrun with people looking for jobs, but you don't have to live like that. You can start a new life. An American dream. However, there are rules that you should know, rules this generation must abide by.*

The voice-over then presented a series of lessons, starting with the importance of obeying authority and being respectful to elders. Then it moved on to the ideal dinner for an American family, where the father comes home after a long day at work and conversations must be kept light and pleasant, with girls and housewives dressed up. I almost spat out a laugh when it said, "We must be silent at the table; let Mom and Dad lead the conversation." But I held my tongue, and as I looked from left to right, I watched the lack of surprise from my classmates. The lessons continued, with rigid rules about behavior. I bristled at the topics being covered: *Be seen and not heard. Don't talk back. Normal peer-to-peer interactions. No misbehaving. Avoid comic books.*

Inside my head I screamed: *Conform. Conform. Conform.*

My stomach turned at the skit of a father talking to his son.

"Dad, all the other kids dress nicer."

"Let's get you some of those sweaters kids wear today. Why don't you watch the popular kids to see what makes them fit in, then follow them? In your own way, of course."

"Gee, thanks, Dad. Jimmy seems to be popular. I have class with him. I'll try to sit next to him to-morrow."

It was no surprise that the girl's conversations with the mother were more focused.

"You don't want to be too popular, now. Parking in cars with boys will just get you in trouble."

The mom then points to a young girl pushing a stroller.

"All the boys parked with Sally. Now look at her."

When the film ended, I expected there to be a burst of laughter. But the teacher went into a discussion without inter-ruption.

"What were the five lessons the movie covered?" Mr. Barger cleaned his glasses as he leaned against his desk.

"Girls who park in cars are easy," a guy with a wide smile called out, and quiet chuckles spread through the class.

"Our decisions have consequences," Allison said.

"Exactly," Mr. Barger said. "Your reputation is important. If you're seen with too many boys, you won't be taken seriously. Your life could be ruined."

I scrunched my face at the word *ruined*.

"You have to present yourself in a certain way to be taken seriously. To get along in society," Mr. Barger said.

"Not being too loud or drawing attention to yourself," a kid in the second row added. "Like all those people in the city didn't seem to care. Going out to party and unable to find work."

"Yes. You can make anything of yourself. You just have to work hard."

I wanted to scream. To throw up my hands and ask what they meant. To question the opinions they'd so easily crafted about the goals, even the opportunities, if you played by the rules only meant for some people. Instead I clamped my mouth and joined the class in taking notes. I shook my head, not only at how strange this all was, but at how it reminded me of my father's new talk at home. Hiding who you were might not have been the *exact* conversation happening in every home in the suburbs, but it might as well have been. I was just passing while doing it.

CHAPTER 5

I WAS A MAGNET FOR UNWANTED ATTENTION. ESPECIALLY FROM MARY Freemen. I ditched her by riding my bike to school yet again, but she was still waiting at my locker when I got there.

She was posted up with Allison and Sarah, who were giggling as I approached.

"Hey, Calvin." Mary stepped between me and my locker. She twirled her fingers through her slick, shiny hair.

"How are you?" I forced out a smile. "Allison. Sarah."

They grinned, bumping into each other.

"You going?" Mary nodded toward a poster on the wall for the sock hop—the school dance.

I felt myself freeze as they waited for an answer. I looked at the poster again, "That's two months away, a little early to advertise." I kept my voice cool.

"Oh yeah." Mary shrugged, then let out an awkward laugh. "Dances are kind of a big deal here. But, yeah, it's forever away."

"Forever," I echoed.

"What about the football game tonight?" Mary said. "I can give you a ride. It's no trouble."

My body stiffened like a coiled spring. I was supposed to make friends, but she wanted to be more than that. I wasn't prepared to get that close to Mary. I had never been a fan of football. It was baseball I loved. But if I brought that up, they'd ask me who my favorite player was. And as much as I'd picked up lying, I couldn't lie about my love of Jackie Robinson, hands down my favorite player. It had taken everything in me last week not to bring up the Dodgers, who'd just clinched the pennant and would be playing in the World Series.

"We're grabbing Cokes at the diner afterward." Allison edged in closer before winking at Mary.

"Of course he's coming." Ben towered over me, with Alex by his side. I was used to Ben popping up, walking down the hallway like he was still sorting out his body.

"Maybe later." I shut my locker and looked at Ben. "I'll ride my bike there."

"Bike?" Ben said. "The diner is out past the Capewoods, close to Concord Park on the west side."

I did a double take. I had been near Robert's neighborhood on the west side and hadn't even realized it. The thought of Robert seeing me pass made my stomach flip-flop.

"What's Concord Park?"

"Levittown's big competitor," Alex said.

"Not really. Some developer's building on the other side of the Capewoods—calling it America's first integrated community."

"No way."

"No one's going to live there," Mary said. "At least not anybody white. There's nothing on that side, and the schools out there are for colored people."

I looked away, ready for this conversation to end. I wanted to know why my dad was putting us through all of this when we could've lived in Concord Park. Could've lived closer to Robert.

"How you think you did on the geography test?" Alex asked.

I gave a smile, grateful to talk about something else. Between Ben and Alex, I felt like I could be more myself with Alex. Alex was kind, thoughtful, and—most importantly—didn't ask a lot of personal questions beyond school-related things.

"Hope I did well. I crammed all night," I lied.

Geography was one of my favorite subjects and came easy to me. It was playing white that was hard.

"I couldn't get the multiple choice right for Africa," Alex said.

"I don't know why we need to know about that place anyway," Ben said.

"Yeah," Mary joined. "Hot sun. Lions. Elephants. Seems like a horrible place to live. My dad said that's the reason Blacks won't go back to their awful country."

"Continent," I couldn't help but say.

"What?" Mary made a strange face.

"Africa is a continent," I said.

"Okay," Mary said. "Either way, a whole week on it. What's to know?"

"It's filled with countries, hundreds of languages, cultures, landscapes, developed cities."

Mary's mouth hanging open stopped me from saying more.

"You know a lot about Africa?" Ben's voice was loud and playful.

"I like geography is all."

"What do you know about this?" Darren appeared out of nowhere. He scratched his armpits and ran wildly down the hall.

Crowds of people in the halls laughed and joked. Darren turned over a large empty garbage can and jumped on top, pounding his chest. Then he ran to me, beating his chest again.

"Any guesses who I am?" Darren nudged me as a crowd began to grow.

I felt my face go hot, ready to disappear. Upon my reaction, Ben gave me a conflicted smile that shriveled up. I noted that he might be a clown, but he was fiercely loyal.

"Come on. Guess." Darren scratched at his armpits and stuck his lip out.

Ass was what I wanted to say.

I didn't hear Darren answer; my heart was thumping too loud. My ears burned like a fever. I could see everyone staring at me, but nothing was coming out except a strange laugh that crept up my throat. The only comfort came when I noticed Alex's eyes flickering in horror as the laughter got louder and louder. And before I knew it, he was gone, giving me a reason to exit.

"School going okay, honey?" Mom said. "You've hardly touched your food."

Mom had changed up her cooking with new recipes that were copies of the food that neighbors had dropped off the week we moved in. Dinners were bland and dry. Mushy casseroles. Dry salt-and-peppered chicken. The last normal thing she'd kept was cornbread baked in a cast-iron pan that had been passed down from her grandmother. That night, it went untouched.

"School's all right. . . . It's hard making friends."

"What about Ben and Alex?" Dad asked.

"They're fine, I guess."

I rubbed my forehead, replaying the feeling from today that was eating me up inside.

Mom leaned in, studying me.

Dad set his jaw; I didn't have to say what happened. He already knew it had to be about race, and he wasn't going to entertain a discussion.

"Not a big deal. Just need time." I swallowed the truth.

Mom's gaze landed on the table where a folded-up letter lay. "What did the letter say?"

For a moment I sat up straight, a list of possibilities crossing my mind. Something from Aunt Vera. Ray. One of Robert's letters finally made its way here.

"Nothing to worry about," Dad said. "Just a friendly reminder about keeping the grass trim."

I gave a puzzled look. "From who?"

"Vernon Realty," Dad said with a smile, but his mouth still pinched at the corners.

"I thought they didn't have an association," I said. A sickening chord was struck at the reminder of what *associations* meant to us back in Chicago. They were at the core of everything that chased us out. It had started with little notes about the rules, then spiraled bigger when Ray came to visit.

"I called him and got it all worked out."

I studied Dad, his flat, matter-of-fact tone. Like he had blinders on, unwilling to see how wrong this move was for us.

"You start work with him this week," Dad said. "It's a trial, but I think they really need the help. You do what you're supposed to do and you'll be fine."

"Why didn't we wait and buy a home in the new Concord Park development?" I had no interest in work. I wanted answers. Levittown was the antithesis of a place like Concord Park, which would be integrated and closer to the communities Black people already lived in.

Dad put his fork down and drank from his glass of milk. "This home not good enough for you?"

"This home is great." I swallowed the knot building in my throat. "It's just . . . in Concord Park, we wouldn't need to play white."

"Race is a social construct. And for whatever reason, Blacks are in a caste at the bottom of the hierarchy. I could buy a house in Concord Park, but our investment would never grow. Sure, they'll live side by side at first, but how'll they act when neighbors get married . . . have kids?"

"If we were closer to Concord Park, we could see Robert." I ached to see my brother. We were close, yet so far away.

"The homes in the new development there are all being built on the leftover land and swamps nobody wanted. Near unmarked graves of former slaves. We don't even know if white people will buy there."

I didn't tell my dad that I'd much rather live over the bodies of my ancestors than blend into a community of people who would burn my home down if they knew the truth.

"Finish your food," Dad said. "Enough talk about Robert. Didn't come all the way out here so you could end up in the same position."

"I'm almost out of school. We could live anywhere."

"We're not moving." Dad threw his napkin down and stood up.

"William." Mom touched Dad's arm. "Be civilized when we talk about this. It's hard for Calvin."

"Living in hell is hard," Dad's voice belted. "We were living with a boot on our necks in Chicago. This is easy. We can be anybody here."

Anybody but Black. My eyes teared at his words. There had to be a better way.

"So at least try, Calvin. Can you try?" Dad's voice settled to a whisper that cracked when he spoke.

"Yes, sir," I whispered back.

"Invite your friends over. Spend time with them." Mom rubbed my back and kissed the top of my head.

I blinked back tears. "Ben and Alex asked me to go to the football game tonight and out for Cokes afterward."

"Go," Mom said. "Calvin can go, William, can't he?"

Dad clenched his jaw and nodded.

But I had no plans to go to the football game.

CHAPTER 6

IT WASN'T HARD TO FIND WHERE ROBERT LIVED—HE WAS RUNNING A small boarding school called Sojourner Music School. I'd learned that while communities might bleed into each other downtown, by sunset segregation was strictly at play. I rode past Abbey Lane, then down toward the parkway. As each car passed, I hid my face, expecting classmates to keep me from my mission and force me to the game. I knew the risk, but I was drowning in lies. And that ache in the pit of my stomach from my unanswered calls to Ray was growing. I stopped asking for permission to use the phone and started calling every day. But it never mattered. Not when the phone rang endlessly.

As I pedaled along Bailey Road, the woods on either side of me grew thicker, casting long shadows that danced across the pavement. I knew I was close to the Capewoods. A shiver ran down my spine, and I felt the hairs on the back of my neck stand on end. The trees rustled in a way that made me feel like I was being watched. I picked up my pace, desperate to get away from the eerie sensation that was creeping over me. Every crunching leaf beneath my tires made me jump; every twig snapping in the distance sent a jolt of fear through my body. But I kept pedaling, hoping to reach Sojourner before anything could emerge from the woods to chase after me. As I looked back over my shoulder, I breathed a sigh of relief. I was still following the directions I'd memorized. Not only had the landscape changed, but so had the people. I struggled to not immediately smile at Black passersby, but I couldn't help giving a nod.

Finally, I made my way down Port Lane, and my heart skipped a beat as I approached my brother's schoolhouse. The three-story structure, freshly painted yellow and with bright white shutters, was surrounded by lush woods. Young maple trees and eastern red cedars, newly sprouting, warmed the house. A barn with flakes of red paint peeling off stood to the right of the house. The backyard was an oasis of young saplings, just adjacent to a thicket of trees that looked like a forest. In the distance, in the middle of the darkened woods, were remnants of a small, old wooden church.

When Robert had first moved to the area, he'd written about how the school used to be owned by Quakers, who'd provided a safe haven for Black travelers fleeing from slave catchers determined to return them to the South. As I stepped onto the same ground, I couldn't help wondering about that history. I was only eleven miles away from home, but my world had shifted into another timeline. One that had slowed down. One where I wouldn't have to lie.

Robert stood at the end of the driveway, talking with a group of boys. It had been almost a year since I'd last seen him, but he looked the same. The same light features, except he didn't shy away from the sun like my mother. The sun browned their skin quicker than it did mine. Robert had his hair picked out long in front and short in back, like the popular pompadour style taking over. He just didn't process it like Little Richard or have the sheen pomade like James Dean. If he'd kept it short like mine, his brown hair with golden highlights, he could have looked like any of the kids in school, as long as he laid it down at night and brushed it one hundred times. But if it grew out an inch, the waves would curl; if the sun kissed his cheeks, freckles would sprout. Even from afar, I could see his brown eyes, still dark and deep.

His smile widened in surprise as he recognized me. My heart pounded as I ran toward him, arms outstretched. When we collided, I flung my arms around him, letting out a deep exhale as I buried my face in his shoulder. He squeezed me tightly. At that moment, everything else faded away as he gave back that same explosive love.

"Brother!" Robert's voice bellowed out. "I can't believe it's you." He touched my slicked-down hair and studied my face like he was trying to piece together the things I was supposed to hide. "What took you so long?"

"You knew I was here?" I asked, watching as the boys filtered inside with curious looks.

"Mom." Robert's eyes were glistening, swirling with happiness. "She wrote."

I could feel a deep sadness in his voice.

"Come," Robert said. "I want to show you everything."

I entered Sojourner School, which looked more like an inn. Music leaped out of the house. *Alive,* I thought. I didn't have to look inside to know it was a Black school. The energy, the warmth, it wrapped itself around me.

"I'm guessing they don't know you're here?" Robert said.

I looked away. "I had to see you. I'm suffocating."

"They should have never asked this of you. It's wrong." Robert shook his head low. He knew all about William Greene's military-style rules of order and discipline since returning from the war.

"You gonna tell 'em you came to see me?"

"I—"

"Don't," Robert said. "I miss you, brother. I like what I'm doing. The teaching. These kids. But it's lonely. I miss the family. I don't want him taking you away from me."

"I miss you, too," I croaked out, my heart throbbing with all the words left unsaid. I wanted to scream out to Robert, to tell him how passing made me feel like I was falling apart, tearing at the seams. The fear of being discovered haunted my every moment, every breath I took. I wanted to let it all out, to share the burden that had been weighing me down, but the words caught in my throat, and I could only stare at him, my eyes pleading for him to know already.

"You playing much music?" Robert asked.

"He won't let me," I said. "He thinks playing jazz could out us."

One Christmas Eve service, a traveling band of Duke Ellington's had come to play "Silent Night" with a full orchestra. At seven years old, I'd never seen anything like that in my life. After the service ended, I walked aimlessly to the trumpet and held it in my hands.

My mother thought it was a phase. That my small mouth couldn't possibly have the energy to make a sound. It took two years, but the second I got the strength to make a note, nice and clear, it was settled. Once I learned it wasn't about blowing the hardest but mastering the lip form to buzz—with or without the trumpet—the notes came.

Robert shook his head. I knew it sounded ridiculous. "You can always play here."

My eyes welled. I bit back that nervous feeling, which had become all too familiar, of being exposed. I glanced over my shoulder, anxious as another student walked down the hall.

"Come," Robert said, breaking me from my thoughts. "See my room."

We scaled the stairs, boys passing us, smiling at Robert, and whispering with curious looks. There was no hiding who I was here.

Robert's room on the third floor had a small bed covered by an ivory quilt. His closet held three shirts and pairs of pants and a single set of dress shoes. I was pulled to his nightstand and a framed photo, which I picked up and held tight.

It was the one of Robert and Charlotte at a summer fair. They were always so mischievous together, egging each other on. I'd often have no choice but to fall into their traps. The photo had been taken just after they'd convinced me to join them in sneaking into the Chicago fair in 1950. We'd walked along Lake Michigan and seen every inch of the fair. It had been worth Dad whipping us within an inch of our life when he found out.

I looked at Robert, unable to avoid seeing Charlotte in his face. It was like seeing the ghost of our sister and the painful reminder of how close they had been. A part of him was missing, and that ripped all my wounds open.

"They don't even talk about Charlotte." I was tired of avoiding her name. Tired of burying the past.

"How is Mom dealing with the move?" Robert sidestepped me.

Places like Levittown weren't new to us. Trumbull Park, our home on Chicago's far south side, was a mostly white, middle-class neighborhood that didn't seem bothered by our arrival. That is until Ray visited me, and his dark brown skin stripped away the thin veil of their acceptance. Dad urged us to keep our heads down when the harassment started, but Robert didn't listen. When the White Circle League of America, an organized hate group, mobilized mobs of neighbors to rally outside our home, Robert got the NAACP involved. And each time we left our house, we were the ones treated like criminals, loaded into a police patrol wagon and driven away for our *protection*. The mob eventually grew to a thousand, and a firebomb ripped through Robert's bedroom. The flames spread as the firefighters stood by, letting it all burn down. Robert wasn't even home, but Charlotte was. And now she was gone forever. A death we could never reconcile.

"I wish Mom could see you." I couldn't answer his question, because I didn't really know.

"Think she's still mad at me?"

"She never blamed you for what happened." Flashes of that night hit me. I focused back on Robert. "She loves you."

"Doesn't matter anymore." Robert shook his head, and a sad smile played at the corners of his mouth. "I have a new family to look out for."

I turned away, unable to meet his gaze because it felt like he'd punched me in the gut.

His room was filled with a heavy silence, a space for everything we had lost, everything we could never get back.

Music floated throughout Sojourner, echoing up the stairs. A group of boys joked and jostled by the balcony until they caught sight of me in Robert's room. Their gaze followed Robert, who turned his back, wiping away his tears.

A knock on his door followed, and my eyes widened at the sight of James, who'd been friends with my brother for years. More than friends. It was just never spoken.

"I heard rumors of a visitor. I knew it had to be you." James greeted me with a handshake I swapped for a hug instead. "I was wondering when you'd make your way out here," James said, clinging to my arms and giving me the embrace I wished my brother had at that moment.

"Now, don't start," Robert said, his voice lightening.

"Oh, come on," James said. "Let me revel in the victory. Your brother here said six months, and I said less than two."

"Enough. Let's feed my brother." With Robert's laugh, it was as if everything we had talked about was bypassed.

When we entered the kitchen, James already had a plate filled, and he shoved it my way.

"I didn't know you were out here." I reached for the food, starved for a good meal.

"I live a few miles out and work in a hardware store not too far from there."

Robert and James paused in silence. A glance shot between them, deciphering my reaction.

I hadn't been the most open when I realized my brother's relationship was more than a friendship. Charlotte used to cover for him. The first time I'd ever seen two men kiss, it was Robert and James behind a store. It had taken me by surprise, and I hadn't known how to react. I'd been recovering from that tension ever since. And the distance between us had made it hard to bridge the gap. Now, as I stood before them, I couldn't help but feel the weight of my unspoken apologies.

"I mean . . ." I searched for a way to mend those wounds. "I wouldn't have worried so much about Robert if I'd known you were here."

Robert's eyes crinkled in a smile.

"You're a good brother, Calvin." James grabbed my shoulder in a squeeze.

I tipped my head in respect before scarfing down the rest of my food.

"You sure y'all related?" James teased.

"I think it's your cooking," Robert said. "Don't embarrass me with those caveman manners. I know you ain't eating like that in your school. Bet you tuck a white napkin in your shirt there."

I was too busy eating to take on my brother's teasing.

"You got friends?" James leaned in closer to me.

"I'm a part of school, but only a sliver of me. Like in *Invisible Man*—people refuse to see me. Or I guess I refuse to be seen. Does that make sense?"

"You're finally reading Ellison, then?" Robert smiled. He'd been pushing the book on me for a few years now. I hadn't gotten it before. Now it was the only thing that made sense. I looked away, swallowed up by the thought of being so run-down by not being seen that I'd choose to hide from everything around me. Disappear until I could rebuild myself into something braver.

"What's it like being at a white school?"

"They got everything, and they don't even know it. They toss their books like they're nothing." I looked around Sojourner School's kitchen. "You're really the one in charge?" I forced down my jealousy of his new life that didn't include me.

"Yeah. It's all dumb luck."

"It's more than dumb luck." James touched Robert's shoulder.

Robert gave a shy smile, shaking his head. "I met a music instructor who knew the state was looking for someone to run a youth home for musically inclined Black students. The state covers funding, and I get some help from teachers across town."

"Why don't they just go to a regular school?"

"Too far out, but mostly it's truancy. Most of these kids lost their parents. Foster kids. Working. Been in juvenile detention facilities. They're no longer accepted or can't make a regular schedule because of work. We also offer music lessons in the evening for the girls in the area."

"They all play?" I pointed to the piano in the main entrance-way. Then I walked to the hall to take a closer look at the instruments stacked along the walls. Numbers were etched on the side to track the rentals. I slid my fingers across a stamp mark on the back of one of the instruments: PROPERTY OF THE AME CHURCH OF GOD.

"The ones who end up here, yes. Last-chance school."

I lifted my eyebrows.

"I know what it sounds like, but they're good kids. Talented. Hell, so talented. Just victims of their circumstances. Sometimes I get a new kid; they resist the rules the first few weeks. But then they realize I'm not kicking them out, and they can rely on me. They know it's safe here."

Before I could speak, I lost all attention to a Black girl about my age passing through the kitchen, not paying us any mind. I shamelessly stared at her. I was so used to ignoring girls from school, I finally got why it was so easy. They weren't like the girls I knew in Chicago.

"You'll be back," a tall boy called to her.

She rolled her eyes. "You can keep talking about what you're going to do."

"What you're doing is insane," he said.

"Eugene, let it go." She picked up her bag and walked toward the front door.

I turned my back, not wanting her to see me. It was too much of a reminder of what I was missing at Heritage. Someone who could *know me*, not like what Mary wanted to see in the image of me.

As she left, I watched her before directing my attention at Robert. He gave a knowing grin that I ignored.

"James and I have to take care of a few things. Let me introduce you to some of my students." Robert pointed toward the boys who had been speaking with the girl.

"These are my two longest students: Eugene Thomas is the oldest, eighteen, and his younger brother, Harry Thomas. Fourteen."

When Robert and James left, a nervous rumble hit my stomach. Eugene was a dark-skinned boy with a slick pompadour hairstyle like Nat King Cole's. My eyes immediately noted his slender hands. I knew he must be a piano player with fingers like that. Harry had a flattop and was a shorter version of his brother. He tapped his hands on everything, in between sentences. I guessed he was a drummer.

"You live out here?" Eugene dangled his fingers across the table and pretended to play the piano.

"Out in Levittown. I go to . . . Heritage." Eugene and Harry froze. I could see them putting the pieces together.

It wasn't smart to let anyone know. But I was tired of the lies.

"So . . . they think you white, then?" Eugene said.

"Yeah."

A silent gasp came from both boys as they studied me. I worried they'd get up and leave because they'd assume I thought I was better than them.

"What's it like to be a white boy?" Harry broke the silence.

"Awful," I admitted. "I can pass, but it's hard to breathe when you're hiding all day long."

"What would happen if they found out you ain't white?" Harry said.

I looked away, worry filling me that maybe it wasn't a good idea to share my secrets so close to home. I hadn't even told Ray yet.

"Not sure why they can't see you Black, though," Eugene said. "It's about as obvious to me as Harry."

"They too stuck in a black-and-white world. Unable to see the range of blackness." Harry gripped my shoulder and then clapped my back.

Relief ran up my spine. I knew what it meant to pass—most often it meant that never the two worlds should meet. It was an unwritten rule to let them be.

"Just don't get too friendly," Harry said. "If they ever find out, it'll be the ones you made friends with that'll be the angriest."

I swallowed hard. Dad had said the same.

"And don't mess with no white girls," Eugene said. "That'll surely get you killed."

"He ain't thinking about no white girl. He still looking out that window for your girlfriend, Lily." Harry let out a deep laugh. One that started to grow on me and reminded me of Ray. I thought I'd caught Harry watching me from the stairs earlier.

Our conversation was like music. The joking around. The ease of it all.

"Was that Lily in the kitchen?"

"Yeah, that's Lily," Eugene said in a way that told me I wasn't the only one who had eyes for her. "She's not my girlfriend, either." Eugene shot Harry a hard look.

"Anyway." Harry ignored him. "Lily goes to a regular school but comes here for lessons. She won't be back, though."

"She'll be back," Eugene said curtly. A glance between them told me there was more to it. Eugene paused, watching me, then lightened his voice. "She sings like Billie Holiday. But she's trying to focus on graduating high school so she can go to a good college."

"Where is she going?" I sat up, hoping what they'd say wouldn't mean she was moving far away.

"Some white school," Eugene said. "But ain't no way white folks gonna let her in their schools. *Brown versus Board* might have just passed, but they take it like a suggestion. Like everything else out here."

"There's a group of white folks around Pennsylvania working on integration in schools," Harry said. "My friend Bobby

Simms registered Lily for this new school, pretending to be her uncle. They signed her right up without seeing her. Just marked her white instead of colored."

"How'd he get away with that?" I said.

"He white," Harry said. "Besides, it's legal. They didn't know any better when Bobby gave them her paperwork."

"Bobby's not your friend," Eugene said. "He's ten years older than you."

"You're just mad he did it on a favor to me and now your girl is gone."

Eugene punched Harry in the chest. Then Harry grabbed on to him. I stood up to give them space, but they were play fighting, and it was over as soon as it started.

"You got family anywhere else?" I asked, hoping to switch subjects.

"Harlem," Eugene said. "And the South, of course."

"You go visit them?"

"Nah," Harry said. "I want to, but Eugene's too chicken to travel."

Eugene socked Harry on the shoulder. "I just value my life more'n making unnecessary travel, especially in the South."

I had no interest in going to the South. I figured that since Chicago grew by the millions with Black folks moving from the South, they were fleeing something worse.

"What do y'all do around here for fun?"

"We throw a dance in the barn every once in a while. When your brother lets us, that is." Eugene pointed to the barn. "We play records and live music."

"In a barn?"

"We make it nice," Eugene said defensively.

"Nah, that's good," I said. "We got a dance coming up at school. Not going, though."

"Maybe we'll hold one the same day," Harry said. "Show them white kids they're not the only ones that can have some fun. The barn is where we hold lessons, classes, and meetings." Eugene slid Harry a look at that last part.

Meetings? "What about in town? You play out there?" I was buzzing, thinking about playing gigs again.

"We get requests to play jazz all the time," Harry said. "But Eugene always says maybe next time."

"We don't have a car, first of all, and how we supposed to get around when you lost your only bike?" Eugene said.

"It was stolen! I told you."

"Nobody riding around on that bike. You trashed it. Probably stuck in a swamp and you'll never get it back."

"I told you it was stolen—they came right out of the church in the Capewoods and jumped me."

"That's too bad," I said.

"You should've seen it. I made custom handlebars, crossbar, and downtube out of old music instruments. And I could still haul musical gear to any gig."

My face drained as Harry spoke. I struggled to keep my composure, my mind racing as I tried to figure out what to do next.

"What?" Harry interrupted my thoughts. "You seen it?"

"Nah." I shook my head. "Would've loved to, though. What

kind of gig requests you get?" I edged closer in my seat, mind still reeling. If I told them I knew where his bike was, then I'd have to do something about it. I wasn't ready for my two worlds to collide.

"Mostly people calling for a fill-in when they can't make a gig," Eugene said. "When you graduate here, you usually go out and work days and perform nights."

"We even got a call to entertain for the regular CORE meetings in Virginia."

Eugene gave Harry a hard look, like he didn't want me to know they might be involved in organizing. But I knew about CORE, and so did Robert. It had started in Chicago as an interracial equality group and now had chapters sprouting all over.

Harry rolled his eyes at Eugene, then smirked. "But Eugene declined. Like I said. Chickenshit."

"I'm not riding through sundown towns in the dark."

"I could do it." I raised my shoulders. "I travel all the time, passing. You stay in the back at sundown, no problem."

Dad downplayed the dangers of passing because I had done it before, slipping in and out of white communities without a care. Mostly it had been just a game, something my friends dared me to do in areas we could only dream of visiting. I got so good at it, they joked that I was their very own *Green Book*. The real *Green Book*, a guidebook for Black travelers to find safe routes along which they could drive, eat, and stay overnight, was something my dad knew all too well. He had worked for it after returning from the war and knew about sundown towns from the Midwest to the East Coast. I had traveled those roads with him, collecting stories like little trinkets to share with my friends. Robert and I had helped our dad scope out safe places to stop, but Robert had had to wait in the back seat because he couldn't pass as easily. If we were accepted, then Robert would join for the next test. Finally, staff would vet the site before adding a place to the *Green Book.*

"You think it would work?" Harry looked to Eugene.

"We don't got a car," Eugene said.

"Bobby does," Harry said. "He'd let us drive it. Maybe even Robert."

"You'd know where to go?" Eugene sat up, taking me more seriously.

"I could do it using the *Green Book,* make sure we weren't out driving close to sundown."

"Yeah. That could work." Eugene rubbed his temple. "What kind of places you been?"

I went through all the towns I'd traveled through. Naming off safe locations I'd memorized from my travels with my dad. The conversation flowed naturally, like with my friends from Chicago.

Robert entered the room, shaking his head. "I leave you for a minute and I can tell you've already been scheming."

"What?" I threw up innocent hands.

"You better hurry on home," Robert said. "Get Ma all worked up and Dad—"

"I'm leaving. I get it." I looked at the time, realizing I'd better hurry back.

"Can we call you?" Harry asked.

I almost said yes, but then I thought about what my dad would say if he answered the phone. Before I could answer, Harry spoke up.

"I can play white too." Harry chuckled, tapping his flattop and running his hands along the sides.

My eyes went wide.

"Over the phone. Come on, man, I can do it." Harry cleared his throat. "Hi, Mr. Greene, what a lovely evening. Is your son Calvin home? I hoped we would be able to study tonight, sir." Harry's voice came out proper and stilted. Eugene and I busted out laughing at his ridiculous but workable impression.

As the night wound down and the boys went upstairs, I hugged my brother goodbye, the loneliness creeping back in.

"I wish you would come see Mom," I said. "She misses you."

"I can't ever come home." Robert looked away.

"They'll always love you."

"He'll never forgive me."

I wanted to deny it, but deep down I felt this to be true. Dad would never be able to look at Robert without seeing Charlotte.

I clutched my brother. "The mob did that. Not you. You were fighting back. We deserved to live there as much as them. How were you supposed to know that night would be different from any other night?"

Robert nodded, but I knew he didn't believe me.

My throat tightened as flashes of memories hit me. Even the sound of something sharp and loud still terrified me. That was one benefit of living in the suburbs: the silence. But it also felt like looming death. The peace and quiet were a constant reminder of what was on the other side of the chaos and violence. Seeing Robert restored all that felt tangled inside me. I'd told myself I'd only visit him once. But now I knew that was a lie. I'd be back. Again and again.

CHAPTER 7

WHEN I ENTERED SCHOOL, I HEARD A QUIET BUZZING IN THE AIR, A stark contrast to the usual raucous voices that echoed through the hall. A group of men crowded the main office, and their presence sent shivers up my spine. I couldn't tear my gaze away from the scene, and neither could my classmates.

With the commotion, a sense of emptiness brewed in the pit of my stomach. While I blended in almost too easily with the white kids, who carried books and greeted me with wide smiles, I felt unseen and disconnected, like a soulless body floating through life. It was as if I were me, but not entirely. I felt like an imposter, a shell of myself. If I hadn't known it before, I knew it after Sojourner. I'd had enough of playing white.

I walked the halls, my hands running clammy. Panic took over—had I been seen on my ride to or from Sojourner last night? Or maybe I'd been outed by someone at Robert's.

I rushed to my locker, no longer interested in feeding into my own paranoia.

Ben stood there, waiting.

"Heard why they're here?" Ben pointed to the office with a knowing smirk. One I was seeing more and more from him.

I stayed head down, but my shaky hands kept missing my combination. I'd jerk my hands up and be met with a big thump before twirling the lock round and round, trying again.

"Who's here?" I said when I finally got it open.

"Mr. Vernon and a few people we call the Association."

I froze. There was no official association, but everywhere I went there were Mr. Vernon's fingerprints controlling this town. If your grass grew too long, you'd get a notice or a friendly visit. Reminders about no trucks in sight or parked cars on the road, only in the driveway. Paint colors should stick within the current scheme. This was all too familiar—I had witnessed the same from the South Deering Association in Chicago. Who were more than happy to rally to violence and intimidation when their perfect community was *blemished* by the presence of Black families.

What weighed on me was that I didn't know what Levittown people were capable of. I worried that if they did find me out, or my parents, it wouldn't make front-page news, not like in Trumbull Park, where the police had been called in to *protect us*. Levittown would move more stealthily.

"Why are they here?" I braced myself for everything to fall apart.

"Your parents must really not know anyone—didn't see you all at the meeting," Ben said.

"The meeting?" I shook my head.

"Someone broke Mr. Vernon's rules," Ben said. "They thought they could hide it from him."

My eyes widened.

"Don't worry, they said they'd handle it."

"Handle it? What—what does that mean?" I stammered.

"They'll make sure they never come back," Alex said behind me.

"*Kill* them?" My mouth dropped. I thought of my parents. My mom, alone at home. I had to know what was going on and if I needed to warn my parents before it was too late.

I studied Alex's glazed eyes; he didn't answer my question. Even he was afraid of Mr. Vernon.

"See you in class," I said.

I ran down the hall, bumping into students as I went against traffic. I rushed into the bathroom and hid in a stall until the bell rang. When the classroom doors shut, I exited the bathroom, pulling at my stomach, and headed to the main office. Mr. Vernon was huddled with three men in the principal's office. I had to find out what they knew so I could warn my family before they showed up at our house. I quickly entered, shielding my face, and turned to the receptionist.

"Can I help you?" she said.

"I feel sick." I touched my stomach and leaned on the desk; it wasn't hard to appear sick. "I think I just need to rest for a minute."

"You look pretty pale," the receptionist said. "Not out here—come with me."

I followed the click of her heels, still hiding my face from Mr. Vernon.

I entered the nurse's office, disappointed it was too far to let me overhear the men's conversation. That is until my chest dropped. Behind the thin white free-standing privacy screen was Lily, the girl from Sojourner. She caught my gaze through the gap and quickly looked away. Relief and worry simultaneously ran through my body.

"Now you just lie down. The nurse isn't in yet, but take this blanket. A garbage is right there if you can't make it." She pointed to the bathroom.

I didn't speak, just took the blanket.

She closed the door behind her. At the soft click, I could hear my breathing, fast and hard. The rest of the room was silent except for the soft tap of Lily's shoes.

"You need help?" My heart was pounding in my chest as I waited for Lily's response. The tension in the air was so thick, I could hardly breathe. And then, after what felt like an eternity, she spoke.

"I can go to school here if I want. It's my legal right," she said, her voice steady and irritated.

"No," I whispered, my voice cracking with emotion. "Are you okay?" I asked, my body shaking with fear and concern. Lily didn't answer me right away, but I could see her peek at me again. As I studied her warm brown eyes, I could see that while she was being brave, she was scared. A feeling that I was all too familiar with.

"You sick?" Lily whispered; I could see her turn to the door to watch in case someone was coming.

"Much better . . . now that I know you're okay."

I hoped my words would give her comfort, but she pulled back, holding her bag close to her. I wanted to fix what I'd said, so she wouldn't clam up.

The door opened a crack, and the principal entered.

"Here's your schedule, Miss Baker," the principal said. "They're gone now, but they'll be back. Every day. Today was quiet because no one knew what was happening, but it'll get harder. Are you sure this is what you want? Your other school is just as good."

"Thank you for my schedule. I'll manage."

Lily stood, gathering her things before walking past the curtain. She turned to look at me, her mouth tight. I wanted to see her smile, but I knew she didn't trust me.

Lily opened the door, then faced the principal.

"My school doesn't have a nurse's office. It's a closet stuffed with cleaning supplies and bandages. The books are old and dated. The building is too small, and the college-going rate is nearly nonexistent. So I think I'll be the judge on what's just as good."

My mouth dropped open.

Lily walked off with her head high, the principal stuck in place.

I stood up quickly, threw my blanket down, and followed Lily Baker.

CHAPTER 8

I RACED TO BEAT THE NEXT CLASS BELL. AS I REACHED THE DOORWAY, I scanned the bustling hallway, desperately seeking a glimpse of Lily. She was nowhere to be found. Each class I attended throughout the morning was filled with the same disappointing absence. During lunchtime, I fidgeted in my seat next to Ben and Alex, eyes trained on the door. I almost jumped out of my chair once Lily entered, led by my first-period teacher, Miss Brower. No personal student escort or buddy like Ben was for me.

Lily's hands were wrapped tightly around a brown paper bag lunch. She shook her head as Miss Brower searched for a seat that wouldn't turn her away. I stretched my neck as far as I could, while saying "uh-huh" and "hmm" as Ben talked a mile a minute, not paying attention to a cafeteria filled with cold eyes on Lily.

Lily pointed to the covered courtyard outside and went to sit quietly on the bench.

I couldn't breathe.

There I was, hiding behind passing skin, fearful each day that I'd be discovered at Heritage, and Lily was out in the open, eating her sandwich, holding her head high, and ignoring the students who gawked at her with cold, soulless eyes. A group of boys nearest to Lily stood up, and Miss Brower mouthed for them to sit. I thought of my father talking about the army during World War II. The military was segregated, fighting against the Nazis while their own countrymen were divided, dripping with fear and hate. But the longer he was abroad, the more he got to see what it was like elsewhere. My father felt freer than he'd ever been. This fooled him into thinking America would be different when he returned from the war. He was convinced we'd do well in Trumbull Park once everyone got to know us. When that failed, he blamed Robert for his *Communist* ways.

My father was still chasing that feeling of freedom. He was a soldier, and I was proud of him, but to me there was no one braver than Lily Baker.

The last period of the day always brought me dread, because it was the one class where I was struggling. All day I'd build up confidence that I was just as good as my classmates, only to crumble in confusion in science. Especially with the upcoming frog dissection.

I sat in the back row, ready to watch the clock like I'd done all day. That is, until Lily entered, handing Mr. Grimes her schedule. Mr. Grimes pointed for her to pick a seat.

I gulped hard as Lily walked past classmates. With each step she took, heads turned and whispers followed.

Lily stopped, deciding between the last empty seats: by me or by Mary.

"Taken," Mary said smugly, then looked at me like she expected me to do the same. Instead, I pulled my things off the extra chair to make room for Lily. Mary's mouth dropped open; murmurs escaped the class. I didn't care. I needed Lily to see that I was different.

I turned to the front of the class, holding my head high. I felt like my brother, unwavering. Like Lily, stoic.

"Let's get to work." Mr. Grimes hit the desk, grabbing attention only for a moment before the rushed whispers crept back. "Okay. How about this, pop quiz," Mr. Grimes said.

With a chorus of grumbles, the class returned to order as Mr. Grimes listed questions on the board about safety rules for the lab. I quickly answered what I could. Out of the corner of my eye, I studied Lily as she tapped her pencil before answering each question.

"Time." Mr. Grimes closed the book on his desk. "Partner up and review."

I turned to Lily. "What'd you get on the first one?"

"What'd you get?" Lily said softly, covering her blank answer.

"True." I showed her a copy of the lab safety guide. Lily hesitantly took notes from my paper.

I wanted to ask her how she was doing. What her classes were. Where she lived. I was even tempted to mention Sojourner. But I knew better.

After we turned in the pop quiz, the lesson continued.

I pretended my attention was locked on class, instead of on Lily.

Ten minutes before class ended, the principal stood by the door as Lily packed her things.

"Everything okay?" I whispered to Lily.

"Head start," Lily said with a tight mouth, then carried her bag of books out the door.

When the bell rang, I sprang up, convinced I could catch her and make sure she got home safely. I didn't trust what Mr. Vernon might have planned for her after school. They might not have stormed the building like others protesting *Brown v. Board*, but they certainly weren't going to drop it.

I skipped my locker, books pressed to me as I zipped through the school's back door, ignoring the hum of classmates whispering Lily's name. I pedaled down Main Street, my heart racing in sync with the whir of the wheels beneath me. My head whipped back and forth as I searched for the path Lily would take home. When I caught a glimpse of her on her bike, excitement rippled through my veins, and I slowed. I kept a calculated distance, allowing her to turn the corner before accelerating once more.

I hit the corner, expecting to lose her in a sea of people downtown. Instead I nearly toppled over her. My tires skidded against the pavement and crashed against the side wall of a nearby building. She stormed my way. Even though I was hurt, I knew a foolish grin was plastered on my face. Bracing myself, I stood up and prepared to unleash all the questions I'd suppressed at school.

Before I could say a word, Lily's hand met my chest with an undeniable force, shoving me backward.

"Why are you following me?" Her accusation hung in the air.

"I . . . I'm not." My voice weakened, losing all courage.

Lily's face showed a flicker of doubt before firming up.

"You are."

I wiped my forehead, catching my breath, and prepared to lie again but went for the truth instead.

"Just making sure you got home safe."

"By chasing after me?"

"By catching up to you." I rolled my bike back to give Lily space. "I didn't mean to scare you."

Lily hopped on her bike.

"Hold up," I called after Lily. "I'm Calvin."

"I know who you are." Lily kept her pace.

"I . . ." I sped up to catch her. "I'll stop, once I know you'll make it home."

"You realize you're putting both of us in danger, right? This is exactly what they don't want. Integration." She drawled out the last word.

"I don't care about what they want."

Lily looked me up and down. I swallowed hard, wanting to speak. To tell her everything. Tell her we could be friends. Tell her I wasn't like the rest. But it all just stayed tight in my throat.

"Fine," she huffed. "But I gotta get home. Don't slow me down with chitchat."

I wanted to shake on it, but I settled for a nod.

Lily rode ahead of me all the way onto the state parkway

and past Bailey Road, which I was now beginning to memorize. This time she rode slower, but just enough for me to know my place. When she reached her exit, she stopped at the line that defined our communities: the start of the Capewoods. She gave me a thumbs-up, but I didn't move. I wanted to know she was safe.

"You could fit in at Heritage," I said. "Maybe all you need is someone to prove to everyone it's not that big a deal."

"Maybe I'm not trying to fit in. Besides, that'll never work."

Lily entered the Capewoods. The sign from the party before school started was prominently displayed. I'd missed it before on my ride out to Sojourner. My classmates had spray-painted *Get out of our town.* My eyes burned, fists turned up, ready to knock out all the guys I could remember being there that night. Lily slipped away from me and headed deeper into the grass toward the woods.

"Can we be friends?" I called out to her. "At school."

Lily stopped in place. I caught my breath and waited for her to speak. She came a little closer so I could hear her clearly.

"Not everyone can play white, Calvin. And not everyone would want to if they could." Lily turned and rode through the woods.

She knew.

CHAPTER 9

I ARRIVED AT SCHOOL THE NEXT DAY WITH SLUMPED SHOULDERS AND A bruised ego. All night I'd repeated Lily's words in my head. *Not everyone can play white. Not everyone would want to.*

An ache sat in the back of my throat as I wondered why even though Lily knew, she'd still kept me at a distance. Her gaze was stuck in my mind. She was fearless in almost everything. Fearless in joining Heritage. Fearless of riding home. Fearless of the Capewoods.

But she feared me. Feared me playing white.

I was heartbroken. *It wasn't like it was my choice—my parents made me.* I wrestled my inner voice, which was screaming, *I could have fought them harder.*

I wanted to speak to Lily again, but her words burned inside me. And besides, what else could I say to her? So I went throughout school pretending I didn't see her. Pretending I was like everyone else.

When school was over, I walked to the town center with Alex and Ben, on my way to my newly accepted position with Vernon Realty.

"What's it like living behind Mary Freemen?" Ben asked as we took up space on the sidewalk and people scattered out of our way.

"It's fine," I said, avoiding his eyes.

"No, really," Ben prodded. "She said you won't ride with her to school?"

"She's not my type," I said quickly.

Ben gave me a puzzled look.

"I have a girlfriend back home, that's all."

"In Illinois?" Ben asked. "You think she's really waiting around for you?"

My mouth went dry answering rapid-fire questions. I hadn't thought this through. There was no girlfriend. The only girl I'd had back home was a crush, Nancy. A crush that Ray and I had sworn we'd never pursue, or our friendship would end. Maybe that was why I hadn't heard from Ray—he'd finally asked her out. I rubbed my temple, stopping at a store I had no real interest in.

"Hey. Didn't mean to worry you," Ben said. "I'm sure she's waiting for you. I'm just messing with you."

I gave a little smile.

"Nervous about working for Mr. Vernon?" Alex said.

I waited for him to explain, but he stayed silent.

"What's Mr. Vernon like?" I asked.

"He's practically the mayor of Levittown," Alex said. "No

one buys in Levittown unless they pass through him. He's the Levitt and Sons whisperer, and he takes his job seriously."

"Serious how?" My brows furrowed. He'd never answered my question about whether Mr. Vernon's "handling" of things at Heritage meant killing someone.

"Well, let's just say there's a reason your house was the first resale on the block," Ben said low.

"Because of the fire?" Mr. Vernon's words about the grass came back to me. I'd told myself it was something small, but maybe it wasn't.

"Ben's just being dramatic. The homeowners were . . ." Alex took a breath and Ben cut in.

"Black," Ben said. "The original owner purchased it, then sold it right under Mr. Vernon's nose. Before we knew it, we had our first Black family in Levittown."

My throat constricted, and I gulped to catch air. "What happened?" It came out a desperate whisper.

"They weren't there long—Mr. Vernon made sure of that," Ben spat out.

Alex shot him a hard look. I filled in all the gaps.

Before I could ask more, my always-roving eyes spotted Lily. I watched the flow of her skirt and her dark brown skin, hair blown out in soft clouds. She didn't see me, because of course I'd blended in. But I couldn't help craning my neck to get a better look. I studied her as she entered a record store.

"Let's check out that record store." Before they could respond, I ran across the street toward the other sidewalk.

I wanted to know more about her, what made her take such

a risk to go to Heritage. When we got within steps of the record store, I calmed my breath. I entered, expecting Lily to look up as the bell rang. But when she did, she looked right past me. I bit the inside of my cheek, disappointed. She knew better than to make eye contact with *me.* I was a leper to her. Not white, and no longer Black. A rock grew in the pit of my stomach. I should've turned around, but I couldn't help myself.

"Hey, check this out." Ben fumbled through the aisles, picking out records on the other side of the store. I fought the pull to go to Lily and followed Ben. But my glance turned her way each chance I got.

When Ben found something of interest, I trailed my way to Lily. "I'll be back. Just want to check out a record for my dad."

I swallowed my fear and boldly joined the end of the aisle that had caught Lily's attention. I inched closer and closer, my fingers floating over the albums, moving with precision, admiring the music that Dad had stripped away from me.

Finally, I made my way around to the section in which Lily was firmly planted. At school I kept my eyes away from her, cautious. But now I had my first chance to study her smooth brown skin and long slender neck. The way her delicate fingers touched the albums slowly, section by section. She had an appreciation for music that mirrored mine.

My heart beat fast as I searched hard to guess what Lily was looking for. I could tell she was focused, the way an artist is when looking for that one specific thing.

I went rigid when the owner walked toward us. I almost

retreated, but stayed, hoping our proximity wouldn't catch attention.

"Looking for something?" His voice was friendly but urgent, like he wanted her business but wanted her to be quick about it.

Her lips twitched. "Can you help me find Billie Holiday's self-titled album?" Her voice was honey, but there was a sadness to it. Like her entire day would be ruined if she didn't find it.

"Her torch songs album comes out next month."

"No, I'm looking for her last one."

"Should be there. If you don't see it, must be sold out." He stood a second longer, gesturing that she was in the right area, before stepping away.

I took my chance and moved closer. My fingers sorted quickly through, flipping album after album. The section was a bit out of order, and I hoped that meant it was still in stock.

A smile escaped my lips when I found it.

My hands proudly touched her precious album. I tried to play nonchalant, but I was too excited at a reason to speak.

"Lily," I said. "It's right here."

Lily squinted at me, irritated again, but then the urgency to touch the album with her own hands took over.

She looked past me.

No, she looked through me.

"I was looking for her new one, but I guess it's not out yet," I say. "I'm surprised you don't have this already."

Lily turned up a surprised smile, meeting my eager gaze. "Played it too much and scratched it, so now it skips."

If I'd been in Chicago, my game would have been smoother. I was rusty. Back home I'd have found some way to get her to listen to the album with me. I wished we were there so she wouldn't think twice about speaking to me.

"That the only one?" Her voice shook.

I thumbed my fingers across the rows of records to check. "Yeah."

Her mouth turned down. I realized she thought I was rubbing it in, that I was buying it.

"No, this is for you. I'm just looking around before my shift at Vernon Realty."

She recoiled. Not harshly, but enough for me to notice she was wary of the name. Wary of my affiliation. I immediately regretted saying it.

I stepped closer, desperately searching for a connection.

"I'm here for the Miles Davis *Blue Moods* LP."

"Miles Davis?" Lily squinted her eyes again. "You listen to that?"

"He's my favorite. I play the trumpet, too." Before I could say more, Ben's booming voice called behind me. I froze, wishing that if I ignored him, he'd go away. But my name rang out, loud and clear.

I turned to see Alex and Ben approach me. Their mouths were wide open with twisted and confused looks. I knew I should drop the album and retreat to another section. But I was lost in Lily's deep brown eyes. The soft smile I knew better than to stare at in class. The familiar scent of her washed hair with oils I'd known from when my sister's friends would come over. Lily Baker was a sight for sore eyes. But Lily wasn't looking at me in the same way. Her gaze had dropped, and she bounced from foot to foot, wanting the album so bad, but knowing she couldn't just grab it out of my hand. My friends came closer. I needed to make a decision.

"Are you getting it?" Lily whispered.

"You can have it."

Lily didn't hesitate. She grabbed the album and practically ran to the checkout line.

I couldn't even pull back my smile when my friends joined me.

"Why'd you let her have it? That *girl* can wait," Ben said in that loud, boisterous tone that now grated against my ears.

"Nah. I'll get it next time." There was no use pretending I'd confused the albums.

"Hey, girl. He was buying that." Ben followed Lily. "Don't rush him so he can't have time to think it through. You can wait while he makes up his mind."

Lily stood frozen; the checker held on to the album, waiting for me. Lily looked at me, desperate for an escape. Desperate for me to explain. I was met with a stare of confusion from Ben.

"Looking for an album for my dad." I pointed to the Miles Davis album. I hated disowning the music I'd just convinced Lily was my favorite. I was also beginning to hate Ben.

"This?" Ben plucked a few albums out, all Black artists. My stomach sank.

Before Ben could make a scene, I shut the conversation down. "It's all hers." Then I left the aisle, dizzy and ready to run.

"Wait up, Calvin. Hey, Calvin," Alex called after me.

"It's no big deal. She can wait," Ben pressed.

"No. It's hers," I called over my shoulder. I didn't want to have this conversation in earshot of Lily. I sped out the front door as quickly as I'd entered it.

"What's wrong with you?" Ben chased after me.

Sweat dripped from my forehead, a nervous kind. I could feel them putting two and two together. The way I'd bristled at the mention of a Black neighbor being ousted. Were they now going to study my mouth? My nose? The freckles that were light because I'd avoided the sun, but just dark enough to be seen up close? I pressed down my hair as if the curls would start showing as soon as they started to think maybe I wasn't white. That's how my nightmares usually started. Something innocent in the day. The mention of someone Black. Then all eyes turning to me.

Behind my friends, Lily walked quickly as she gripped the album tight to her chest as if someone would rip it away from her. She looked at me, catching me watching her, and gave me a smile, mouthing, *Thank you.* I knew right there that my nightmares would be worth it if I could speak to Lily Baker one more time.

CHAPTER 10

I WORKED TO LOSE BEN AND ALEX. I'D MAKE UP A LIE LATER TO COVER my quick departure. I weaved into a store and hid behind a display. When they passed without seeing me, I followed an older lady out and slipped back onto the sidewalk. I'd picked up tricks like this in Chicago. How to disappear in an instant.

Through the crowds I searched for one more glance at Lily. But she was long gone, so I let Lily's smile linger in my mind. Somehow the prospect of friendship with her made my heart flutter with new possibilities of how I could survive Heritage.

I checked my watch. Miraculously, I was going to make it on time for my first day of work.

Mr. Vernon greeted me a few moments later and showed me around the front of the office.

"You'll mainly be here helping customers fill out applications and sign up for visits. Weekends are busy—that's when

Sharon and I take them out to walk through the homes. When we first started, we used to fill a town hall of people interested in buying, sight unseen."

I bit my lip, fighting to keep from asking about the history of my house.

"I'm thankful for the opportunity," I said instead. "I don't know much about real estate."

"You know your way around a map, north and south, east and west?"

I nodded. Although now this all carried a different meaning. Two sides of my existence, from Levittown to Sojourner.

He pointed to plans laid out on a display table. "Just keep track of what plot numbers are open—that's all you really need. The houses are all the same size; they sell themselves."

"I can do that."

I studied the maps, fascinated by routes and roads, street names, and the way the homes were easily plotted out to avoid the congestion of highways and parkways. The lots were efficiently laid out, like wooden blocks lined up in rows. *Grass. House. Grass. House. Grass. House.*

I ran my fingers along the master layout and pointed out the homes still for sale.

"Look, Sharon, he's already a pro."

I hadn't expected to be at the center of filtering clients. My gaze bounced between the two options. Black and white. I couldn't help but linger at the homes that sat near where my brother lived.

"Is this Concord Park?"

"Heavens no," Sharon said. "Mr. Vernon doesn't sell integrated homes. Market's too risky for that."

I gave her a puzzled look.

"But there are fine enough options we provide for colored folks nearby there. We hired Barbara to handle *them* so we could focus all our time on Levittown inquiries."

Sharon pointed toward the back corner, where a Black woman in her thirties sat.

I forced a smile. When I'd helped with the *Green Book*, my work had been about expanding safe places for Black families. Now I was ensuring the opposite.

I followed Mr. Vernon, handing out applications and picking up on how to greet people with a smile but also making eye contact with Barbara, who would quickly escort any Black customers to a private office in the back, which also served as the cleaning-supply room. When they left, they didn't get the nice folders with all the options, just a single sheet of paper, while the white patrons were allowed to gather inside and ooh and aah over the visual displays, sample flooring, and color options.

When Mr. Vernon left to help a customer, I snuck a folder and shoved it into my leather-strapped backpack. I wanted to know more about homes in Levittown. As much as I wanted to leave, to tell Dad this wouldn't be a fit, I couldn't. Besides, deep down I already believed my dad had bought our home knowing exactly what had happened. He never went into anything without research. It was those details that had made him so good for the *Green Book*. If my dad wasn't going to tell me what had happened, I'd find out on my own.

CHAPTER 11

I FOLLOWED SOJOURNER'S GRAVELED PATH, WHICH HAD PAVED THE way for so many others. My time with Eugene and Harry had flipped a switch in me that had needed lighting; the pressure on top of my chest had released. Then I'd met Lily, and it felt like she was a sign that things could get better. I'd slept well for the first time in weeks.

That's the thing about being in your own skin: nothing else fits the same. Living out in Levittown left me off-kilter. Twisted inside. At Heritage I swallowed my identity and emerged as something new. At home, I was consumed with thoughts of how I'd cease to exist if I spent all my time passing. Sojourner drew me in, simply to replenish myself.

As I got closer, I recognized Robert on the porch, wedged in a corner, lost in a book. James was dutifully by his side, looking out at what I'd learned was the other end of the Capewoods, before catching my arrival and nudging my brother. Robert tilted his head, surprised, then glanced at James, who instinctually went inside to leave us alone.

Robert and I had been close until the year of the riots in Trumbull Park. After that, I couldn't explain our distance. Why Robert couldn't just be himself with me. But after only a few weeks in Levittown, I finally understood what it was like to hide a piece of yourself. Robert could be whole here. And for whatever complicated reason he couldn't be with my parents, I didn't want that to define us.

"Brother." Robert stood with open arms. "Back again, huh."

I wanted to tell him everything but felt stuck in silence as we hugged.

I was always that way when something was on my mind. Robert never rushed me. The kind of approach that would make him good at running Sojourner, a place with young people filled with life stories that they would rather leave untold. He could make their walls come down and build trust. Robert unraveled their stories. He'd keep their stories tight to him like armor, committed to helping each and every one of his students. I hoped this would include me, even against my parents' demands.

"What if I live with you?" I stared out at the Capewoods, not looking at my brother. I knew the answer, but I also thought that if I was persistent enough, maybe one day Robert would allow me.

"Why?"

I huffed, frustrated that he was going to make me spell it out. "I can't do it anymore. I don't know why I can't live here and go to school. Mom could visit every week if she wanted. No one would know."

"Because you need to go to college." Robert paused. "And Dad would never let it happen. Not after—" Robert stopped hard.

"Why can't I go from here? I could audition for a music school. Where I came from wouldn't matter as much as how I played."

"You've got options, Calvin." Robert stepped closer. "You're musically talented, but you're also brilliant. I don't agree with them, but staying here would be a mistake."

"I can be myself here. It makes me feel whole." I turned to Robert. "Alive." My vision blurred. I'd been forcing myself to hold everything in for so long. To do what I was told to survive. But then Robert had found another way. We didn't have to live like this. "Every day I'm afraid someone's going to find out the truth. I can't even make real friends."

"I'm sure that's not true."

"It is."

"Calvin." Robert shook his head.

"I was with friends." My eyes watered. "Then Lily was at the music store. I followed. . . . It was stupid. I could've been caught. . . . I ran away like a coward."

Robert gripped my shoulder, forcing me to be silent.

"You just started school," he said. "Things will get easier. One more year and you can be out of here. Then you can be white. Black. Whatever you want. But if you leave now, Mom and Dad will cut you off. Not because they want to, but because they're stubborn. They're so deep in it. One day Mom's going to wake up and realize she won't be able to see Aunt Vera, our cousins. Anybody back home. They need you. And even if you don't believe it, you need them for at least a little while longer."

"What about you? You run a school you love. You don't have to pretend to be anyone else."

"What do I really have here?" Robert spread his arms wide. "The top of my class and I'm running a halfway house, fooling myself to think I'm running a school. I'm babysitting, Calvin. Most of the people who live here won't be making music when they leave—they'll be working backbreaking jobs, wishing for gigs on the weekends."

I understood what Robert was saying, but passing wasn't the answer.

I didn't speak. I knew that if I left for Sojourner, I couldn't go back to Levittown. Mom would be heartbroken. No Robert. No Charlotte. I was all she had left, and even though I knew this, I also knew it wasn't my fault we'd upended our lives.

"Listen," Robert said. "You can come here anytime, okay?"

I nodded, watching the sunset and picking at the rail with my fingers. "It's not just that. It isn't safe."

Robert sat up, mouth turned down. "What do you mean?"

"I heard something from my friends at school. The previous owners of our house were run off. . . . They were Black. My new boss is a part of making sure the community stays white. Did you know about this?"

"No." Robert shook his head firmly. "Things are separate

here. And that kind of thing wouldn't have made the news. They operate differently than—"

"Back home."

"Yeah," Robert sighed. "You spoke to anyone back home?"

The way Robert asked sounded strange, like something had happened. I went to push for more, but he spoke again. "Calvin, you gotta be careful out here."

"You think I should quit my job?"

"No. Don't do that. Just watch yourself."

I nodded.

"Here, too," Robert said. "You go back and forth, people start talking. . . . What do you think would happen if it got out?"

"It would be catastrophic," I said. I'd thought about the eleven miles between Sojourner and home. Downtown sat right in the middle of my two worlds. I couldn't flip-flop between the two there.

I'd have to choose.

It had already been chosen.

Robert let me have silence. He didn't make a move as the tears escaped from my lids. I looked toward the Capewoods, a place that tempted me to scream until my throat was raw. Suddenly, movement amid the trees caught my attention. There was a flicker, something flashing. I blinked forcefully, questioning whether my eyes were deceiving me. The branches swayed, and shadows of faces danced across the trees, approaching with an unsettling pace. As they neared, I could sense a rush of fear building within me. Before I could ask Robert whether he'd seen the same eerie sight, Eugene and Harry emerged from the dense foliage, running as if their lives depended on it. The terror in their faces gradually faded as they reached the safety of Sojourner's steps. Robert moved closer, and I instinctively followed.

"What y'all running from?" I said when they made it to the porch, bent over breathing hard and sucking in air.

"Came back from town—something strange is going on. White folks acting weird," Harry said.

"Weirder than usual," Robert said with a chuckle.

"Yeah, this news has them all worked up," Eugene said.

"No news talk here." Robert cut him off. "You safe?"

"Yeah, we're fine. The Capewoods got Harry freaked more than normal."

"It was getting dark," Harry said. "More cars on Bailey Road, yelling out to us, calling us names. So we made a run through the woods with my bags. Then I heard something."

"What bags?" I looked at an empty-handed Harry and an out-of-breath Eugene.

"Back there." Harry pointed to the trees. "I dropped them."

"You gonna get them?"

Harry looked out at the woods, then shook his head. "Nope."

"I didn't see anything," Eugene said.

"Then why were you running?" I was now amused, holding in fits of laughter I wanted to bellow out.

Robert gave me a smile and clapped his hand on my back before going inside.

"Harry took off, and I wasn't about to stick around to find out why," Eugene said.

"What is the deal with the woods?" I stepped onto the gravel and faced the trees.

"Haunted," Harry said.

"It's not haunted," Eugene said. "People just be living out there."

"Why'd you run, then?" Harry said.

"People living in the woods are a whole lot scarier than some ghosts."

"You didn't feel that cold shiver? Like someone was chasing the back of your neck."

"That was me trying not to get left, man," Eugene said.

Harry's shoulders relaxed; then he piped out a chuckle.

"Why do you think it's haunted?" I asked.

"You spend enough time there, you'll think it's haunted too," Harry said.

"Nah. It's just always been like that. Forbidden. Makes it easier for us to stay here and them over there." Eugene pointed toward what had to be Levittown. "It shaves off twenty minutes of walking if you cut through. But these woods are ours."

"There's a white kid who sometimes hides out in the church, drinking," Harry said.

"See. And how many times have I told you to stay outta there. That thing's practically ready to collapse."

"I'm not going there! Not anymore," Harry said. "But there's ghosts. I swear. I've heard 'em."

I wasn't sure what to believe, but I was convinced I wasn't going to take any chances. Haunt or no haunt.

"Didn't know you were coming by again," Eugene said.

"I didn't plan on it. Just had to get away." I shoved my hands in my pockets. I kept my gaze down to keep the sadness to myself.

"Things getting hard?" Eugene said.

I nodded.

"You watch the Yankees?" Harry's eyes went bright. I was happy at the shift in conversation. "Think they're gonna make the World Series and play against the Dodgers?"

"Definitely. I'm rooting for the Dodgers," I said.

"Yankees all the way," Eugene said. "You know why Jackie was first. He didn't scare those white folks. They could stomach him being their Black player."

"That's how it's always been," I admit.

"Willie Mays is my favorite player," Eugene said.

"Don't get me wrong—Willie Mays ain't nothing to snuff at. He's a hell of a ballplayer. I just like the way Jackie plays. It isn't easy being first to break out of the Negro Leagues."

"Yeah. Sure ain't."

"Boy, I wish I could see them in the World Series, against each other. Now that'd be some baseball."

"I'm still thinking about that catch by Mays in game one of the series last year," Eugene said.

"That was some game," Harry said.

"If they can, you know they're gonna bench Jackie when it counts," Eugene said.

"They wouldn't." I shook my head even though the same thought had crossed my mind. They wouldn't want him on a game-winning record.

"I'm rooting for Jackie," Harry said. "Just play all night long. Tire out them white boys."

I chuckled at the thought and followed them inside.

We found ourselves in the music room. I picked up a trumpet, settled my fingers, puffed my lips to stretch them, then perked my lips in form as I did a buzz routine before even putting my mouth to the trumpet. I'd forgotten how much I loved to run through exercises for full range of motion: low loud to high soft, back-and-forth zipping. There was a band at school, but I knew it would be another reminder of having to hide my real interests.

"You gonna pick up and play or just let your mouth do the work?" Eugene said.

"Give me a minute. Go on and start playing something."

"You want to choose?" Eugene said.

"I'll catch up." I gave a cocky grin.

I zipped through a few more exercises while Eugene played the piano, Harry falling into beat with the drums. It took me a second to pick up Eugene's pattern, but once I had it, I put my trumpet in play.

Eugene tossed his head back to look at me when I let my horn draw on and paced my finger buttons through the scales, trying to catch on to Eugene's notes. Swinging the beat that would complement, not mimic, the same chords.

"Well, goddamn, boy. You can play." Eugene picked up his pace, improvising.

Being a good jazz player, especially a trumpet player, was about learning the structure of notes first, then breaking all the rules. The act of improvising had taught me how to operate within a box so I'd know how to match someone else's playing.

I tapped my foot, not taking my lips away from the trumpet.

My ability to play had been years in the making. Once I'd learned to let myself feel the music, it became like an out-of-body experience.

We'd just started playing together, but I knew that if we spent more time, like how Ray and I had spent hours, we could be a real trio. No set would ever be the same, because the music would push us to a moment of improvisation.

After an hour, my worries had dissipated. My chest was filled with harmonic sounds that lifted my spirits. Other students floated past the stairs to listen. Every once in a while, my heart jumped at the thought that Lily might appear any second. But she wasn't anywhere to be found.

I played until my mouth ached and my fingers crinkled up. Until I forgot about Mr. Vernon. About Alex and Ben.

On my way home, an eerie feeling prickled my skin as I passed the woods down Port Lane. I flicked the light on my bike as I looked down the dark road, trees blocking the moonlight. I knew that if I was found on this side of town, there'd be scrutiny into my travel, who I was, and what exactly I was doing here. Port Lane was dark as night until I reached Bailey Road, where streetlights were spread.

When I hit the parkway, my body relaxed on the homestretch. I formed my mouth to make zipping sounds, running through trumpet exercises while the wind and air carried my sound down quiet streets.

Muggy air rushed in as I sped closer to home. At night the indicators that helped pinpoint which way to turn were few and far between. I repeated street names, trying to retrace my steps. But I was turned around. *A left or a right, is it?* I'd said too many times. Finally, I saw my dad's car, parked in our driveway. Strangely, my dad was standing next to a car parked on the street in front of our house. The way my dad leaned forward to the window, I could tell he was angry, in heated debate.

I hopped off my bike, walking it quietly in hopes I could hear what my dad was saying. He caught my eye but kept speaking in a whisper. I was relieved that he wasn't out searching for me. But from the intent look in my dad's eye, I could tell he had something more pressing on his mind.

CHAPTER 12

THE NEXT MORNING, I WAITED FOR MY FATHER TO ADDRESS MY LATE arrival the night before. But he kept silent, eating breakfast.

"Morning." I touched my mom's hand.

"Morning, Calvin," she said. "How was your first day at work? Came home a bit late?"

Hesitantly, Dad lowered the paper. He wouldn't be able to avoid talking about last night, because when Mom spoke, she was staring directly at him.

"It was dark." Mom's voice was shrouded with warning.

"It was busier than I thought it would be."

"I just don't want you out so late."

"I want you back before sundown," Dad said.

I'd traveled enough with my father to know how dangerous sundown towns could be; we'd always been cautious when we were far away from home on the road. And no doubt I'd been terrified leaving Sojourner the previous night, but Dad didn't know about the risks I was taking.

What bothered me more about this was that Levittown wasn't just a sundown town; it was a sundown suburb—seventy thousand strong. One we were smack-dab in the middle of.

I looked up, hard-faced. *He put us here.* "Time just flew, plus I'm still learning how to get home."

"But nine p.m.?" Mom said.

"Alex was downtown, so after work he showed me around." I looked down, hoping that lie would land.

"That's good," Dad said. "And I'm glad you've got yourself a job. Learning about real estate is a good opportunity, too. That's how wealth is built."

"I don't like it," Mom said. "There's just something about this neighborhood. It's too quiet. Too many people watching who's coming and going. No more late nights."

I knew what she meant. I hated riding through the streets, nothing to set apart my neighborhood from another. I'd been turned around several times, getting lost down wrong streets. But it was more than that. At night I would pass the homes with neighbors in their windows eating dinner, stepping outside on their porches to watch me. It was dead silent, with only the cicadas swarming. Streetlights covering only part of the road, leaving corners dark. It was too quiet. Too easy to get comfortable.

"You hear me?" Mom interrupted my thoughts. "Until we get used to it out here."

"Don't make it a habit," Dad cut in. "He'll be safe, Ann."

I bristled at Dad calling her Ann. And, worse, Mom didn't even flinch at her new white name.

Ben and Alex were huddled outside school with a crowd of boys. They were easygoing as they let laughter escape, something amusing catching their attention. I almost let a smile slip, but I watched the way the group shifted. Laughter building into venom. It was a difference I'd learned all too early in life. Sometimes joy was at the cost of something else. Sometimes it was cruel.

Darren waved me over, pointing at something in his hands. I wanted to walk right past. Skip up the steps and go straight to class. But that's the thing about a surging mob: it grows by feeding on curiosity and a burning desire not to miss out. It was this flame that I followed, pushing forward until a path cleared. Almost like it had been waiting for me.

The words that escaped were a swarm, difficult to decipher, but enveloped in the circle of greedy eyes studying something. Then it was too late for me to turn around—they were waiting for my reaction, like all the others who had joined before me.

A sickening ache dropped inside me once I recognized the familiar small size of *Jet* magazine in Darren's hands. My parents had subscribed to it for years. Something they couldn't continue now in Levittown.

The issue was open to the pictures of the open casket of a fourteen-year-old boy murdered for talking to a white woman. The magazine called him by his formal name, Emmett Till. But I'd known him as Bobo. I was in a daze, like my soul had been pulled from my body and I was watching from above, unable to respond.

"Nasty!" a kid I didn't know said before I could react.

"My dad said he tried to rape that lady," another boy said.

"No. It says that he just spoke to her," Alex said.

I couldn't understand what was happening, because the face of the boy I'd known almost my whole life looked different. I ripped the magazine out of their hands and flipped through the pages. Tears welled in my eyes as I studied my best friend Ray's cousin Bobo. But he didn't look like Bobo. Not any longer. The ache took over, uncontrollable, tears dancing at my lids. I wanted to scream out a guttural cry. I scoured every word, hoping there was a mistake.

But I couldn't deny the photo of Ray's aunt, in shock. Devastated. I could almost hear it through the pages as I studied the schoolboy image of Bobo. Emmett had only lived a few blocks from me and Ray.

Ray had to have assumed I'd heard. He hadn't answered my calls because I'd left him to deal with this alone.

The magazine fluttered out of my hands as I staggered backward. The swarm of boys didn't notice the tears dropping from my eyes. I wanted to call Ray to confirm it wasn't true. Beg for forgiveness for not being home in Chicago and for missing Bobo's funeral, even if the thought of an open-casket service terrified me.

I fought the urge to run home. If I did, I'd have to look Mom in the eye and learn that she'd known for weeks. There was no denying that. Aunt Vera would've called my mother the second she heard what had happened. They'd have been on prayer calls.

My parents had lied to me. But what hurt worse, Eugene

and Harry had talked about the town being worked up because of news, and Robert had cut them off. Robert knew too.

I knew I was supposed to push through the school doors wearing a mask of whiteness like I'd been playing. But that day it was impossible.

Instead I left school and rode toward town, then on to Bailey Road as I headed to the path that would take me to Sojourner. I expected to be alone, but ahead in the grass toward the entrance of the Capewoods was a shadowy figure swaying with the early fall wind, which still felt hot and stifling. The stories came to mind, and I prepared myself to fight a person or a haunt.

As I got closer, I rubbed my eyes. It was *Lily*. She didn't notice me, because she was crying. It took me a few minutes to reach her, and she still didn't hear me approach. I wasn't sure if I should interrupt her. But I was hurting inside, and I needed someone to talk to.

"Lily," I croaked out.

She lifted her head, tears dancing at her lids.

"What are you doing here?" She stood up, turning away to stare out at the woods.

I tentatively stepped closer. "I . . . I couldn't be at school today."

"You came looking for me?" Lily met my eyes with hot anger. But also with fear.

"No. I was going to see . . ." I stopped. I didn't know if I should say it, but Lily was shaking, and I'd have to trust that since she knew my secret, she wouldn't out me. "My brother . . . runs Sojourner Music School. I couldn't stay at Heritage."

Lily studied me; then a small smile turned her lips. "Robert."

"Yes." I smiled at the sound of my brother's name. Of being known.

"Wow. I can see it now. I mean, now that you say that, you really do look like him—maybe that's what gave me a clue about who you were. . . ."

A pause took over.

"I'm not supposed to see him."

Lily didn't object as I stepped closer, my hands shoved in my pockets. I circled around, making my way to a spot near her.

I liked that she didn't ask me why I shouldn't see Robert.

"I go there for classes, to play music for their open lessons. I've never seen you before."

I swallowed. Unsure if I should admit I had seen her before Heritage. I held it back.

"We moved in August. Robert was here first, before us. No one's supposed to know I'm not—"

"I would never tell anyone." Lily paused. "I didn't mean to scare you by saying I know. I was angry. But I'd never . . ."

"Thank you." I rub my temples. "It's complicated."

"I'd say so."

"It's not like I had a choice."

I defended myself, but I didn't feel judged. I wanted Lily to know I wasn't like others who passed. Who wanted to walk away from their community. I'd had no choice. I studied Lily's eyes and her soft, pouty lips. How could I explain?

"Where do you live?" I asked.

"Right in the middle of where they're building the Concord Park development."

"They let you transfer that far?"

"The school district thought they were doing me a favor, helping me get out of the 'integrated schools.'"

"Well, I guess they did." I chuckled.

"Your parents don't know you've been seeing your brother?"

"No." I paused. "Why'd you stop going to your old school?"

"I deserve to be at Heritage. I got tired of talking about it being a better-resourced school, so I decided to just go and try to integrate." Lily looked away. "But now after this Emmett Till news, I don't know if I wanna be at Heritage. This morning they were passing his photo around like it was just another one of their trinkets, their lynching postcard."

At the mention of Bobo my throat got tight. "That's why I left. I didn't know where else to go."

"Me either," Lily sighed. "If I tell my parents, they'll make me stop going."

We sat, hidden together behind the grass. Silent for a few minutes.

Then I told her the truth. That I knew Bobo. I put my head in my palms and cried. Lily placed her hand gently on my back. When my tears were dry, the lump in my throat slowly shrank, becoming smaller and smaller until there was nothing left.

"What's it like being at Heritage . . . you know, being white?"

I twisted a long strand of grass between my fingers. "I didn't want to move. Didn't want to—"

"Pass."

"Not if it was about hiding myself. It's weird. Even when

things seem like they're going fine, I'm waiting for the ball to drop. I can't even play my music at home."

"They won't let you play?"

"I mean . . . they would. But my dad forbids me from playing jazz or any of my favorite artists. I'd be playing what everyone else listens to out there. My mom had to fight him just to let me keep my trumpet."

"You really play the trumpet?" Lily sat up. A lightness filled her voice.

"And you sing."

"You've heard." She let a small smile slip out. "Singing won't pay the bills, but it's what's let me think there's something bigger than myself out there. And staying at my old school won't break me out. Won't give me a shot to get out of here."

"Sing me something."

"Play me something." She tapped my leg.

"Kind of need my instrument." I opened my empty hands wide.

"Well then, I guess we'll listen to the birds."

We were quiet again, waiting each other out.

I couldn't take it any longer.

I formed my lips and zipped a tune in and out, letting the vibration of my breath dictate a sound. Lily looked at me and laughed. But I didn't stop. I knew she loved Billie Holiday, and all I could think of was Bobo. How his life had been unjustly taken.

I began the intro, pushing out the sound for "Strange Fruit." I caught the flicker in Lily's eyes when she realized what I was setting her up for. I ran through it again with my lips, buzzing through my mouth and releasing a sound like my horn would play. Then I paused as Lily began.

Southern trees bear a strange fruit
Blood on the leaves . . .

At the break of the verse, I zipped again, louder. I felt like we were in a music hall, not hidden among the trees and the willowy grass. The breeze whisked around us, like the trees were hanging on our last breath. Lily ended with the last words of the song. Then silence again. This time it was healing. Music was what brought us together, the thing that wrapped everything between us into making sense, and we spent hours talking.

When two p.m. hit, we squeezed hands before we both headed home. I knew she'd creep into my thoughts for many nights after. A girl who'd fight her way into a school that didn't want her. How she was braver than me. Shame crawled through me. I'd never deserve Lily. Because if she came back to my school, I couldn't ever look her in the eye. Not when I was passing.

CHAPTER 13

I'D FOUND A SAFE PLACE TO MOURN WITH LILY. A PLACE WHERE I DIDN'T have to pretend. A place to grieve. But as I rode home alone, it didn't take long before all the heaviness and pain came tumbling back.

I was unhinged. A sickening feeling bellowed in my chest like a raw wound left exposed. Betrayal flashed before me because the news about Bobo hadn't come from Ray. From my family. Or, for that matter, from anyone who knew my truth.

By the time I reached home, I was depleted. My mom stood by the window, watching as I walked up the driveway. Rage blazed inside me. I wanted to hurl my accusations at her so she could feel the whiplash that had spun me out of school. The glossy look in my mother's eye stopped me. The unfairness of having to be cautious around her twisted inside me.

Her eyes bounced back to life when she caught sight of me, her shoulders settling in relief. Like she was coming alive after holding her breath all day. The rosiness in her cheeks returned as she hugged me. She hadn't heard I'd ditched, or I'd have been peppered with questions about my whereabouts.

"How was school?" Mom released me from her hold.

My shoulder blades tightened. I'd been fully prepared to lie before stepping into the house. But the anger crept in.

"I didn't go." I flung my leather backpack in the corner of the entryway.

"What do you mean, you didn't go?" Her voice quavered.

"I mean . . . I went, but when I got there, a group of boys . . . No." My voice sputtered out, unable to contain the venom of accusation in my tone. "The supposed friends you and Dad want me to have were waving *Jet* magazine around, entertained by Bobo's murder. Like justice was served instead of a horrific crime against a . . . kid."

Mom moved to touch my arm, but I shuddered away. Her body stiffened.

"My best friend's cousin was murdered, and I didn't even know it. How long have you been hiding this?"

Mom opened her mouth to speak, and the truth rippled across her face.

I couldn't watch her crumble at having to answer for herself. I brushed past her, but she latched on to me.

"I didn't know what to say," she whispered. "What could I say?"

"What could you say?" My voice cracked. "The truth. This is national news. What must Ray think? That I didn't care? That I was calling with excuses for why I wasn't at the funeral?"

"I'm sorry," Mom said. "We were just waiting for the right time."

"Keeping me away from news back home won't hide that these things still happen to *us*. You can't put me in a bubble of white walls and think that's somehow going to protect me. I'm in disguise, but it doesn't erase who I am. You can't erase me. I won't let you."

"I needed time."

"For what?" I spread my arms wide.

"Time to heal . . . from Charlotte. Things happened so fast, and your father—"

"He's not thinking rationally, Mom. He's acting like he saved us from war by bringing us here, when really it's ripping us apart."

"That's not true."

"Tell me you don't hate it here. Tell me you don't miss Aunt Vera. The church. The sounds of our old neighborhood. How free you could be. Getting your hair done at the salon. The house ringing with calls from friends and family." I pointed to the phone. "It doesn't ring here. You're alone every day. No work. Only nosy neighbors knocking, who you ignore. And you can't stand it."

Mom leaned on the couch to steady herself before covering her face with shaky hands, sobbing out, "What choice do I have?"

"Any choice. All choices but this." I pointed to the outside. "It's not real, Mom. I need to talk to Ray," I begged.

Mom picked up the phone. It took several rings, like she had a code to use so they'd know it was her, not someone harassing the home. Now my unanswered calls to Ray made sense.

"Cora," Mom said, "it's me. Agnes. Yes, so good to hear your voice. Did you get our package?" Mom went on, talking to Ray's mom before finally handing the phone over.

"Ray." My hands shook as I waited for him to speak. "I'm so sorry. I didn't know. I swear I didn't know until today."

"Where are you?" Ray said. "When you coming back home?"

I looked at Mom, wanting to answer. She shook her head firmly. My eyes welled, and I wanted to yell out the truth.

"I can't say. But I'm not far." I looked to Mom, dared her to stop me from telling him some truth. "We're passing, Ray. I don't know when I can visit. But when I can, I will." My voice dipped, cutting in and out with each word.

"I heard that rumor. Didn't believe it. But when I didn't hear from you . . ."

"I tried," I said. "I called, but the phone just rang."

"Yeah, ever since I got back . . . things have been scary."

"I still can't believe it. I'm so sorry about Bobo. About what you've been through." I waited a beat for him to tell me what happened. How scared he was. But it was silent on the other end.

"You still there?"

"Yeah," Ray choked out.

"Do you want to . . . talk about it?"

"Not now." Ray paused. "They took him. They took him and I couldn't save him."

"I'm going to visit. I'm going to see you."

110

"Yeah, okay, Calvin." I thought he might have hung up, and my chest sank. Then finally he spoke again. "Can we talk about anything else but this? Something funny, like none of this happened?"

"Ray . . ." I stalled, sorting out what I should say.

"Yeah."

"You ain't go dating Nancy, now, are you?"

Ray gulped out a hearty chuckle before saying, "We practically married."

"You wouldn't." I laughed, wiping away a tear. "You can see her. I'd rather it be you than anyone else."

"You not gonna take that back, are you? I mean, fair is fair."

"I'm not gonna take it back."

"That mean you not coming back?"

"No. I'm coming back." I looked at Mom again, making sure she heard me.

"You got a girlfriend, then? Some white girl?"

"Not a white girl." I caught Mom's eyes flickering in my direction before I turned to whisper in the kitchen about Lily.

We talked for a full hour. Long distance was adding up on our bill, but I didn't know the next time I'd have this chance. Finally, Mom twirled her finger, urging me off.

"I gotta go, Ray. I'm sorry you went through all that without me. It never should've happened. To you. To Bobo. You be careful."

"I will. You be careful too."

I hung up, and Mom gave me a hug before we shuffled to the family room. The lump in my throat ached. Without

111

having to ask, I turned the television on and sat next to my mom. We watched in silence the news about the horrors of what happened to Emmett Till. Both shocked at how the news was taking a sympathetic turn to the tragedy. Our cries tore through the house, breaking the fragile walls we'd tried to hold up for appearances.

When my dad came home, I swear he could feel the cold, crisp air of the house signaling that something monumental had happened—and he had missed it. He stood looking at us, then at the television with the news my parents had been hiding from me. Finally he slumped in his seat, with his hand gripped on my shoulder, shaking as he broke down watching part of the country mourn, and the outrage growing over a beautiful young boy who had lost his life.

With heavy hearts, we took turns calling more family and friends we hadn't been in touch with, sharing the pain the community was suffering back home. And when we were done, Dad pressed his lips on Mom's forehead and said, "Good night, Ann."

A blur crossed my eyes, because the message was clear: we'd have one night to be devastated, but nothing was going to change.

CHAPTER 14

MY STEPS QUICKENED IN ANTICIPATION OF MEETING LILY. WE'D MOVED into a pattern in the past two weeks. We'd reach town after school separately, and Lily would walk her bike and I would follow with mine until we were at the edge of town, out of sight.

Lily's brown skin and full, pouty lips called me from a distance. I couldn't deny I was mesmerized by her. The way her skirt would flutter as she walked. The catch in her voice when she spoke to me. Moments that gave me hope I stood a chance at winning her heart.

The first day, she'd caught me by surprise around the corner. Now we'd found a routine, a safe way to meet. One that also paralyzed me in fear it would end the day Lily couldn't take having to hide our relationship and I'd become another white boy she'd have to avoid.

Guilt swirled in my stomach because I knew things were getting easier for me at Heritage. Lily had given me something worth looking forward to. And the spotlight that had once shone on me as the new kid had shifted to Lily. The difference was that what I was trying to hide, she boldly carried on the outside.

The principal had said Mr. Vernon and his representatives would be back. But they hadn't been. It was almost worse not knowing what they were up to. That was the undercurrent that threatened our relationship. Threatened Lily's safety and her family's.

I edged closer to the street corner, catching a flash of Lily's blue skirt. I ignored the cars and passersby. The only thing that mattered was her.

As I approached the curve, I could feel the quietness of the road. The wind blew, shifting the grass, and we caught each other's eyes as she glanced back to see if I was still coming. We shared anxious smiles from a distance. Normally, we pretended to be strangers until the bend of the road curved away from town. Lily would cut down a trail, hidden by overgrown grass and willow trees. It was there we'd meet eyes as the blowing grass uncovered Lily waiting for me. Then we'd walk at a snail's pace with our bikes. I could feel that bubbling excitement grow as my thoughts raced. I swallowed my bursting eagerness, but inside, my body rattled.

Before I could speak, my view was cut off by a white boy pulling his car to the side of the road and getting out. It was Lily who alerted me. Her sudden flash of recognition made her face turn blank. I lost my smile. Without a word, Lily cut onto the trail early, bumping over tall grass and piled-up dirt.

At first I thought it was a coincidence. But then I realized she was still being followed. It was undeniable. I had been too busy thinking about catching up to her to realize it earlier. I'd gotten too comfortable.

It was the flash of blond I saw first: Darren.

Without hesitation, I picked up my pace, cutting through the grass. I moved with shallow breaths, hoping Darren would go off on his own in another direction—to party near the Capewoods, to stop, to slow down—but he was hot on her trail.

Darren had no reason to head to that side of town. Fear gnawed at my insides.

Lily pushed her pace and he kept up, closing the distance. My chest burned as I watched Lily, who didn't stand a chance of getting away.

I was catching up, but not before Darren grabbed at her shirt, causing her to crash onto the grass.

"Get over here." Darren tugged harder as Lily flung her arms, slapping him away.

My chest tightened, but I pushed past the pain so my bike could fly. I hopped off and started running. My arms whipped quickly at my sides as my legs tested the limits of my body.

I sprang on top of Darren as soon as I was in reach. Caught by surprise, he threw punches. Until he recognized me. His face relaxed, as if he thought I was there with the same intentions as him. But I didn't let go. Darren's smile turned into a sharp snarl.

Lily slipped out of reach and took off with her bike.

"Get off me," Darren said. "She's getting away."

I didn't speak—I pulled Darren's arm and forced out a stunning punch to his jaw. He was taken aback, but then he hooked one arm around me before punching me in the stomach and kicking me down. We rumbled on the ground. The longer we fought, the more danger I'd be in, so I stopped defending myself, letting Darren get several cheap shots to my face. When I didn't hit back, he stopped.

"What's wrong with you, man?" Darren took a heavy breath, sucking air and brushing dirt off his clothes. "I got a game this weekend."

"What do you think you're doing?" I said.

"Me?"

"You're going after a girl."

"What's it to you?"

My head was throbbing as I thought, *Stall for Lily. Keep her safe.*

"My boss is Mr. Vernon from Vernon Realty."

"Okay. And we're friends." Darren rubbed his jaw, his neck flushed red from the punches.

Friends. How could I be friends with Darren? I quickly mustered an excuse.

"What were you thinking?" I said. "You're gonna chase her down to her side of town, then end up alone with no backup? Besides, you're supposed to let them handle it—weren't you at the meeting?"

I tried to throw everything at him that would get him to listen. The way Ben had described the meeting in town the night before Lily started school, Mr. Vernon and the men who had joined him planned to manage things. And Darren had to know this.

"Doesn't look like they're handling it." Darren pulled at his jaw, clearly sore.

"Let's see what Mr. Vernon has to say about this." I turned, walking back to the road, hoping Darren wouldn't call my bluff.

"Wait," Darren called out.

Thank God.

"You're really going to tell them?"

"Depends." I slowed so he could catch up. "You gonna leave her alone and let them handle it?" I braced myself for a sickening response.

"What's with all the questions?" Darren asked. "What were you doing out here anyway?"

"I—I was headed to town," I stammered. "To work at Vernon Realty, when I saw you going out toward the parkway. I thought you were headed to the Capewoods to hang out again."

"I wasn't going to do anything!" Darren looked away before running his fingers through his hair.

"Well then, you should be on your way before I have to explain why I'm late for work today. You know there's a reason Mr. Vernon trusts me. Why we live in our house." I pushed another lie, hoping everyone was scared of Mr. Vernon. By the widening of Darren's eyes, I could tell it had worked.

"You gonna keep this between us?" Darren stepped closer to me, attempting to act tough, but something flickered across his face. Fear.

Mr. Vernon had the power to force residents to move in

the middle of the night. What else did Darren know that I didn't?

"Yeah." I paused. "It's between us. As long as I don't see you do anything like this again. That means no harassing her at school or anywhere else."

I stuck my hand out because it seemed like the kind of thing I should do.

Darren shook my hand, then jogged toward his car. I watched him pull away and drive out of sight.

Then I raced after Lily, jumping on the trail, pushing through grass and over rocks. I found Lily hidden between two trees. I shouldn't have been able to catch her camouflaged there, but since I'd first met Lily Baker, she seemed to be the only thing I could see clearly.

I cut through the grass that whipped at my spokes. My head no longer throbbed; all my worry was on making sure Lily was safe. Her hands gripped her handlebars, ready to ride. But she was waiting for me.

I pulled up alongside her, reaching out to see if she was okay. She slapped my hand away.

"That was stupid, you know," Lily said.

"I . . . wait. What?"

"I could've handled it myself." Her voice rose.

"You're right." She was wrong, but it seemed like the right thing to say. Her eyes were glazed over. Her body shaking.

"He won't do that again." I hoped this was true. "Got him afraid Mr. Vernon would be after him."

"Why would that scare him off?" Lily said.

I didn't know where to start. I wanted to warn Lily about Mr. Vernon, but wasn't sure if she trusted me enough yet to listen.

"Let's get you home," I said. "Can we avoid the main road?"

"This way." Lily walked further through the grass between some trees, so we were far enough away that cars flying by wouldn't notice us.

When we were out of sight, I felt looser being able to walk beside Lily without worry. Lily's shoulders relaxed as much as mine. She gave me a slanted smile when our bikes bumped into each other.

"You're bleeding." Lily touched her hairline and her eye, pointing out my injuries.

I touched my face, wincing. The pain automatically kicked in as my adrenaline crashed.

"Hurt much?" Lily went through her bag and handed me a handkerchief.

"Not until you told me I'm bleeding to death."

"You're hardly bleeding to death. Maybe a quart of blood lost." She gave a sly smile.

"A quart!" I went along.

"Okay, maybe not that much."

"Does it look bad?"

"It's swelling. Maybe if we get ice on it?"

"My dad's gonna kill me." I put pressure on my eye, hoping that would help before I got home.

"I'm okay from here if you need to go."

"Nah. I can stay. How much farther?" I was excited to finally get a closer look at Lily's neighborhood.

"Just right through there." Lily pointed to a large entrance to the woods.

I recognized that this must have been the entrance Eugene and Harry took to cut through the Capewoods. I could feel an eerie breeze. Like secrets kept inside wanting to make their way out into the open.

"Okay." I swallowed hard. I didn't want Lily to leave. But the thought of cutting through the Capewoods terrified me to the core.

"I'm fine, you know. Really. Get some ice on that."

"I can't let you go through there alone!"

"Why not?" Lily's shoulders rose up defensively.

"Because it's—"

"Haunted."

"Yeah . . . that."

"I'm not worried about the woods, or who lives there."

"So, you don't think it's haunted?"

"Maybe a little. Besides, the dead are gone even if their presence is there." She gave a dry laugh. "And if there are ghosts, I don't bother them, and they certainly don't bother me. You should go home, Calvin. You shouldn't be seen with me anyway."

I gave her a frenzied look. But I wasn't about to let her think I was a chicken. And not just about the woods. The world, too.

"I'm not worried about being out here."

"Not because of that, Calvin. Because of me."

"I want to see you. I shouldn't have to avoid you."

"It's getting dangerous. We won't be able to meet again. I'm sorry, Calvin." Lily cut through the Capewoods, disappearing through the trees.

CHAPTER 15

WITH A CHILLY GAZE, MARY STOOD ON THE CORNER SCANNING ME from top to bottom.

"What happened to you?" she finally said.

I felt the blood trickle down my forehead, blurring my sight. "Trouble on my way home."

"You should be careful, Calvin." Mary's voice was smooth, but there was a hint of an edge. "You could always get a ride home with me."

I nodded. Ready to run inside my house and shut everything out.

"Where are you always rushing off to anyway?" Mary said. "You don't even take the right route home."

I paused, answers floating in my head. I didn't want to get caught in a lie. I bit my lip. "Just going into town."

She looked at me, puzzled.

"I gotta go." I left before she could ask more questions.

When I stepped on the porch, the door swung open. My

parents rushed me inside. Dad gave glances at Mary, waving as he forced the door closed behind me.

"Oh, Calvin," Mom cried. "What happened? Who did this?"

"Out of the view." Dad closed the drapes after taking one more look outside.

Mom snatched a bag of frozen peas and gently pressed them over my throbbing eye. At first it was a shock; then came soothing relief.

"Who knows about us?" Dad said.

"Please, God, no," Mom said. "I knew it was too dangerous— we're lucky you weren't killed."

"Did they find out?" Dad shook my shoulders.

"No, sir," I said, closing my eyes to stop my head from spinning. "Nobody knows. I just got into a fight is all."

"What could you possibly be fighting over?" Mom said.

I paused, the day swirling again.

"There's a girl at school. She was being followed home, and I stepped in." I hoped that would be enough to appease my parents.

Dad let go of me and stood by the window. "Please tell me you weren't helping who I think you were?"

"What are you talking about?" Mom turned to Dad, then to me.

"A new girl at school." I saw the look in my father's eye. I could never lie to him. I knew what the repercussions were.

"It was the girl integrating Heritage, wasn't it?" Dad said.

"Why didn't anyone say anything about this?" Mom's gaze locked on both of us.

"You seeing her?" Dad said.

I paused because I wanted that to be true. "No. Darren was going to hurt her. She was minding her own business, riding home."

"How did you know where she was headed, and why were you anywhere near her after school?"

"I—"

"This why you've been late coming home?"

"No. Dad, I . . . She needed my help."

"I don't want you seeing this girl." Dad firmly grabbed my arm.

"I'm not seeing her. She just started school. I—"

"You stay away from her."

"William." Mom put her hand up to Dad. "Come here, Calvin. Let me see."

Mom wiped the last of the blood, then lifted my chin to place the frozen peas on my head so they formed around my eye. I winced at the cold, but then my jaw relaxed as the numbing kicked in. Dad paced while mom checked my face and cleaned the blood in between rotating the ice pack. My eye pulsed, puffy and sore.

Dad poured whiskey into a glass cup and swirled it before drinking, his hands shaking as he watched the door. Like he was expecting a mob on the other side. The room was silent until Dad gulped the rest of his drink and turned to us.

"You'll understand when you get older. I know what's good for you."

"I just don't get why you're mad. Why we're even living here if it's so risky for the truth to come out."

"Because they think they can leave us out of this American dream by a caste system. I fought for our place—I won't let them take that away from us."

My head throbbed at Dad beginning one of his philosophical lectures. "You act like you hate being Black. Hate who we are. Like something's wrong with us."

"Something's wrong with the world, and I don't know how to fix it, damn it." Dad slammed his hand down. Then he lowered his voice. "I love where we came from. But I love us more. Don't turn this around like I made the rules—I'm just trying to survive."

"I just don't believe it's the answer." I sat on the couch, nursing my eye and trying to make sense of things.

"We can't ever get ahead, because the deck is stacked against us. I'm buying us time to climb a hill before we fall back down. We're caught in a scam that has the bottom half bamboozled, believing that the American dream is achievable by those who deserve it. Work hard enough. Then they justify burning up our justice. Our access. Our dream. The very thing this country was created to uphold. But this country only knows how to rule in terror and by blood. The physical and the metaphysical. The hate that has now fueled this country against us is as visible as skin color and as invisible as the soul."

I sucked a long breath in. My father was the smartest man I knew, and while what he shared was true, I could never agree with his solution.

"If we'll never be at the top, then why would we want to play by those rules at all?"

"Did you know Hitler and the Nazis studied the United States?" My father leaned closer.

"We won the war, Dad." I threw my hands up, irritated at his tirade. It was always about the war with him.

"I fought a war so ugly, so destructive, only to come home and find out we were fighting overseas so we'd be too tired to fight at home."

"That doesn't mean we should try to be a part of this pyramid and wall ourselves away from who we are. We could've stayed in Chicago. Made it together."

"Could have stayed?" Dad slammed his empty glass on the coffee table.

"William." Mom put her hand to her temple. "Let's just stop this."

"I'm not finished," Dad said. "Calvin, there is no hope for us. Our history is we've been slaves longer than we've been Americans. And we're now told, 'You're free. Be off and make it.' As long as we stay within glass walls." My father turned his glass over and covered a spider crawling on the table.

I watched the spider freeze, then work to escape, gliding up the glass and back down to the table. Stuck with nowhere to go.

"We're as helpless as this spider. We can see freedom. We can see opportunity. But we have this glass ceiling. These glass walls." Dad picked up the glass and the spider scurried away. "What I did is simply remove the glass. Remove the man-made barrier. The construct of race. So, son, I'm not saying you have to hate who you are. I just want you to have a chance to see what it's like when that glass isn't controlling you. What you can build. So, yes, this is about the war. We'll never stand a chance in the war at home until the masses turn the pyramid upside down. I'm scrambling to the top as fast as I can, until there's enough of us to turn it over."

Dad grabbed his keys and stormed out of the house.

He might not have come back from the war with visible injuries, but his scars were wrapped inside him. He was in battle. His vision focused on us, here and now, and nothing else. It terrified me. Ripped me that the country he loved so much had done this to him. To us.

I opened the drapes, staring out at the rows of houses as my dad drove away.

"You really think I should've left her alone and let someone hurt her if I could stop it?"

My mother paced, then clutched her hands to her chest. "No, honey. If someone was in danger, I'd want you to do something. Your father . . . your father needs this right now. He wants to be free. To see what life he can build, so you can walk away from it with more than we started with."

I swallowed hard. Watched my mom bite her lip, holding back tears. She was shaking, like so many nights when she'd gathered our family in the kitchen because it was blocked from any glass that could be shattered by the riots outside our door. We didn't meet eyes again—we knew where this was headed.

CHAPTER 16

MY FATHER GROUNDED ME FOR TWO WEEKS. WITH EVERY ORDER HE barked, my only option was to respond with a *Yes, sir.* The first week he dropped me off and picked me up from school, and on the days I had to work, he took me there, too. By the second week, his chauffeuring routine had ended. Paranoid he was following me, I kept my strict schedule. No deviations. But I was growing tired of avoiding Lily beyond the small exchanges we had in science. And it had been too long since I had traveled to Sojourner to see Robert. So when Saturday came, I lied about my work schedule and left early in the morning.

When I arrived, a handful of cars were parked there, more than normal. The door was unlocked, so I entered the house and headed to the kitchen to drink straight from the tap.

"Calvin," James said. "What in the world are you doing?"

"I'm sorry," I said with water dribbling off my chin. "Long bike ride."

James grabbed a glass from the cabinet and filled it up with water before handing it to me.

I guzzled while saying thanks in between breaths.

"Here for the meeting in the barn?" James gave me an eye, surprise glimmering on his face.

"That where Robert is?" I looked at him, puzzled.

"Robert? He's not into organizing anymore."

I lifted my eyebrows. *Organizing.* Robert had been all about this—*before.* I grew curious. I wanted to see Robert, but I also wanted to know what this organizing business was. I washed the glass, then stepped outside.

The barn door creaked as I entered, and I shuffled to an open seat in back. Eugene stood at the front of the room with a few older boys, closer to Robert's age. I blinked twice when I noticed there were a handful of white people in the room.

I whispered to a kid next to me, "What's going on?"

"CORE meeting about Emmett Till." He handed me a flyer.

The ink on the flyer was light, the faintness of it sending a shiver down my spine. Almost like the ink was a whisper, a warning that what was happening was dangerous and required discretion. I pulled the paper tighter, like if I were to show it to anyone else, it would disappear.

"This is different," Eugene said. "The country is changing. We must take this opportunity to do something. He could've been one of us."

Eugene lifted the copy of *Jet* magazine and pointed to the photo of Bobo with his bright smile, placed next to the horrific image of him bloated and disfigured. My stomach churned as I looked away.

I wanted to remember Bobo like he was, let the name Emmett be someone I'd never met. But I couldn't ignore the image of his body; it was branded in my mind.

"What are we supposed to do about that?" a girl with braided black pigtails asked.

"Join me."

I knew that voice. I looked up to confirm, searching for Lily.

"I can't be at Heritage by myself," Lily said. "They'll just get rid of me. Scare my family. Whatever they can do to use me as a lesson to keep us down."

I felt guilty because I was caught between two worlds. I wanted to be brave like Lily, but all I could think about was what would happen if word of my passing got back to Mr. Vernon. My parents could lose their house. Worse.

"If I go back for more paperwork, I'll be caught." A white guy in his early twenties spoke. He looked to Harry, then Lily. "They already suspect I'm the one who did it. That puts everything I'm trying to do at risk. I have to focus on fixing the housing situation."

I sat up in my seat, wondering what they'd been planning.

"You don't get to tell us what to prioritize, Bobby," Eugene said.

"I'm alone at school." Lily drew attention back to her. "But if you join me, we could change things."

I couldn't help but see the way Eugene looked at Lily. I knew that feeling.

"We should all be able to go to Heritage," Lily continued. "The Supreme Court passed *Brown versus Board.* We have a right to be in the same school. They restrict where we live. We might not be in Mississippi, but they do it in their own way just the same. Making sure homes cost more for us. That our schools aren't equal. We've got to fight for our rights."

"Our parents can buy homes in Levittown," Eugene said. "We've already done it again since the Sampsons—they just don't know it yet. Why not us, too?"

Eugene looked at me. I felt dizzy as heads turned. I wanted them to join me at Heritage. But our family had tried this before. It cost us everything. Cost us Robert. Cost us Charlotte. I knew why Robert wasn't here. He knew what this was like, to drive a group for justice and have it hit you back hard. We couldn't do that to our parents. Not again.

"Calvin works at Vernon Realty," Eugene said. "They're the head of the snake for housing segregation. Calvin could be our inside guy. Tell us everything they're planning."

Everyone looked at me like I was a secret weapon leading some underground mission to turn the tide of segregation in Levittown. I held a fake smile watching Lily, who was smiling back at me, hoping I believed in what they were doing. And I did. I just didn't want to be a part of it.

But then Lily was looking at me, begging, *Please.*

"I'll do it," I said.

CHAPTER 17

SWEAT RACED DOWN MY BODY AS I PACED IN THE BACK OF THE BARN. My regret at being so easily swept up in the conversation mounted. I hated myself for volunteering. Hated that I wanted to burst out of the barn, but that my burning desire to see Lily, to prove myself, anchored me in place. Lily made her way to me.

I ached to smell her skin again, to be caught up in her laugh. To hear the vibrato of her voice singing. My insides bounced around, that is until Eugene and Harry followed after her. A rush of attendees left, except a few students picking up chairs. Eugene stepped in front of Lily and my eyes flickered away from her. He gripped my shoulder in a friendly way.

"Thanks," Eugene said. "You helping will make a huge difference. I didn't think about it before, but you're the perfect cover for us."

I nodded.

Lily shot me a crooked smile.

I swallowed my excitement, to not let Eugene know how it felt to see Lily. But it all rushed out of me when she spoke.

"You came!" Lily flashed me another smile, and it was a chain reaction to let my face drop all swoony and out of control.

"You've met?" Eugene said.

Lily looked away, flicking an invisible hair off her face, and cast a glance at Eugene.

"At school, of course," Lily said.

"You mean what you said?" Harry broke the tension.

"Yeah." I swallowed hard, still trying to remember what exactly I'd agreed to.

Eugene smiled back at me, with the same look in his eye that Robert had had the night of the fire. I'd begged Robert to listen to Dad and stay home. Robert had tugged at his sweatshirt and pulled it over his head, talking a mile a minute about how what he was doing was going to fix everything.

I'd never felt that way before. Where an idea would spin so hard in your head it was like you were above all harm. The sort of thing you saw in leaders. In the barn, I could feel that energy. It was intoxicating. That was the high that Eugene was chasing. But the excitement of working with them began to dwindle. I was scared. Now the only thing left was reality. I could feel the paralyzing effect of fear writhing through my veins.

"Calvin?" Eugene said.

I was so deep in thought that I missed his question. I gave him a dazed look as I recovered.

"Can you stay?" Eugene repeated. "There's some things I want to talk to you about."

Lily smiled, her eyes crinkling. God, I'd been waiting for her to look at me like this. I just hated that she was doing it because she thought I was brave.

Back at the house, the four of us took the steps upstairs. I tiptoed, as if my brother could identify my footsteps over everyone else's and yank me to the ground. To safety. To hiding.

On the third floor, I entered Eugene and Harry's room, which was across from Robert's. They had two single beds, a small closet, and one dresser that they shared. I expected to sit, but I noted that Harry was racing to pull on a string from the ceiling to bring down the stairs. We climbed up quietly like the world was waiting for our plan.

I was blown away by the size of the attic, which covered the length of the house. I walked across beams to reach the small window, the weight of the world on my shoulders. I looked out to the Capewoods.

"You think we could get people to actually try and go to school at Heritage?" Lily said.

I turned to her—her arms were crossed over her body like she was giving herself a hug. I wanted the answer to be yes, so she wouldn't feel so alone.

"If we can get applications for admittance, they legally can't deny anyone," Harry said. "You got in."

"On a favor," Lily said. "Bobby Simms got me the registration paperwork for school. Legally I can sign up because my address is drawn within the school district. It was an error made when they first started building a new property near our neighborhood. But I could never get the district to hand me the registration paperwork."

"Bobby's not gonna do it again." Eugene threw his hand out to Harry in irritation.

"Bobby will help again." Harry stood up taller. "I'm the one that got him to do it in the first place."

"He won't," Lily said. "You heard him. He's afraid that too much upset at Heritage over Black students trying to integrate there will scare away the white folks who are open to integrating in Concord Park. We need you, Calvin."

"Well, I'm glad we agree on something," Eugene said.

"That's where you come in." Lily turned to me. "If *you* went."

"If I went where?" I swallowed hard.

"You could pick up the registration paperwork at the district office," Lily said.

"You think they'd give it to me? What if anyone finds out I'm the one that did it? I shouldn't even be here—my dad wants me to lie low, not draw more attention."

"I get you might not feel close to this kid Emmett, but I do," Eugene said. "I feel like it could've been Harry. All of them times he wanted us to jump and run to find our dad back South." Eugene looked at his brother.

My eyes stung from restraining the tears at how much I *did* know Emmett. And it hurt like hell. Lily touched my elbow, and our glances locked. I sensed her unspoken words, as if she wanted to assure me that everything would be all right.

"Just listen. It's all over the news." Eugene turned on a small radio and adjusted the dial to get good reception until he found one of the channels covering Emmett's murder. I recognized Emmett's mother's voice right away.

My throat felt like it was closing, unable to speak Emmett's name. We all huddled, surrounding the radio, listening quietly to the incantation of her voice.

After a few minutes, I couldn't take it anymore. I had to turn the radio off.

"Why'd you do that?" Eugene said.

"You should tell them." Lily nudged me.

I didn't want to—I'd planned to keep that a secret—but as Lily stared at me, I couldn't hide any longer. I looked at Harry and Eugene through cloudy eyes.

"What, man?" Eugene leaned closer.

"I knew Emmett back in Chicago." I cleared my throat. "We called him Bobo. He was my best friend's cousin. He grew up a few blocks from me and Ray. I hadn't heard from Ray in forever; I thought he was mad at me for moving. For . . ." I couldn't help but touch my own skin. "For playing white. I didn't know what happened until I saw the magazine at school."

It felt good to share the truth, to let it out. A trip to Chicago ached in my chest. My mom missed Aunt Vera, but each time she mentioned it, my father changed the subject. The secret of passing was that once you crossed that line, it was hard to turn back. Too dangerous. My father had promised we could visit, but that had been another lie of his.

"I'm sorry. . . . I didn't know." Eugene covered his mouth and then shook my knee.

I nodded, choking back tears.

"You want to do something about it?" Harry broke the silence.

"I could introduce you to some people." Eugene perked

up. "You could tell your story. Tell them about your friend's cousin. Maybe give them ideas on how we could organize bigtime. Not just here."

"We could help Emmett's memory," Harry said.

I could feel myself shifting. Eugene was contagious with inspiration. He started to talk more about being the youth organizer for CORE for Pennsylvania. I took in everything Eugene shared with me. How he'd been holding meetings for over a year.

"Would you go to Virginia?" Eugene said. "Meet some organizers?"

It sounded like such a simple question. One that I couldn't find a reason to say no to. What would be wrong with a meeting? I looked at Lily before I answered. Locking away the alarm bells ringing in my head.

"Yeah. I could do that," I said. "If you don't tell them about how my family got to live in Levittown . . ."

Eugene smiled. It felt good to think I was helping. That is, until Eugene spoke again.

"Sometimes the CORE group in Virginia opens up meetings for people to join outside the area. They might have ideas about how to help us with integration here. If you take us, we could make it safely."

I knew what this meant. But the way Eugene was speaking, playing white would mean something different. It was for something bigger than all of us. Virginia would be dangerous to travel through, but it sounded a lot better than making plans in my own backyard, where getting caught could hurt my family.

"I know it'll be hard to get away," Lily said.

She was trying to give me an out, but that only made it easier to agree.

"We need you," Eugene said.

"Yes." I answered before I could change my mind. "I could do overnight if I tell my parents I'm staying at my friend Alex's house. The night of the dance at Heritage."

I looked at Lily, wanting to take her to the dance but knowing I couldn't.

"What about Robert?" Harry said.

"We could do it the same day if we're smart about it." Harry and Eugene looked at each other, then Eugene stood up. "Last time we held a dance, Robert went out of town so we'd be forced to clean up the next day. Had a little vacation. He hasn't gone anywhere in a long time with James."

I couldn't help but notice a beat of a pause at the mention of James. They all seemed like family, and James was there often. But I still couldn't tell if they talked about my brother behind his back.

"Yeah. I could start dropping hints to James about how Robert needs to take a break every once in a while," Harry said.

"Could you really get away?" Eugene pushed to nail down an answer from me.

I had to think. A day trip could work, even though coming home past sundown frightened my parents a little, but overnight? No way they'd let me unless I convinced them I was finally fitting in. The upcoming dance could work—maybe make a weekend out of it. I'd need Alex to cover for me one night, so if our parents ever asked about my staying the night, it wouldn't be a lie. But would Alex go along with this, not knowing all the details?

I'd traveled enough with my father to know I could make a long-distance call to check in. If I kept it short, I could afford to make a call on a pay phone, and my parents wouldn't know the difference. In some way, deceiving them was payback for their keeping Bobo's murder from me.

As the morning got later, I could feel time wisping away, calling me to head to work. I hadn't even seen Robert. Not so long ago it was Robert making plans like this. Those days were over.

We left the attic, passed Robert's closed bedroom door, and went down the few flights of stairs. Eugene and Harry hung back on the porch as Lily and I left Sojourner.

Lily looked to the road and then to the woods. More nervous than usual.

"I could ride home with you before I go in to work," I offered.

"No. It's too dangerous."

"Too dangerous?"

"I mean, with me at Heritage, there's a trickle of people already stalking my street."

"How long has this been going on?"

"They've been doing it for a while now. Nothing to worry about. They're just trying to scare away the white folks considering buying in Concord Park. And they want to make sure no one else who's Black thinks about going to Heritage."

A trickle had turned into a mob numbering as high as a

thousand back in Trumbull Park. I shuddered at the thought of living through that again.

"I can't let you go by yourself. I know what it's like to have your home feel like a prison when a mob gathers."

Lily studied me, like she was searching for what my words meant. "I can't be seen with you, Calvin."

"I can't believe you think it's safer to cut through there." I pointed at the woods. I was joking, but when I looked out, I swore I could see movement.

"I'm not superstitious."

"Haunting lore doesn't just come out of nowhere," I said. "Usually there's a reason. A lesson. Either case, I'm not letting you go alone—at least let me get you close."

She nodded, and my face warmed at her agreeing to an escort.

"What do you think will happen if our plan works?" Lily asked as we walked our bikes down Port Lane. In no rush at all.

"I don't know. Riots." I laughed, but Lily kept quiet. "What do you think?"

"It could be hard. But then maybe it would settle. Maybe—"

"Maybe we could be friends at school, too?" I said, stopping myself from saying *more than friends.* I liked that thought.

"Maybe."

"Maybe." I took Lily's free hand, and the sparks flying almost shocked me. I had to let go, but not before catching a smile escaping Lily's serious gaze.

"Eugene thinks we can change this place. You believe him?"

"I don't know. You know Eugene better than me. Did you two—"

"Long time ago." She looked away.

I wanted to pry. She was only seventeen, so what was a long time ago? Were they serious before? Why did it end? A thousand questions bounced in my mind. I swallowed them up as Lily hopped on her bike. I couldn't tell if she was worried about being late or if she had had enough talk about Eugene. After a half a mile, she slowed her pace.

"You should stop over there. It'll be safer." Lily waved her hand at me to say goodbye.

I hadn't been this far into the woods before, but I wanted to get closer to her home. "That yours?"

"Yeah. Don't worry—it's just a handful of people."

A group of white people were yelling and making noise on Lily's front lawn. I shook my head at her, letting her know I had no intention of leaving.

"Have it your way," she huffed. "We can cut through some neighbors' yards to get to the back."

We weaved down the street to a small strip of lots that hadn't been developed yet. Soon there would be properties, flyers made for home sales. I bristled, knowing how bad the fight for integrated housing could get.

We rode over dirt roads and made our way to a construction area that blocked us from view.

"This better?"

Lily nodded, then got off her bike. This time I made sure we didn't have bikes in between us as we walked at a snail's pace. We caught each other's glances when our shoulders were touching.

I stopped. Lily did too, as she looked out to her backyard. I'd kissed girls before, but I'd never met a girl like Lily, and it made me nervous. I also had this feeling that I wouldn't be able to take back this moment. That if I kissed her, I'd be unable to physically ignore her at school. I'd need to be by her side, walk her to class. I looked away, hurting inside because all I wanted was Lily. Before I could change my mind, Lily reached toward me as she leaned her bike along a pole, and I put my kickstand down. I was caught up in her so much that there was no other possible use of my arms but to hold them around her.

Lily lifted her head, and it was like the universe was pulling me to her; I was unable to resist my own destruction. My lips touched hers. Everything in my body radiated, like an electric cord was at the tip of my tongue. Then we paused, slightly pulling apart before crashing into each other again, lips moving together. Arms fumbling to hold each other. I reached for her face to hold it so close to mine, careful not to make a mess of this moment, but desperately wanting her to know I didn't want to stop. She pulled away, and I felt like my chest was ripping apart; then she rushed back to me, leaving me undone. Unable to fight any remnants of reasons we shouldn't be together. Lily tugged on me one more time, and I could feel that our morning was ending.

"I have to go," Lily said.

"I know."

We repeated these words, walking. Until we were practically in Lily's backyard.

"Now you have to go." Lily playfully shoved my chest. "My little sister probably has her head out the window, waiting for me to arrive."

I took a breath, in a trance as she made her way to her back door. She placed her bike next to the steps, then tapped quietly for her family to let her in. When her mom opened the door, I ducked out of sight and jumped on my own bike, racing to Vernon Realty. My chest beat hard, my mind occupied with what I needed to do in order to see her more. Tear up Mr. Vernon's office for anything I could use against him to help Heritage and Levittown become more like Concord Park. Then I could see Lily Baker every day.

CHAPTER 18

AT VERNON REALTY, SHARON WENT OVER MY SCHEDULE FOR THE DAY, but I couldn't help letting my gaze go to Barbara. Working with someone else who was Black was an easy way to be outed, which was why I didn't tell my father about her.

I watched Barbara throughout the day, how she'd come from the back when a Black customer entered for an appointment, and how she'd quickly usher them out of sight. At three p.m. she packed up her things and tilted her head, saying goodbye. Nervously, I prepared myself to speak to her, but anxiety clenched my throat, as I feared I might inadvertently offer a warm greeting that seemed too familial.

When I was getting ready to finish up my shift, three white men entered the office. I wasn't sure, but they looked like the same men who'd been in the school office on Lily's first day. I gulped hard; typically, it was families who visited Vernon Realty.

"Can I help you?" My voice shook. "We're closing up now."

"Got a meeting with Mr. Vernon."

"He'll be here shortly, running late," Sharon added behind me.

Sharon walked the men to the open back room, where a long table stood that we typically used for lunch breaks. I watched them as they whispered, glancing at me, before launching into their business.

Sharon paced, checking her watch. After fifteen minutes, she turned to me.

"Think you can do me a favor?"

"Yes, ma'am."

"I need to get dinner ready for my family." She twisted her fingers. "You see, my husband won't let me keep this job if I don't have dinner ready by six. Can you stay? Get these documents to Mr. Vernon?"

"Of course," I said.

Sharon's ask was emblematic of Levittown. Around Vernon Realty, these messages were in all the materials highlighting the kind of life you were promised. Illustrations of women dressed in heels, parading around the kitchen and doing laundry, ready to greet their husbands home from work. Erased were the women who'd worked during the war. For Sharon, working was something she wanted to do but needed permission for.

I had noticed the Levittown effect on my mother. She didn't seem to know what to do with herself. At first she'd been busy setting up the house, but in a brand-new house there is only so much you can do. Several times when I was coming home, Mom was waiting by the window. I could sense her relief not only for me being home safe but so she wasn't alone anymore.

When Sharon left, I sat at her desk, which was cleared except for a couple of folders for Mr. Vernon, a notepad, and three pens. There was nothing personal.

I tapped my fingers on the folders, curiosity building because they weren't labeled like the other Vernon Realty folders I'd been handling since I started.

I couldn't help myself. First I nudged the top folder. When the papers finally slid partway out, I opened it.

I filtered through the papers and read the documents. A signed letter from the National Association of Real Estate Boards caught my interest.

> The Brown v. Board of Education *decision will have significant impact on the sales of real estate. To avoid financial implications and ensure confidence in the market, it will be imperative that properties shown to customers not disrupt the balance of the neighborhood. The Federal Housing Administration will not underwrite mortgages that have risk of incompatible racial groups living in the same communities. Note that while* Shelley v. Kraemer *required the change of NAREB Article 34 of the Code of Ethics, we continue to follow our professional obligation to never show a property to a member of a race or nationality whose presence will be detrimental to property values. Please utilize the*

attached map of redline districts for your area to avoid
profit impacts from sales to non-white clients.

My mouth dropped open. I recovered, then searched through the second folder, rushing because this was exactly what I needed to bring back to Sojourner. I looked closely at a letter written on Levitt & Sons letterhead by the developer of the Levittowns in Pennsylvania and New York. In plain black-and-white, he stated that the company had been charged for being out of compliance. But it wasn't a letter outlining how to change—it was a how-to guide for operating while they managed any legal concerns. Step one: direct all inquiries by Black residents to a designated set of offerings just outside the Levittown neighborhoods. I scoffed. Barbara's role had started six months ago, exactly at the time of this letter. The *Brown v. Board* ruling wouldn't make a difference in a place like Levittown. Not when the government, the banks, the real estate agents, were all working hand in hand to make sure their communities stayed white.

I was ready to stop looking when I pulled out a document on school district letterhead.

We must not elicit violence or any front-page news
by restricting entrance. There are other means to
dissuade colored students from entering our schools.
Our efforts toward developing a Levittown Association
are underway. Visits to the home have been a big
recruitment strategy of like-minded individuals. Many

are willing to be present round the clock at the homes of potential students.

—Michael Vernon, Vernon Realty

I heard an engine and looked up to see Mr. Vernon exiting his car. With shaky hands I neatly tucked the documents back in the folders.

Mr. Vernon shared a brief greeting before scanning for Sharon.

"She's having me lock up." I stood up. "You have guests in the back."

"Good. Those for me?"

I couldn't speak—I just touched the folders.

Mr. Vernon smiled, then picked up the folders and sorted through the papers. My head spun; I was close to passing out as profuse sweat ran down my brow.

"You can go now." Mr. Vernon walked past me, dropped one of the folders onto his desk, and headed to the back.

I couldn't help but wonder which folder Mr. Vernon had chosen for his meeting—the letter from NAREB or Levitt & Sons. I picked up my things and made my way to Mr. Vernon's desk as he greeted the three men. On top was the NAREB letter. I turned, watched the men, and listened closely.

"Relax," Mr. Vernon said to a tall, heavyset man. "We can't cause chaos. It'll hurt my business, and an officer of the law can't be seen to be involved. The meeting went fine yesterday. I'm sure we'll be okay. Everyone's on board to let us handle it."

I stayed still, straining to listen. Then the room went silent.

Mr. Vernon turned around and looked at me.

"Good night, sir. Locking up now."

Mr. Vernon waved, and I left with unsteady feet.

I rushed out the door and bumped into Alex. I'd forgotten he offered to swing by and get me if he was around when my shift ended.

"You waited for me," I said, gathering my bike.

"You okay?" Alex said.

"I think I'm coming down with something."

"Put your bike in the back, come on."

"Thanks." I shoved my bike in the back of his car, feeling shaky, wishing I had been able to stay and catch Mr. Vernon's conversation.

We rode about halfway home before Alex spoke. "This is different."

I could see a smile tugging at the corner of Alex's mouth.

"What?" I asked, intrigued, wanting to know more about Alex.

"I've just never been in the car this long without someone speaking."

"You weren't talking." I squinted my eyes, trying to catch what was on his mind.

"I've been giving Ben a ride all around town for a year, and I forgot what silence sounded like."

My smile loosened. "What's it feel like?"

"Good. No, great," Alex said. "I can hear myself think."

"I'll be sure to stay silent the rest of the ride."

"No." Alex put his hand out toward me. "I don't mind it. But refreshing for a moment."

"I get it."

"Ben's great, don't get me wrong."

"He is. . . . But he's a lot."

"Yeah. He can be. What do you do for fun?" Alex said.

I paused. I wanted to tell him the truth, the actual truth. "I hate football."

"That why you don't go to the games?"

"Yeah." I looked away, then said, "I'm a baseball fan."

"I hate sports." Alex's shoulders relaxed a bit. "But I don't mind hanging out at games."

"What do you like to do, then?"

"You're gonna laugh," Alex said.

I sat up, leaning closer to the dashboard. "I promise."

Alex was quiet, but I waited him out. "Comic books. I used to collect them."

"That's not weird."

"No? Ben always gives me a hard time."

"I play jazz," I said out loud before I could pull it back. I waited for the sky to collapse. For things to turn on me like Dad had said they would.

"Really? That's cool. You should join the band."

I nodded. Still expecting something to change between us. For a question to lead us down a rabbit hole.

"You like working for Vernon Realty?" Alex said with an edge he seemed to fight covering.

"It's fine."

"What's your work schedule?"

I hesitated, unsure if I should share my schedule in case it got back to my dad.

"It changes all the time. When I'm needed."

Alex pulled up to my house, and Mr. Vernon couldn't leave my mind. I wanted answers about what Mr. Vernon was up to and about what had happened to the previous owners of our house.

"What really happened here, Alex?"

He looked away.

"Alex. I live here, you know. I'd rather hear it from you."

Alex turned back to me and swallowed hard. "It started almost a year ago. With the house being sold under Mr. Vernon's nose to a Black family, the Sampsons. There was outrage, crowds of neighbors every day. Then Mr. Vernon called a meeting, said that's not how he'd handle it."

"Was the whole town angry?"

"Not the whole town," Alex said. "But enough. The angriest were the loudest. A few families helped the Sampsons clean up all the trash that kept getting thrown on their yard. Some neighbors started a group of community meetings to support them." Alex took a long pause; I clenched my fists nervously. "My dad was one of the people who tried to help the Sampsons."

I looked at him, my eyes tearing in relief that he hadn't joined in. He wasn't like the people at Trumbull Park.

"What about the Freemens and the other neighbors?"

Alex looked up, gripping the steering wheel. "They all

watched it happen. Started a fire that burned up the yard. The only thing that stopped it from burning down the house was the neighbors worried about it catching onto theirs."

"Then what happened?" I leaned in.

"Things got pretty serious after that. But in a different way. Like quiet. Neighbors shut the blinds and acted like they didn't see them. Then they were gone." Alex looked away and wouldn't meet my eyes.

"So they moved?"

"Mr. Vernon said they did." Alex looked away again.

"But you don't believe that."

"Not exactly." Alex paused. "I heard there was an accident. Mrs. Sampson was cleaning up the house after the fire, but she got hit by a car, in the middle of the day. No witnesses. Next thing you know, house was for sale, and you moved in."

My mouth dropped open. When Dad bought the house, he must have known about what had happened. But did my mom?

"I gotta go." Alex tapped at the steering wheel.

"Thanks, Alex. I mean it." I stepped out of the car.

"Calvin," Alex called out to me. "You can't tell anyone I told you. My dad's on a list Mr. Vernon keeps. We almost had to move."

I nodded. "I'll never say a word."

CHAPTER 19

SUNDAY MORNING, DAD DROVE ME TO WORK WITHOUT SAYING A WORD. It was as if he was silently demanding the truth from me. As he parked the car, a sense of urgency filled the air, and I instinctively made a move to jump out. Before I could act, his hand swiftly reached for my arm.

"Let me talk to you for a minute."

A cold wave of fear washed over me as I sat back in my seat. Dad probably knew everything.

"The last thing your mom needs is to worry about you," Dad said, his voice laced with concern and exhaustion. "You need to be safe. Stay outta trouble." His hand tightened its grip on my arm as if to emphasize the importance of his words.

"Yes, sir," I said, twisting in my seat.

"You've never caused us any, not like your brother."

The mention of Robert stirred a mix of emotions within

me. I wanted off this topic immediately. "She gonna try church again?"

Another Sunday had passed without a whisper from Mom about getting ready for church, as if the mere thought of it had vanished from her mind.

"I don't know." With a sigh, he continued, his words punctuated by deliberate pauses. "Just don't think she's ready. . . . She's been invited to a few other churches, but . . . we'll see."

Passing in front of God's sanctuary was a lie too much for Mom to keep. The absence of praising like she'd known all her life was like playing my trumpet without the finger buttons.

I watched my dad, thinking about what I'd learned about Mr. Vernon. About the Sampsons.

"Do you know much about the house before we bought it?"

"Before . . ." Dad took a long pause. "Nothing, really. Just had our name on a list, and we got it. Pretty quickly, too."

"You ever wonder about that?" I prod again.

"Wonder?"

"Just . . . at Mr. Vernon's there are a lot of people interested in homes, and it seems competitive."

"Told you. An army buddy helped me. Besides, Mr. Vernon usually sells new plots. He only brokered the deal with the house—it was a resale."

I studied him. He'd known. He'd had to. A white army buddy got Dad the VA loan and happened to get him connected to a house previously owned by a Black family. But if my dad was so desperate to move us to Levittown, why would he take that kind of risk in a home already under scrutiny?

"You just make a good impression with Mr. Vernon."

I left Dad's heavy words, wondering if he was using me as a cover so Mr. Vernon wouldn't suspect anything about us. Or, worse, maybe Mr. Vernon had only hired me to get close to our family. To not get fooled again.

As soon as I entered Vernon Realty, I was greeted by Sharon.

"Oh good, you're here," she said. "Today's another busy day! I'm going to need you to greet customers and usher any of Barbara's customers to the back as soon as you see them." I nodded as she went through the sign-up sheet, then gathered the list of tours and materials.

After an hour, the walk-ins slowed down like usual. I'd refilled a pot of coffee while looking at the list of names of people who had signed up to visit homes.

I filled a cup of coffee, adding sugar and cream like I'd seen Barbara do. Then I made my way to the back office. I approached the door, which was slightly ajar. Barbara was biting down on her pen, reviewing the two applications that had come in for her. Stacked in the corner were the bathroom cleaning supplies and rolls of toilet paper.

"I refilled the pot," I said, and held out the cup to her. "I used the last bit of cream. We'll have to get more."

Barbara looked a few years younger than my mom. She was the kind of woman I could see in my old neighborhood. But when she looked back at me, I knew the feeling wasn't mutual.

"I . . ." Barbara hesitated.

She looked like she was weighing her options. Levittown wasn't the kind of place where kindness was created for her, but for her to deny a drink could be offensive.

"That's okay," I said. "I can drink it if you don't want it."

"Thank you, Calvin. I'll have some." She studied me more, like she wasn't even blinking. But then in a flash she was back to normal.

"Slow today." I pointed to her papers as she took the cup of coffee from me. I'd made a promise to Eugene and Lily that I'd try to get information to help them. And if anyone knew something suspicious was going on, it would have to be Barbara.

"Slow every day. These will probably get denied by the bank." She waved the applications. "I'm surprised I still have a job, but I . . ."

Barbara didn't finish. She didn't have to.

"Well, at those prices, I'm not sure how he expects to make sales," I said. "If he'd offer the new developments in Levittown, there would be plenty of buyers." I wanted her to know what I really believed.

"You're an interesting young man." Barbara turned her lips up and studied me again. "Where you say you from?"

I hesitated. "Illinois."

"Illinois, huh. What part?"

"Ch-Chicago, ma'am." I looked away.

"Hmm." She took a sip of her coffee, but before she could speak, the bell above the front door rang.

I greeted a white customer out front, going over the lay-outs of the homes I'd studied. I could feel myself bouncing around, itching for them to leave so I could talk to Barbara more. Finally, they settled on an appointment with Mr. Ver-non to visit the property site, leaving with an application in hand.

It was only a few minutes before the bell rang again. I perked up when a Black couple entered. I raced to greet them before Barbara could get out of her seat.

Barbara smirked, enjoying the rebellious side of me, but the moment was short-lived as she shut the door behind her.

With no one at the front entrance, I passed Sharon's desk and settled in Mr. Vernon's seat. I felt a pull to learn more. If what I'd found yesterday had been out in the open, what was hidden away?

I searched through each drawer. At first cautiously, then greedily, as I counted down the minutes before Barbara would be done. But there was nothing out of the ordinary. Even the folder from the previous night was gone.

I watched the office door. If she kept her typical length of meeting times, I had a good twenty minutes.

I passed the office, walking through to the back room where Mr. Vernon had held his late-night meeting. The filing cabi-nets were stacked neatly together. I held my breath as I opened the first drawer and ran my fingers over folders. Searching for something, anything. But all I could find was loan applica-tions and signed documents.

The files were arranged by year, then alphabetical. I searched through the drawers, which yielded nothing, until I got to the bottom file cabinet. Locked.

I caught my breath and tugged at the drawer to make sure it was locked and not just hitched wrong.

Without hesitation, I rushed to Mr. Vernon's desk, where I had found a small set of keys I was hoping I'd find a use for. My heart thumped hard, panic rising, but I knew this was my shot. I snatched the keys and slid past the office, no longer caring if Barbara opened the door. I tried each key, waiting for a fit. Success on the fourth try.

The files were like the others, but in the very back, I found the two folders Mr. Vernon had received from Sharon yesterday. With shaky hands, I grabbed for more files, pulling them out and deciding to put them on the table so I could keep things organized.

I almost gave up, until I found a brightly colored folder with the heading INTEGRATION.

Inside, chicken-scratch handwriting on a piece of paper. At the bottom of the folder, a stack of white index cards caught my eye. Mr. Vernon's talking points, held neatly together by a blue rubber band.

I studied each word, things circled and underlined. My gaze stopped on the third note card: *Our last resort will be to push them out of their home however necessary.* The word *necessary* was double underlined.

Those were tactics I knew all too well. The veins in my neck tightened. Violence was in the air you breathed in Trumbull Park; you could suck it down with each inhale. Here in

Levittown, it was covert. No repercussions from breaking the law because there was no one to enforce it.

The rest of the note cards were filled with warnings to not draw attention. These carefully crafted words sanctioned actions as a business decision, nothing to do with race.

I flipped the last card over. *Sampson home, 1954.*

The ringing of a bell jerked me to attention—then Sharon's laugh, joined by Mr. Vernon's boisterous voice. I hurriedly threw the materials together, stacking the note cards. My brain was sluggish, unable to remember the order of the files. My heartbeat thrummed in my ears. At the sound of footsteps, I pushed the drawer closed, but it kept hitching, since the files were sloppily put back together. I gave it one last shove.

As I reached for the keys, I felt a shadow. A tingle ran up my spine.

Barbara stood watching with her arms crossed.

My mouth hung open, but my words stuck in my throat.

"Found him yet?" Mr. Vernon called.

Barbara hesitated before speaking. "He's finishing up in the restroom, sir."

Barbara waved her hands for me to join Mr. Vernon. I wanted to lock the drawer, but then I'd have to explain what I was doing with the keys. I left them out in the open on the table and headed to the front office. When I turned, I watched Barbara lock the files and pocket the key.

I waited for the sky to fall. For Barbara to pull Mr. Vernon aside. By the last hour I was pale and sweating, but Barbara never said a thing as the room cleared or as she returned the keys to Mr. Vernon's desk.

At the end of my shift, I said goodbye, forcing the shake in my voice to sit buried in my throat as I gave Barbara a ghastly smile before turning away.

CHAPTER 20

OVER THE NEXT FEW WEEKS, I WAS IN A HOLDING PATTERN WAITING FOR the CORE meeting in Virginia. Eugene emphasized that my job was to gather information. But at work, Barbara had her eye on me. We never spoke about her covering for me. It was understood that she'd keep this a secret. But also that I'd better not do it again. I knew I needed to act like everything was normal, but I couldn't let go of the churning feeling in my gut that Heritage wasn't safe. My roller coaster of emotions was at the mercy of someone whispering Emmett's name. I didn't like the power that held over me. What pulled me to school was Lily. How we'd kissed. How she'd kissed me back. For the first time I felt like passing didn't matter. That she wasn't going to hold it against me. But our chances to be together were getting fewer and fewer, so she was what lifted me at school—even if we couldn't speak.

I weaved down the hallway, floating on that high I got

seeing her each school day. At my locker, I met Ben and Alex, who had ridiculous grins on their faces.

"What?" I said.

"Nothing." Ben shrugged, fighting off the goofy look that grew.

Seconds later, Mary joined us, and before I could find an excuse to run off to class with my friends, Ben and Alex scattered.

"Haven't talked to you in a while," Mary said.

"Yeah. I've been busy with work and school; it feels like I don't have any time to myself."

"Hmm. Well, I'm sure the dance will be a nice break." Lily walked by behind her, and I couldn't help but immediately smile, thinking about Eugene and Harry putting on a dance in the barn that same night. Lily would be there.

"Calvin."

I shook my head, brought back down to earth.

"Yeah . . . the dance. Should be fun." I nibbled on my lip, thinking through approaches for how to use the dance as a way to sneak to Virginia.

"Who are you going with?" Mary leaned on the locker next to mine.

I looked up at her, catching sight of Ben and Alex standing off in the distance watching us. Giggling like a couple of schoolkids. Then it hit me. She was waiting for me to finally ask her to the dance.

"Um, no." I felt my face drain. "I hadn't really thought about it. I mean, I'm not even sure I can go."

"Oh, come on." She tapped my shoulder. "You have to go. Everyone goes."

"I . . ." My brain froze, and under my shirt I felt clammy and hot.

"Let's go together. I'll pick you up at seven. We could do dinner, or meet up with Ben and Alex and their dates."

"I . . . er . . . um . . ."

Before I could answer, we both turned to look at a commotion across the hall. In the middle was Lily, circled by a bunch of boys. I slammed my locker and left Mary behind.

"Where you going?" Mary called after me.

Darren led the group circling Lily. The boys were chanting and teasing; she was bouncing around like a Ping-Pong ball as she tried to break the circle. Lily bumped into Ben accidentally, and he bounced her back into the circle, looking at Darren for approval.

I whipped my head around, searching for someone to step in. Dad's warnings whirled in my brain. I looked for a teacher to call out the rowdy classmates who weren't following Levittown's sacred rules, but no one was there. And everything inside me shouted the truth: They ran to Levittown to get away from Lily. From me. And nothing about picket fences and backyards was going to tell me different. Teachers conveniently locked in their classrooms. Bystanders all around. A utopia only for some.

I pushed my way through the growing crowd.

"Just let me go," Lily cried out.

She held her books firmly to her chest. Darren swiped her hand down, sending books flying everywhere. Lily dropped to the floor to pick them up. I stepped closer and caught her eye, saw the tears held at the cup of her lid. I scrambled next to her, helping her gather her books up. We didn't meet eyes as I piled them tightly together.

"Lily," I whispered.

Lily didn't answer. She kept her gaze on Darren as she snatched the books from my hands.

The crowd began to break up. At first I thought the incident was over, but then I recognized Miss Brower rushing down the hallway, shaking her keys to catch everyone's attention.

"What's going on here?" Miss Brower said.

Lily didn't answer. I stepped forward, but she shook her head, warning me to stay out of it. Reluctantly, I stepped back, until I caught Darren's grin—he knew he'd get away with harassing her.

"Why don't you tell her, Darren?" I said.

"What?" Darren's eyes went wide. "It's my fault she's clumsy?"

A few chuckles released from the crowd of kids. Ben included. My veins burned in anger.

"Get on to class," Miss Brower said. "All of you."

No one moved.

"Now." She raised her voice, and with the snap of her finger, everyone got going.

"Lily," Miss Brower said, "did someone bother you?"

Lily shook her head. Her body was trembling. You couldn't look at her and not know she was terrified and angry, all swirled together.

"I tripped," Lily said. "Not feeling well. I'm going to check in with the nurse."

I looked at Miss Brower, ready to tell her everything. Miss Brower had a flash of pity cross her face, but Lily didn't wait for permission; she was already halfway down the hall as the final first-period bell rang.

"Calvin." Miss Brower touched my shoulder. "Please tell the class to read chapters five to seven on their own."

"Yes, ma'am," I said.

"Tell them . . . tell them if I even hear a peep down the hall, everyone's writing a ten-page paper on the subject of my choosing. Put it on the board."

"Yes, ma'am."

Miss Brower followed Lily.

I stepped into class, shaking so much I could barely repeat Miss Brower's request. I wanted to follow Lily into the nurse's office, like on her first day.

As I stood at the front of the classroom, eyes bored into me. I fumbled, repeating the assignment, then writing out the exact chapters, underlining the ten-page-paper threat. I kept my head high, like I was Lily. The class followed my lead.

Miss Brower didn't return. I went to my next class, hoping to catch Lily in the hallways, but she was nowhere to be found. During lunch, I walked the aisles between the tables, searching. She was nowhere.

By my last class, I'd given up.

I watched the clock like a hawk, waiting for school to be over. When the bell rang, I wanted to rush out of school and search for Lily, but I knew better. She had left long ago. She wasn't going to be waiting for me behind the trees. So I did the next best thing and knocked on Miss Brower's classroom door.

"Yes," Miss Brower said with a voice that bled exhaustion.

I pushed the door ajar. My walk was as heavy as the weight of the secrets being kept inside me.

"Is she okay?" I whispered.

Miss Brower put her papers down and leaned back in her chair.

"What happened this morning?" She studied me.

"Lily didn't tell you?"

"No. She didn't."

I paused. This was Lily's story to tell, but not speaking up for her felt wrong. I was one of Heritage's "own" as far as they knew, and if I couldn't stand up for her, in this place of privilege, then I wasn't worthy of her anyway.

"I walked in late," I said. "But there was a crowd around her, and Darren . . . he was blocking her from entering class."

We both fell silent. My words caught in my throat.

"Lily went home today." Her voice shook.

I looked up with blurry eyes, studying Miss Brower.

"She shouldn't be the one to have to go home," I said. "It should be Darren. Ben. Anyone who harassed her."

"Did you attend an integrated school before?"

I shoved my hands in my pockets and stared out the window before answering.

"Mostly segregated there, too." I looked away.

"This community isn't ready for change. There are a lot

of people fighting to keep things the way they are," Miss Brower said.

"Why can't we still make it change? Just because people don't want it doesn't mean you have to let the behavior go."

"I'm afraid this town just isn't ready."

"What about you? You don't follow the Levittown prototype." I pointed to the fact that she wore pants instead of dresses.

"That's different. Women have been waiting a long time for this—half this town is women. We'll push our rights here, make changes. Let them see that women are just as good as men. One day people will also be ready for integration."

"Lily's a woman. Half the town going to support her equal rights?" I knew the answer. I just wanted her to say it. For her to realize what she was saying.

"Lily is bright. I told her just as much. But being here could end up hurting her if she wants to go to college. It's better if she finishes out in her neighborhood and goes off to college and makes a difference there."

I bit my tongue. She wanted Lily to wait to be treated fairly. She knew it was wrong, but she also wasn't willing to go beyond her own fight.

"Lily's brave," I spat out.

"I'm afraid Lily won't be enough. She'll need a lot more support. I'm sure by the time you have kids, things will be better." She gave me a righteous smile, like I should be satisfied with her answer. And I was certain other people would have been. But I could never.

I swallowed hard because I wanted to say more. She wanted to wait an entire generation. I couldn't wait that long.

"You're a good kid, Calvin. I've seen the way you look out for Lily. Being the new kid must be hard, but saying this kind of stuff can get you in trouble in this town. It's not normal."

I'd thought Miss Brower would be the one I could confide in. The propaganda films replayed in my mind: *Be popular. Fit in. Blend in.* Disappear.

I'd been so close to telling Miss Brower the truth. She had been the only one looking out for Lily, but even she didn't think Lily belonged. She wanted Lily to finish up elsewhere. Try somewhere else, not stain the *perfect* Levittown community that she lived in. I didn't like that plan. And I was ready to prove her wrong. Prove that it wasn't just white women who deserved their rights. I'd get the evidence from Mr. Vernon's files that everything they'd been doing was illegal. Then I'd get the registration papers to Eugene. Get all of Sojourner and anyone within the area to fill out this half-empty brand-new school.

CHAPTER 21

MY GRANDMOTHER USED TO SAY THERE WERE PEOPLE TIED TO A DES-
tiny. That life was threaded around so tight that once you'd set
on a path, it was almost impossible to pull away from it. In our
family, that thing was grief. Never untangled enough to find
a way out to the light. Her voice knotted into my chest at the
end of a painfully long week. Lily hadn't returned to Heritage.
Or to the trail. Not even to our tree stump hidden by a thicket
of trees.

The truth hit me hard: Lily wasn't coming back.

When my parents were asleep, I called the Sojourner house,
searching for ways to drop Lily's name to James. To Robert.
Even to Eugene, who quickly cut me off, either from irritation or because he wanted to move to the topic of Virginia.
We were a week away from the CORE meeting, and I hadn't
gathered anything more substantial than that first file I'd read.

I danced around his questions like he danced around mine.

Finally, we landed in the same place. If I wanted Lily back at Heritage, I needed to help Eugene and finally secure a cover so I could go to Virginia for the meeting. A path that would lead us to something we both wanted. But when I spoke, I could hear my grandmother's whispered warnings.

I was riddled with guilt when I asked Alex for a ride to work Saturday and promised we could hang out after. Using someone was against everything I believed in. And Alex was the only person, other than Lily, who I felt safe with at Heritage.

Alex arrived promptly at nine a.m., greeting my parents as he stepped inside our home. My mother closed her robe tight before pouring a cup of coffee for Dad.

"Sure you don't want any breakfast?" Mom nudged me again.

"I'll grab some toast to take with me."

"All right, then. Have a good day at work." Mom paused. "Alex, you sure your parents don't mind having Calvin over for dinner after?" Her voice was light, but the question sounded strange coming from her.

"They don't mind at all."

"Maybe I could even stay over sometime?" The words slipped out of my mouth, my voice slightly shaky. "Or here."

"Yeah. Of course," Alex said.

Mom almost overpoured her cup of coffee, but she nodded.

I needed that seed planted, and it landed perfectly. My parents were forced to act like it was no big deal.

The office was busy, with a line of people waiting to get them-selves on the showing list. Sharon had me pass out clipboards with forms to fill out. I couldn't help but notice that I'd yet to see Barbara come out of the office. I occupied the time talk-ing to customers, pointing out where people could wait before they reviewed the plans. Once Sharon and Mr. Vernon col-lected all the paperwork, the office quieted as they prepared to go to the first showing.

"Calvin, I'm gonna need you to lock up," Mr. Vernon said. "I've got a meeting after work, so I need to head straight there."

"Sure. Should I stay later? I'm on until three p.m."

"It should be quiet. Right, Sharon?"

"Should be."

"Close up at three, then. Just make sure Barbara leaves with one box."

I nodded, confused. As soon as the door shut, I rushed to the back office, knocking until Barbara answered.

"Come in," she said quietly.

I opened the door slowly, not sure where to start. Barbara was packing up the trinkets that typically took up her desk.

"You leaving?" I bit my lip.

"Don't need me anymore. Got the boot."

"What? No way. What about the customers?"

"Black customers are no longer welcome at Vernon Realty. I'm supposed to cancel these applications and take my things and go."

"Since when?" Instinctively, I looked out the door toward where I'd broken into the files. Then I blinked quickly, looking to Barbara.

"Since a girl from one of the homes I helped sell near the Concord Park community wasn't dissuaded from attending Heritage."

"Lily Baker?"

"You've heard the name?"

I know her.

"Got a class with her. What's that got to do with you, though?" I pressed my hands on her desk, desperate for answers. I hadn't seen Lily in days, and hoped this was a sign she was coming back.

"Well, for some reason Mr. Vernon didn't realize these homes here were districted to Heritage. A little loophole." Barbara smiled like she'd known all along.

She pointed along the map on her desk. It covered the outline of homes just along the Capewoods, where Lily lived.

"These are Levitt and Sons homes?"

"No," Barbara said. "Mr. Vernon can fire me, but he's not going to stop the sale of these houses outside the properties he represents."

"Well, if he doesn't sell those houses, then who will?" I said.

"There are a few agencies. Clayborn and Sons. They hire a Black and white staff and don't sell in Levittown. They also sell exclusively for Morris Milgram, the developer of Concord Park."

"My father works there," I said, confused. Dad was helping build up an integrated community, yet he chose to live in Levittown instead?

"Hmm." Her eyebrows rose.

"What?"

"Does that explain what you were doing in those files over there? A little infiltration?"

"I—uh—"

"You know what, don't tell me." She stacked more papers. "I'm in trouble enough."

"What do you know about their plans to stop integration?" I leaned in closer. "Do you have anything to prove they're doing illegal things?"

She took a long pause. "What trouble are you up to?"

"Is there something in his files that would make it hard for Mr. Vernon to keep doing what he's doing?" I lowered my voice. "If it got into the wrong hands, that is."

"Stay out of that business." Barbara leaned over the box. "Whatever you're up to, that's the last thing you should be doing. You are too young to be caught up in something like this."

Barbara studied me up and down. I could see her looking over my features—she knew the truth about me. She had to.

"What about near Lily's neighborhood? Any other loopholes?" I pointed to the map, circling my finger around the Capewoods, which sat between Levittown and the Concord Park development. "Tell me about here."

"The Capewoods? Well, you're full of all kinds of surprises. You hearing haunting lore at your white school?"

The way she said "white school" made the hairs on the back of my neck stand up. Like she'd purposefully said that to call me out.

"Something like that."

"Every piece of land has history, Calvin. This is part of the Lenapehoking, the land of the Lenape people, who were the indigenous people here. But this land is also known as the site of several Underground Railroad stations. Long ago, a massacre occurred by slave catchers in the Capewoods. Right near that church, where everyone thought they were safe."

I remembered what Robert had said about the Quakers owning the schoolhouse. I followed Barbara's hand as she pointed to the church and explained where there might be hidden tunnels. "I couldn't let that land be taken up by people who wouldn't appreciate that history. So I stomached working here and used all my connections to process whatever paperwork I could."

"What about the Sampsons?" I couldn't help but tie this conversation back to me, to my house.

"The Sampsons?" Barbara sat down, and I sat across from her. "You know about them?"

"Not much. Other than that my dad bought their house."

"Is that what has you trying to go through files? You want to figure out your neighborhood secrets?"

"What really happened?"

"They were chased out. I started working here shortly afterward."

"Why?"

"I needed a job." Barbara laughed. When I didn't respond, her voice turned serious. "Black people needed homes, and I wanted to make sure they weren't run out of this community. I convinced Mr. Vernon that homes near the Capewoods were a good option for selling to Black families. He didn't look into details of districting—just assumed it would make the Concord Park developer have a hard time convincing white folks to buy there."

I studied the map of Pennsylvania, plotted out to show who could live where. Barbara had outlined the sections where she could confirm sales for Black families and the areas that Mr. Vernon and Sharon could sell for white families. No color code marked the acres of Capewoods that went untouched.

"You think it's haunted?" I pointed to the undeveloped land.

"Anything that old will have echoes of history, if it was bad enough. I think they want us to think it's haunted. So we don't pass the line to the other side of town. It's so close, one day it'll become part of either the Black side of town or—"

"The white side."

She nodded.

"So the Capewoods will stay untouched."

"Until they can't build out anymore. Eventually it'll be owned by somebody—for now it's vagrants. People caught in between who can't own but grew up near that land."

"What do you think Mr. Vernon's going to do about the Black people who bought homes near there?"

Barbara stood, thinking over something as she bit at her lip.

"What is it?" I wanted to know if she'd made a connection I hadn't yet.

"You've got a lot of questions for a seventeen-year-old white boy talking to a Black woman." She studied me again, casting a knowing look at my eyes and hair.

"I'm sorry I—"

"How about I pack up my things and just don't happen to pay attention to you rifling through those files again."

Before I could even answer, she carried her box to the front of the office. I followed her, then went into Mr. Vernon's desk to grab the key.

Barbara didn't even look up when I rushed back to the filing cabinets.

Once I was in the files, I took my time reading through more conspiratorial letters and notes. Talking about *Brown v. Board of Education* back in 1953 before the Supreme Court had made its decision. Detailed plans around how to stop integration because of worry it would slash the growth of property values, with examples from other communities that had fought off integration. I moved on to the files of Levitt & Sons, the developers of Levittown. They explicitly stated that the homes should be for whites only and gave detailed guidelines about how they'd navigate the law.

I skimmed through contract after contract. Every purchase requiring Vernon Realty not to sell their home to anyone non-white. The deception was so blatantly obvious that it didn't matter what legal policies were accepted at the federal level, because the developers, real estate agents, and bankers were plotting at the local level. Housing discrimination. Education discrimination. Levittown was white utopia disguised as an American dream.

Anger roiled inside me. With each file, I questioned if this would be enough to take to that CORE meeting in Virginia. I pulled out another folder. Inside were meeting flyers for the proposal of an association for Levittown. I'd heard the names before—they were the men who'd been there that night waiting for Mr. Vernon in his office, and at Heritage on Lily's first day. But this time I knew more about what they did in the community. An entire system committed to breaking the law to keep segregation.

The last file was called RESEARCH, its folders labeled with last names. It was like a case study with photos of families— opposition research. My mouth dropped when I read the last name Washington. Alex's last name. A photo of his family slipped out of the folder. Notes scribbled to the side questioned if their lineage was Jewish. Relief settled inside me that the case was marked CLOSED. Like they'd decided they couldn't prove it or were willing to let it go. As long as no one else found out.

I swiftly pulled out another paper with the name I'd been searching for: Sampson. It was all here: details of a partial house fire, and an apology note saying that Vernon Realty took care of it. The paperwork was dated 1955, a few months before we purchased our house.

I pulled the papers out and placed them in a brown paper bag, which I folded up and taped closed as if I'd received a package. Then I tidied up.

By 2:59 p.m., Barbara was long gone and I was already locking up and running to the record store to find Alex. Anger coursed through me, and I was eager to quit working at Vernon Realty, but I couldn't. The pressure to do something with this information tightened up on me.

CHAPTER 22

"I WAS THINKING." ALEX SAT ON HIS BEDROOM FLOOR, FUMBLING around with his words. "That time we were in the record store . . . You know Lily Baker . . . from school?"

"What about it?" I kept my gaze down, trying not to move.

"You just . . . I don't know. When you're around her, you're different."

"Different? What do you mean? Because I don't treat her badly like everyone else?"

"No. I mean yeah. But the way you look at her. Even when Darren was giving her a hard time. Your face, it was like . . . pained to see it. And in the record store you were smiling and talking to her, but then as soon as Ben and I got there—"

"Listen. I'm not sure where you're going with this, but where I'm from, there's not the kind of divide of Black and white like here. I'm used to seeing all types of people. . . ." I didn't know how I should describe my people. Negro. Colored. Black. I didn't know what white people said in public. "Out here it's, like, not okay to be different. You ever notice how everyone dresses the same? Drives the same car."

"Shops the same place. Talks the same way," Alex added.

This lightened the mood and we laughed, going back and forth talking about all the things that made Levittown strange, including the indoctrination movies at school.

"Where'd you grow up?" I wanted to know more about Alex.

"New York City," Alex said. "We moved right after the war."

"Do you go back?" I was glad we could shift our conversation away from Lily.

"I have a lot of family still there. We usually stay longer over holidays. . . ." Alex's voice trailed off.

I thought about the papers I'd carefully wrapped in a brown paper bag. Alex's family might be keeping a secret. Or just trying to fit in, like Ben. Like this entire town was emulating commercials and TV shows about what life was supposed to be like. It felt like we'd entered another dimension. A simulation.

I picked up Alex's copy of George Orwell's *1984* and flipped to a line I'd been memorizing. Repeating before I went to school.

> *And if all others accepted the lie which the Party imposed—if all records told the same tale—the lie passed into history and became truth.*

"You ever want to move back?" I leaned against the wall.

"I don't know." Alex shrugged. "My parents were always

working extra hours when we were in the city. Family moving in when in need. There was always something happening. I like the quiet."

I used to feel that way at my Aunt Vera's. After the war, money was tight, with rations restricting how much gas, sugar, supplies we could buy. We might have more space here. And money, but there was also a cost. And not everyone could have this life. Not Eugene. Harry. Or even Lily. The doors were still closed for them. Society could judge what happened abroad in the war. Our fighting against the Nazis should've tied us all together. But it was just used to craft a lie about who would get real freedom. A lie that had brought me here. A lie that was sucking the air from my lungs.

Alex pulled a shoebox filled with comic books out from under his bed, then placed them in between us. He flipped through *The Crypt of Terror.*

"This goes against our educational movie training," I chuckled, snatching the comic and flipping through the pages. "You like the dark stuff?" I made a gagging face, pointing to the zombie with a hollow eye socket on the cover.

"Try these." Alex searched through the bottom of his box and handed me another comic.

I slipped it out of its case. A 1941 story about Captain America punching a Nazi. Robert had had stacks of collections of these. All of it was lost in the fire.

"How many you got of these?"

"My dad got rid of a bunch before we moved here. But I kept some classics."

We flipped through pages, interrupting each other to share certain scenes.

"This one's a good one." Alex flashed a scene to me. A zombie herd practically jumping off the page.

"Aah, get that outta here." I slapped it to the floor, exaggerating. Then bending over laughing as Alex flung himself down, reenacting my gag reflex.

"It wasn't that bad," I said, laughing in between trying to be serious.

"Yeah, it was. I can't believe you were so grossed out. You should have seen your face."

"I was not."

"You were," he yelped. "Almost as bad as what your face does every time you see Mary Freemen." Alex was crying with laughter now. Showing me another one of my exaggerated terrified smiles. "'Hi, Mary. No, I'm busy.'" Alex's eyes widened, and his mouth flexed hard. "'No, Mary, this seat is taken.'"

"Stop." I couldn't even pretend it wasn't funny. My stomach jumped up and down as I gasped for air between fits of laughing, scolding him for parroting back our conversations.

"I'm sorry. I'll stop," Alex said sarcastically before screwing up his face. "'Mary, yeah, I'll be riding my bike.'"

"Okay. Okay. I get it. But she's my neighbor. I can't get away from her."

"So you going with her to the dance?"

"I thought I dodged that bullet. Is that a thing I should be prepared for her doing again?" I felt my face drain.

"You should practice the right response now." Alex made another gag face, then got up, pretending to be me dodging

Mary as he moved around his bed. I was in a fit of laughter again.

"Who you taking?" I paused, getting the courage to bring up the possibility of using him as a cover so I could leave for Virginia the next day.

"Allison. I asked on Friday. Ben is taking Melody."

"With the big head from first period?"

"No, the one with the small head." Alex threw a sock at me.

"I didn't mean it like that," I said. "I mean it's just a bit larger than average. She's got a great personality."

"I'll be sure to tell Ben."

I lunged for Alex to hit him on the arm but missed. Finally giving up, I took my seat on the floor.

"People usually have a date out here," Alex said. "Are you still going if you're solo?"

"Yeah, I'll join you." I gave a smile.

We joked around for another hour. When it was time to go, I knew I couldn't wait any longer to ask for a cover for the trip to Virginia next week.

"I hate to ask this, but if I go to the dance, can I stay at your place for the weekend?"

Alex gave me a puzzled look.

"It's just, my parents are strict. They have to leave early the next morning and will make me go with them. But if I stay with you . . . they'd let me go to the dance."

"Yeah, I'm sure it's fine. Me or Ben."

I bristled at the mention of Ben. There was no way I'd ever set plans to stay there, even if I was going to cancel last minute. I couldn't trust that Ben wouldn't say something to my parents.

"Just you," I said. "Can you ask if it's okay?"

"Of course." Alex squinted like he was thinking over what I had said. I almost spoke to cover my agitation at the mention of Ben, but Alex said, "Ben's been a jerk lately."

I nodded. "Has he always been like that? You know, think like that?" I couldn't say it. Didn't want Lily to be brought up again.

"Not always," Alex said. "He doesn't mean it. He's just trying to fit in."

"Are you okay with that? Like, having a friend that can change on you any minute."

"No. But if you don't have friends out here, it always brings up questions. Being an outsider isn't easy in a place like this."

I understood. I had my reasons for choosing the friends I made. But that wasn't what was getting me; it was the way Alex said it. He *needed* a friend for cover too, only I knew his secrets and not the other way around.

CHAPTER 23

I BUTTONED UP A WHITE COLLARED SHIRT AND FLUNG ON A DARK GRAY jacket that matched my slacks. An old outfit of Robert's he'd outgrown finally fit me well. My plan was in motion with Alex and Ben arriving with their dates for the dance. I'd planned to complain about being a fifth wheel and squeeze in the back— setting up my excuse to leave early for another ride home and ditch our overnight plans. My parents none the wiser that I was slipping out and making my way to Sojourner.

At the knock on the door, I smoothed down my hair one more time, being careful as I walked not to scuff my freshly shined shoes. Down the hall I heard a girl's voice speaking to my mother; I expected to catch a nervous smile from Alex or Ben as my parents interrogated them and their dates. But when I rounded the corner, Alex's face begged for forgiveness.

"There he is," Mom said. "I think Calvin left out the part about his date picking him up. So glad to see you."

"M-Mary," I stuttered out, on shaky legs. My eyes zipped between Alex and Ben. I dedicated my wrath to Ben, who practically floated with exhilaration at my discomfort.

"Gosh, Calvin. You look really handsome." Mary blushed.

"Thanks." My head was spinning. "You all look great," I said before my glance cut to Ben for a death glare.

Ben's face drained with the realization that his scheming plan had failed miserably. I was *not* pleasantly surprised. I felt a thrumming in my chest, and the tips of my ears burned hotter and hotter. It was one thing to ditch my friends with dates. It was a whole other thing to have Mary follow me around like a puppy dog when I had no interest in her at all. Especially when she already watched my every move.

"We'll be late." I urged them along so it wouldn't come up in conversation that my parents were not actually going out of town. I pointed in the direction of the door. Alex's car was parked outside, and Ben had his dad's car. I felt my plan blow up from the inside.

Allison and Melody joined Mary at the front door, whispering and giggling to each other. I passed Ben and tugged tightly at his arm in a death grip. "I will not forget this."

Ben began a chuckle that turned sour at my crushing squeeze. Then I headed for Alex's car.

When we got to the dance, we walked down the school halls, in lines of twos. It was becoming painfully obvious how much I would've stuck out as a fifth wheel. The smell of hairspray and fragrances slammed the air. Now my mind scraped at how not to alert my date when I made my early exit.

Tony Bennett's "Rags to Riches" played in the gym before

transitioning to "Shake, Rattle and Roll." But it wasn't the rendition by Big Joe Turner, who I'd watched on the show filmed at the Apollo at his release of the song last spring. The song had already been copied by white artists like Bill Haley and His Comets and Elvis Presley. This divide in music was too clear a reminder of race. Our churches were segregated. Our music, even when eerily sung the same way, was segregated.

By the entrance to the gym, I studied my classmates' style of dance. They'd tap their foot in place, step to the side, tap the other foot, then walk forward through a heavy swing. Spinning faster and faster. A few kids attempted to swing their partners over them. It was a quick and easy pickup for me; I'd known these moves, with slight differences, in Black dance halls.

The crowd roared when the next song was Bill Haley's "Rock Around the Clock."

"Come on. Let's dance." Mary dragged me across the floor. I tried to keep in the same pattern as everyone else, leaving out elements of flair that I'd usually relish doing to compete for girls' attention back home. I gave Mary one dance before returning to Ben and Alex.

Dean Martin's "That's Amore" was next, and a small crowd began belting.

"Come on, everybody!" Ben called out as he swayed. "'When the moon hits your eye like a big pizza pie, that's amore.'"

The crowd crooned, and I couldn't help but join in. Music always did that. Let everything dissipate. I flashed a big smile as Alex flung his arm around me, working to lighten my sour mood.

"'That's amore!'" Ben's voice shook longer at that line, and Alex and I were in stitches.

My laughter slowly faded as I caught Mary smiling at me. I knew I had to leave. I looked for an exit. But the music slowed down, and our once-crowded-together group morphed into couples, locking me in with nowhere to run but right into Mary.

"Young at Heart" played, by Frank Sinatra, an artist my father loved lately and I had begun to take a liking to. It felt like everyone was watching me. But it was just Mary.

Alex nudged me. "I'm sorry. It wasn't my idea. But it's not Mary's fault."

I swallowed and let my liking for the song warm me up a bit. What was an innocent dance? I thought of my father playing the LP in our living room. He'd corner my mother in the kitchen until she agreed to dance to my dad's new style of music. Everything and nothing about it reminded me of Chicago.

Mary pulled closer to me before I could make an excuse to run to the bathroom. She leaned in, so I took her hand and began a slow two-step. She took a long breath in, putting her head on my shoulder. I closed my eyes, pretending I was dancing with Lily. The next song rolled right after. I was ready to pull away, but Mary was locked on my shoulder.

"I was waiting for you to ask me." Mary's voice was soft. "I was surprised when Ben called, sharing you were too shy to. You looked surprised to see me; I almost thought it was a joke."

My face went hot. "No. I'm . . . I'm sorry. I didn't know you'd said yes." I bit my tongue, torturing myself for how easy lying had become.

She looked up at me. "Your eyes. They're such an interesting color of brown." She lifted a hand off my shoulder and twined her finger through the side of my hair.

I bristled at her touch, awakened like a porcupine ready to attack. I turned her quickly, so she'd hold on to me for balance and let go of what she thought was a passionate moment. My shoulder blades tightened, a tense pain running up and down my neck. I loosened my collar, trying to suck in more air.

"I'd like to do this again. Well, not the whole dance, but my weekends are always free." Mary kept a smile. "You're always busy, though. Late nights."

I held a tight smile, studying her eyes glistening. She was over the moon, and I was a wreck. I couldn't let her keep thinking there was something between us. The dance was one thing, but what about after?

"Mary, I have to be honest." I paused, bracing myself for how this would go. "I have interest in someone else. I think you're great. I really do."

"I feel stupid." Mary slowed, stopping in the middle of a crowd of swooning couples. "Why'd you let me keep going on and on?"

"This really doesn't have anything to do with you."

"Were you using me? To cover for you?" Her voice went cold and dry.

"I— What? I don't know what you mean."

"For that Lily girl. We see how you look at her. Ben's been saying you have a thing for her. Is that where you go out at night? When you come home late."

"What? No." I fumbled over my words, shaking. "Where did you get that idea?"

"I see the way you watch her. It's like your eye is always looking for her."

I dropped my hands from Mary's waist. She'd been watching me at school. The way she talked, she was disgusted.

"Because I'm dating someone else, you throw that at me? Make things up in your head as the reason why I'm not interested in you? Frankly, Mary, you're just not my type. I tried to go about it nicely, but to do this? To let the nasty ways of treating people make you feel like you're so much better than someone. Why would you even want to go out with me if you believed all that? If you're so disgusted by the thought, go with Ben." I stepped back, bumping into couples dancing.

She grabbed at my arm and whispered, "You're making a scene. I just thought maybe it was true."

I pulled her arm off me. "I'm leaving. Get a ride with Alex. I'll let him know."

I stormed off, a flush of hot and cold running across my face while I prayed that I'd never have to worry about Mary again.

I weaved through the crowd until I found Alex.

"I'm not staying." I leaned in close so his date wouldn't hear me.

"What? You have to," Alex hushed out to me. "What about staying at my house?"

"I've already told Mary. It won't work out. I have other plans tonight—don't tell Ben." I paused, gripping his arm, tight and desperate. "Don't tell my parents, either."

"How will you get home?"

"Don't worry, I've got a ride. I'll come by this weekend, promise."

I jogged off the dance floor and pushed through the back door of the school, the fresh air rushing to my lungs and cooling my skin from the muggy hotness of the gym. I wanted to scream out in anger. At how people were watching me for things I shouldn't feel guilty for. I was swept up in wanting to destroy something. Punch my hand into the wall. Anything to dull this aching pain in my chest that stopped me from breathing every day I lived this lie. I searched for an answer, until I saw it.

Harry's bike lined up on a rack. Ben had left it after school. I took my knapsack from Alex's car, then rolled back the bike. I hopped on and formed my lips to zip out whooping victory sounds all the way to Sojourner.

CHAPTER 24

AS I GOT CLOSER TO SOJOURNER, THE MUSIC BOUNCED OFF TREES. THE distinct jump in rhythm called me. I'd felt undone at Heritage, fighting off expectations of being with Mary. I was so far from myself. But as I drew closer to Sojourner, I could feel myself pulling back into place. I stretched my hands out free, riding Harry's bike, letting the cool night air and the music release me. Whatever had happened before at the dance didn't matter; all that tension riding my shoulder blades was letting down.

The barn door was open, and lights were strung from the house to the barn, touching across the trees, lighting the entire place like a carnival. I parked Harry's bike by the side of the house, grinning just thinking about his reaction to getting it back. The door was unlocked, so I headed to the kitchen to drop my bag. Close together were James and Robert at the table, sipping on whiskey. Their heads leaned in. I didn't mean to watch, but it was nice to see Robert happy. For so long, those last days after Trumbull Park had been seared in my mind. Robert was so distraught, and the arguments and fighting with my parents were constant, amplified by the loss of Charlotte. There was no joy in our house. Now, watching Robert, I could see his spark was back in him. He had done some healing.

"Brother," Robert said. "Didn't expect you to be here. Snuck away, huh?"

He was buzzed. Too slow to pull away from James like he would have done before. We were still learning how to be here, away from our parents' judgment. We were free at Sojourner.

"Rode here, wasn't going to miss it." I washed my hands, then ran a wet cloth over my face and around my neck. I avoided his gaze, not wanting to give any clue that the dance was a ruse to distract him.

"Glad you made it," James chortled. "Not showing up might just let a good thing slip away to another suitor."

I whipped around to Robert. My face was flaming hot in embarrassment. I'd only mentioned Lily a few times, but I should've known he'd see right through me.

"Don't be mad at him. Your nose is wide open." James chuckled before clinking his glass with Robert's, then downing the last of his drink.

"Want some?" Robert lifted his bottle.

"Better not," I said. I was surprised by his offer. When we were back in Chicago I'd be in and out of bars and clubs, underage, playing my music. Robert had warned me about staying away from that scene. But he didn't need to; I'd been sobered by witnessing the adults around me whose way of life fell out during a depression. Musicians were too prone to that life.

Robert drained his drink, then pushed the bottle away. "We got an early morning tomorrow—I'm headed on a trip with James, who'll be taking me far away from you all!"

I smiled. Our plan was working perfectly. Through the window I spotted Lily, dancing in the barn.

"Wish me luck." I made my way to the door.

"Bit of advice." Robert tugged at his jacket. "Keep it on until you see her. Then take it off."

"I can handle myself." I shook my head but noted it was the kind of thing I'd seen in the movies. I trotted out the door, moving to the *rat-tat-tat* of the music. I hadn't noticed when I'd arrived that they'd made the barn look, well, actually like a barn. Stacks of packed hay were set up like benches, occupied by rows of people taking breaks between songs. Inside, my roving eyes stuck on Lily, until my view was blocked by her partner swinging her around: Eugene.

"You made it!" Harry jump-started my broken heart. "Eugene thought you'd chicken out."

"Took longer than I planned." I wiped my brow nervously, watching over Harry's shoulder. "But I told you I'd do it, so here I am."

Harry snuck a glance at Lily and Eugene, then back to me. "We all get along. Everyone dances with each other."

"Good. Because I plan to dance with every girl in this place." I chuckled, reticent to admit the jealous bug I was fighting.

"How'd you make it out here?"

"Hitched a ride on a musical two-wheeler."

Harry squinted his eyes, confused. I gestured for him to follow me to the side of the house.

"What! No way. You did not." Harry grinned from ear to ear, then tapped my chest with one hand, waving wildly with the other at his bike. "How?"

"Let's say whoever stole it has a long walk home," I said.

Harry raced to his bike, hopped on, and then let out a series of whoops and hollers as he did three figure eights before taking off down Port Lane. I turned back to the barn; Eugene was waiting in the doorway.

"What got into him?" Eugene said.

"Got his bike back." I grinned, proud, before slapping hands with Eugene and giving him a side hug.

"Thought you were a no-show."

"I heard."

"Don't worry. I kept your girl busy." Eugene tapped my chest and chuckled.

"I saw." Then I hopped away toward Lily, calling out, "Thanks for warming up her feet. Hope you didn't step on them too much with those heavy toes."

"Not as heavy as your mama's feet. Let me call her right now."

I resisted getting into a dose of the dozens with Eugene. The night was already slipping away.

I slicked my hair back before running my hands around Lily's waist. I wasn't sure what had gotten into me. Whether it was feeling like I was back home or riffing with Eugene, like the good old days with Ray, I was riding high.

"Let me see how it's done, white boy," Lily said with a playful smile.

I took it as a personal challenge, twirling her around, stepping back, and showing her my Chicago bop, which I had perfected while hanging out late in clubs, trying to keep up with older women who thought it was their life's mission to make sure that while my melanin was low, my rhythm was high.

As I watched the other couples dance, I saw some take on the signature East Coast swing, which must've reached Pennsylvania; others danced the older jitterbug, the style that still dominated the blues and jazz clubs I'd frequented in Chicago. Back there I'd pull out my trumpet, dance around like Cab Calloway singing and directing his band. Zipping my horn while I danced. I watched Lily do a slightly different version of the bop. I caught the swing but couldn't help showing her the smoother step of the Chicago bop: step in front to the right, step in front to the left, then kick-kick. I held Lily's hands, and when she picked up the steps, she put one hand on my shoulder and the other in my hand, and we moved across the dance floor.

"Roll with Me, Henry" by Etta James came on, and I twirled Lily again. Etta had the mix of rhythm and blues and rock and roll, one I'd loved because while Chicago had jazz, it really was more the blues that music was birthed from.

"I hope you can keep up." I grabbed her waist, then picked up my feet to get into step. We were gliding; I caught her smile as I threw my jacket on some hay without missing the turn. Ray Charles's "I Got a Woman" had everyone crooning, but it was "Speedoo" by the Cadillacs that got the entire barn filled with sweat and bodies stepping, swinging, and kicking.

When the music slowed, I was dog-tired, but I didn't let go as the Platters sang "Only You."

"'Only you,'" I crooned in Lily's ear, "'can make this world seem right.'"

"You are a whole fool, Calvin Greene."

"You think I'm messing with you?" I turned her slow, dipped her, then pulled her back up before saying, "I am not."

We slowed at Al Hibbler's "Unchained Melody." The song was followed up with another Platters release, "The Great Pretender." We danced closer together. I could feel her heart beating fast against me. She laid her head on my shoulder. I rested my chin by her face, smiling until the words sank in more. The words about pretending took on a new meaning. *I'm the great pretender. . . . I seem to be what I'm not, you see. . . .* I felt the mask I'd been wearing take over me. I knew who I was, and yet Levittown had twisted that all around. I rolled back on my feet. Sweating.

"You look pale," Lily said, touching my face. "You okay?"

"Think the ride's catching up with me. I need some fresh air." I grabbed her hand, and she linked her fingers in between mine. We stepped outside the barn, and I felt like everyone was watching me. Whispering at how I was pretending to be white. Pretending to be Black.

"Here, follow me." Lily led me to the side of the barn, the

lanterns' light dimming the further we walked. I combed my fingers through my hair and took a seat, taking in big breaths of air until my pulse slowed.

"Thanks." I met Lily's gaze. "I'm not sure what happened."

I lifted my arm to put it around her, and she scooted closer.

"School tough?" Lily whispered.

I shook my head, then took her hand and held it. "I feel like I keep losing myself. Not knowing what's real. I—"

"Because of passing."

I swallowed hard.

"Calvin, I can't imagine what that must be like."

"It's . . . awful. It's truly awful." I choked out a laugh to cover how upsetting it really was. Then cleared my throat. "I can do it, is the thing. I wish it wasn't even an option I could take. It's too easy. On the outside, that is. But the better I am on the outside, on the inside . . . I'm ripped to shreds. Every piece of me eating itself. Waiting on defense to not let my guard down. Even innocent things are hard, like going places. Then I think, I wish I could take you. Or Eugene. And I realize that this whole big world . . ." I dropped her hand and extended my arms wide, like when I was riding toward Sojourner. "It's so small for us. So many spaces that are confined. And . . . it's suffocating."

"To feel all the potential by going to a school that has everything"—Lily took a long breath—"is hard. I wanted to know what it's like to just have things be. At school. I want that for everyone here, to not have to think how can I squeeze in, but to think the world is mine."

Lily pulled me closer. Her warm breath was near me.

"Are you sure you should take Eugene and Harry to Virginia?" Her voice quavered.

"We'll be fine. I promise." I held her tighter.

"Let me go with you. I feel like I should be there."

"It's safer with just the three of us. I promise I'll fill you in."

"Sunday. I'll meet you here at Sojourner," she said.

My chest fluttered at the thought of another confirmed time to see her, but I knew I wouldn't be able to sneak away again this weekend.

"Monday. After school."

"I'm not going. My mom won't let me."

I put my head down, heart sinking at the confirmation that Lily wouldn't be back at Heritage, ever. "Then after, near the Capewoods." I threaded my fingers through hers.

"Tuesday works. In our spot." She held her head near my neck, and I kissed her forehead, letting silence take us over as the music in the background floated all around us.

"We should conquer the world." Lily's voice sounded like she was uttering a dream.

"The whole world," I choked out, wanting to sound funny and failing. "Just for us."

"No, I mean it. I don't want to live like I'm in some small box. I want to fight to have the whole world, even if I can't have it all. I want to know I tried."

I put my hand to her face, holding it there. Watching as her eyes, big and wide, filled with possibility.

Our gaze locked. I felt my heart beat faster, my legs wobble even though I was sitting down. But it was a kind of feeling that was rushing energy, not draining. Her lips quivered for a second, and I instantly kissed her, pausing to see if I was reading things right. Before I could pull back, Lily caught my lips between hers, nibbling at me playfully. Then I leaned in closer. Rushed kisses, then long and slow. Kissing to the beat of music floating into the Capewoods.

CHAPTER 25

WE LEFT BEFORE SUNRISE IN ORDER TO RETURN THE SAME DAY. ROBERT was already long gone with James, with a return planned for the next morning. And as far as my parents knew, I'd stayed at the dance and was planning to spend the weekend at Alex's while pulling an all-day shift for Mr. Vernon.

I knew that ditching Alex the way I did was wrong. His eyes had been bright with excitement at the dance; he'd been ready to poke fun at me with Mary by my side like he had at his house. But that friendship was for another time. Maybe another generation.

Virginia was a seven-hour drive, and even though I'd been on long routes, this was different. No Dad along with tips for *Green Book* travels. This time *I* was a guide for Eugene and Harry. Their safety depended on me.

"Ready?" Eugene opened Robert's car door, smile wide as he handed me the keys and hopped into the back seat.

Harry flashed a smile of excitement: he'd be riding in the front.

"Slow down there, James Dean," Eugene said. "In the back with me."

"Staying in the back the whole ride?" I said, even though I knew the answer.

"Yup. I'm not sitting up there with you."

"Why can't I?" Harry whined.

"It's the daytime," I said. "It'll look suspicious if you're both in the back."

"We can duck in the back if we have to. Ain't no way we're riding in the front with you." Eugene pointed at me.

Things were more openly segregated the farther south you went. Sundown-town signs would be up, and we'd have to be out before sunset.

We pulled onto the road, Chuck Berry playing over the radio, and I hardly noticed I was riding solo in front.

"'Maybellene, why can't you be true!'" Eugene twanged, singing along. Then Harry called out, "Lily B., why can't you be true!"

We sang our hearts out until the song ended, and the radio jockey spoke:

> Ladies and gentlemen, listen to your airwaves. I've had the pleasure of hearing this live in a small club, with some interesting lyrics. This is a catchy one. Little Richard—"Tutti Frutti." Everybody—wop bop a loo bop a lop bam boom!

"Turn that up!" Harry rose from his seat, pretending to play the drums.

By the time Little Richard repeated the second verse, we had the chorus memorized.

"Tutti frutti, oh rooty!" we called out loud at the top of our lungs, windows down.

When the Penguins came on singing "Earth Angel," we quieted down. More cars were on the road, so we made sure to keep a low profile.

I picked up my *Green Book*. I had to take a roundabout route to make it through safer stops on the way.

"What we stopping for?" Harry said.

"Gas is safer here, according to the *Green Book*." Even though the tank was halfway full, I didn't trust stopping for gas farther south.

Harry grabbed the book and looked at the city page. "Let's eat," he said.

"We should go." I looked at my watch.

"Come on. This is our first road trip together. And I'm starving."

"That's what we packed food for," I said.

"All that bragging about passing—let's see it in action." Harry clapped the back of my seat.

I could tell Eugene wanted to get back on the road as much as I did, but he'd never let Harry know that. I was now used to playing white full-time in Levittown, and I knew I'd perfected it. But this time I wasn't alone, or with my father: I was traveling with two darker-skinned boys.

The closer we got to the diner, the more rigid Eugene and Harry became. Each time I was ready to turn back, Eugene pushed me forward. We entered the diner, where a young white girl was the waitress. She picked out three menus, then walked us to the very back. I studied the restaurant, relief floating in me when I saw another Black family eating there. Eugene and Harry saw them too, and their bodies relaxed as they scooted into the booth.

"You got money to pay for your meal?" the waitress said to me.

"Yes, ma'am."

"Check your wallets."

I laughed, then rifled through my pants when I got she was dead serious.

"You two." The waitress pointed.

They flashed their money at her, and she gave us the menus before walking off.

"This kind of place gets the okay to be in the *Green Book*, where they make you show your wallets?" Eugene said.

"They let us sit down, didn't they?" I shrugged at the harsh reality. "The real test is if we get our food on a plate and not boxed, burned, or messed with."

When our food arrived, Harry was the first to pick up the bun of his hamburger. Satisfied it looked good, he scarfed it down. We left exact change with tip and got back on the road.

We reached downtown Central Point, Virginia, where more traffic began building up. We drove through a few streets, searching for the restaurant that was hosting the meeting. When we found the right place, I parked in front, then carried my things in while Eugene and Harry followed.

We were greeted by a white manager as we rushed to use the bathroom. I was halfway down the hall when I realized Eugene and Harry were gone. I turned and looked left to right, confused at how easily I'd lost them.

"Where'd y'all go?" I asked when they approached me.

Eugene shook his head, and my gaze followed Harry, who gestured down the hall. They couldn't use the WHITES ONLY bathroom. I hadn't even noticed.

I watched Eugene, who was seething. Finally, I spoke. "I'm sorry. I didn't know."

"The sign was practically flashing!" Eugene said. "I thought they'd throw us out on sight."

"Sorry." I tried to apologize, but he was already heading to the meeting room upstairs with about fifteen Black youths from the East Atlantic region of CORE. We sat, the room abuzz. My gaze went straight to the back, where there was a fair-skinned gentleman dressed in a suit and hat. He looked familiar, like I'd seen him before. But before I could figure out who he was, we were ushered in to get started.

One of the leaders, who introduced himself as Virgil, was tall and slender, about a few years older than me. He had us go around the room and say where we were from, and what, if any, leverage we had to make a big move.

"It's our time," Virgil said. "We need a catalyst. There's a man named Martin Luther King Jr. who's talking about a new strategy. Our chapters of CORE are closing down left and right. We need something big to happen for people to believe we can win this fight. Dr. King said he's looking for the right moment to seize on. We saw what it did, making the world understand what happened to Emmett. People are paying attention."

"We shouldn't have to have a messenger," someone said. "There's injustice everywhere."

"I don't make the rules, but we gotta know the game. We need to use strategies we've never tried before. That's why we're here. What possibilities are there in your towns?"

Groups of people went through their ideas. When it was our turn, Eugene stood up. "Our town is segregated. Whites-only clauses in housing. Segregated schools. We're going to register Black students at the school in town."

I gulped. Hearing him say this out loud in a group, I knew I couldn't turn back if I ever wanted to change my mind.

"We've got good grounds for a fight there," Virgil said, then looked to the back of the room, where the man I'd noticed earlier stood. "*Brown versus Board* was passed. But we need people helping integrate schools. We can't live like this no more. We got a Supreme Court that said it's not lawful—the court is on our side. But we got to stop being scared. We got to pull our organizations together. CORE, NAACP. Get on the same page."

"How you going to get the registration paperwork?" someone asked.

Eugene looked at me. "Calvin here is passing in his neighborhood and at the school, even works for the head real estate agent who's key to making sure segregation is happening."

I'd begged him not to tell anyone my story, where I was from. Coming to this meeting was one thing, but I couldn't let it hurt my family. A long hush took over. I couldn't hear what they were saying, but inside I knew they were questioning whether they could trust me, since I was passing.

"Tell them about Emmett." Eugene nudged me.

I stood to speak. "I grew up with Emmett. We called him Bobo. When it happened . . ." My voice choked up. "He was away with my best friend, his cousin. They took him. . . . Things need to change. I can't go back home, but I can do something here. I work in a real estate office with files showing what they're doing is illegal. And we know a girl that tried to integrate into a school. She's not going back even though she lives within the district. There are more people like her that want to go but are afraid, and the administration won't give them paperwork." I sat back down, my throat raw from emotion.

The fair-skinned man with the suit and hat spoke up. "You have a legal right to go to a school that falls within your community line. If you have problems or proof of wrongdoing, any of you, just let me know."

He spoke with authority before exiting the room.

"How we supposed to do this? We can't fight them to get the paperwork," another person from the group said.

"No. Dr. King said we can't fight. Not like that."

"The hell we can't," a guy next to Virgil said. "This Dr. King wants us to get beat and not fight back."

"Reggie, he's trying something new. They'll treat us like animals either way—whether we fight or not. He's working on a new strategy. Looking for young Black leaders with immaculate stories that can draw more sympathy. To take a stance, make national news. And when they see how they're treated not fighting back, the country will have to stop and listen."

"Like who?" Eugene said.

"Mothers. Teachers. Preachers. All nonviolent."

The crowd murmured. How could they possibly not respond and take the beating or abuse we knew was coming? The repercussions were always bloody. Virgil tried to get the crowd going, but there were concerns all around. I couldn't speak. I was paralyzed, doubting my choice to drive Eugene and Harry, exposing myself and my family to danger. My heart pounded, and panic set in as I stumbled toward the window, gasping for fresh air.

CHAPTER 26

HARRY JOINED ME IN THE CORNER AS I WORKED TO CALM MY BREATHING.

"You did good," Harry said. "I know that was hard . . . to share about your friend."

"Thanks." I paused. "I don't know if any of this will make a difference." I felt defeated, unable to picture changing how things had been for so long.

"It will." Harry playfully hit my arm. "It has to, right?"

The meeting room transitioned from serious tones to fits of laughter. A buzz danced across my skin, and I took in the harmony that floats to you when you think the world might just be a little bit better. I could see that Eugene wanted to draw out the day, but as a slow trickle of people left, it was a reminder of our limited window of sun.

"If you can get the paperwork at the school district, we could do it before Thanksgiving," Eugene said. "After December fifteenth, we'll have to wait until next fall."

I nodded. The energy in the room had convinced me I could do anything.

I was feeling more settled, loosening up with all the smiles in the room, until a loud crash snapped us into focus.

"Hear that?" Eugene said.

"Sounded like glass. Think there was an accident?" I stepped closer to the door to listen to what might be going on downstairs. It was eerily quiet.

"It's outside." Harry pointed to the window, and we jumped to see.

There was a racket outside that didn't carry the same beat of exaltation from inside. Cars rushed to leave as three white boys circled an empty car and gestured to the building.

We were trapped inside.

"We gotta go," Eugene said, leading us downstairs.

In the bar, the leaders from earlier argued. As we got closer, I caught scattered words. I rubbed the back of my neck, forcing a warning tingle away. Eugene and I looked at each other; he shook his head. We both knew this wasn't good. Eugene protectively put a shaking hand on Harry's shoulder.

"Let's find out what's happening," I said, then entered the bar.

"You had your last drink," the white owner said. "I need you to get out of here before they come into my place and tear it up. I won't have that."

"What's the problem?" I said.

Harry squeezed in between us and peered out the window.

I looked outside. The trio of white boys looked slightly

older than me. Word must have got out about the CORE meeting. One guy planted himself on the hood of a car, a gun at his side and a cigarette in hand.

"How we supposed to get out of here in one piece?" Virgil said to the owner.

My head whipped back and forth between their conversation and Harry giving us the play-by-play out the window.

"That's not my problem," the owner said. "The only color I care about is green. But not if my place is in danger."

"We're in danger," Virgil said. "And I've got to get him out of here." He looked to the fair-skinned man who'd spoken earlier from the back of the meeting room.

"What are we gonna do?" Eugene whispered.

I wanted to shrug my shoulders, but I knew the look in Eugene's eye all too well. We needed to act fast.

"I can drive your car," I said. "They might let me pass."

"Son," the man said. "They're after me."

I studied him, puzzled, then turned to Eugene. He seemed conflicted about what to say. I took a breath, forcing bravery.

"I'll distract them, get them to leave. Then I'll come around in the alley and give you a ride. My friends will be able to get out then too."

"You'd do that?" the man asked.

I swallowed hard before answering. "Yes, sir."

"You sure about that?" Eugene whispered. "We said we'd stick together."

"Worried about me?" My joke came out shaky.

"Self-preservation. Worried I'll be kicked out of Sojourner

if I come home without you," Eugene said with a smirk, but his lip quivered.

"I can handle myself," I said before I could change my mind.

"We need to keep Mr. Marshall safe," Virgil said with reverence.

Then it clicked.

I blinked hard, realizing that the golden-tan man I was speaking with was none other than Thurgood Marshall. I knew why he'd attracted attention: Mr. Marshall had led the suit to send *Brown v. Board of Education* to the Supreme Court. I'd listened to the radio with my family, my father so in denial that Mr. Marshall, even as smart and sharp as he was, would win the case for the country. But I'd believed it with all my soul. I'd shaken at the sound of Mr. Marshall's voice, convinced everything he said would be possible. That no one could argue that impoverished Black schools were equivalent in resources to white schools. How could a community rise after slavery, through Jim Crow, when schools were unequal? A man like Mr. Marshall wasn't afraid. But schools around the country weren't taking the law as law—just as a suggestion. A man like him was enemy number one to folks against integration. I had to keep him safe.

"I can take your car, meet you around back. Check you in to where you are staying."

Mr. Marshall looked hard at me, then around the room for approval.

"What about them?" Mr. Marshall pointed to Eugene and Harry.

"You all can't stay here waiting," the owner said.

"Give me twenty minutes. Then I can meet them down the alley." I wasn't sure I could do either of those things, but I knew I was the best chance of getting us out safely. Too much was riding on this.

I snatched the keys out of Virgil's hand and left the building.

"Anything else open around here?" I went head-on to address the white guys surrounding Mr. Marshall's car. "This place is closing to prep for dinner."

I shoved my hands in my pockets to keep from fidgeting.

"Closed?" One white guy with a cap on looked to his friends. "What about the group of coloreds that were meeting in there? You with them?"

"Nah. My buddy works there. Think they all left. Headed home, I guess."

"What? You fooling with me."

"Told you we should've had someone hang out at the back." Another guy kicked the tire.

"What, and have someone jump one of us? This is his car he was riding in."

"This car?" I pointed to the ride I was supposed to take with me. "That's the owner's loaner. I'm about to go pick him up right now." I flashed the keys, swallowed hard, and prayed that they'd believe the owner's car was a loaner and not something Thurgood Marshall was driving in.

"You sure about that?" The boy, maybe twenty, stood nose to nose with me. I wanted to look away, but I knew that if I spoke confidently, I'd stand a chance. And right then, I needed every ounce of confidence I could muster. Any second they could call my bluff. Mr. Marshall had risked his life so many times just to fight for justice. I had to be brave. Had to make meaning of all this privilege I'd been parading around with.

"Positive." I squinted my eyes together and chuckled at them. "Why would they park out here if the colored entrance is in the back? Y'all have a good evening."

I knew they wanted to stop me, weren't sure if they believed me. My shaky hands unlocked the car door, and I flung myself inside.

One step closer to safety.

In the rearview mirror, I watched them get in their cars, then tail me until they finally turned off. With them nowhere in sight, I backtracked and made it down the alleyway of the restaurant, honking the horn.

Mr. Marshall, Virgil, Eugene, and Harry broke out the back door. Mr. Marshall got in the front passenger seat and Virgil got in the back. I waved to Eugene and Harry that it was safe to get into Robert's car and follow us.

I knew this wasn't the end—we were all packed in the cars, unable to hide. We could easily be spotted. I drove to Mr. Marshall's motel, one noted in the *Green Book*. My eyes were on alert for the white boys in case they followed Eugene and Harry.

"Thank you, son." Mr. Marshall and I both stepped out of the car, and I handed Virgil the keys. "You need a place to stay tonight?"

"We're driving back today."

"Drive safely." Mr. Marshall shook my hand. "In case you

need me out in Levittown, take my card. You and your friends take care."

I nodded, then watched Thurgood Marshall walk to his room. His card weighed heavily in my hand. A card I hoped to use one day.

CHAPTER 27

THE TENSION OF BEING LATE HUNG HEAVY IN THE AIR. A SCHEDULE made me feel in control. Now off our plans, I was unsteady. Unsure what was ahead of us.

"Let's go," I said.

Eugene jumped into the back seat and urged Harry to quit stalling. But I could see Harry's face: he was just as terrified and didn't need much pushing.

"I don't have a good feeling," I said when we were all in the car.

"I don't either," Eugene said.

We met each other's eyes. Both still shaken from the earlier encounter.

"I'm sorry," Eugene said behind me.

"About what?" I flashed a glance in the rearview.

"I was worried you wouldn't come back," Eugene said gently, looking out the window.

Harry was curled up against the window, quiet as I'd ever seen him.

"Nobody comes back for us. The last time Harry and I were on a trip, we were supposed to meet our father. He'd gone down South, hopping states looking for work. He'd send money to our mom when he could. Then she passed away." Eugene's voice trailed off.

He'd brought me into their circle, but at a distance before. There was so much more to their story. One Robert knew, one I was beginning to understand.

"We got a ride from my uncle, all our belongings packed. But by the time we arrived, we heard Dad'd been in an argument. His employer shorted him on a check, and he wanted his money. They called the police. By the time my uncle got there, Dad was already dead."

I slowed the car. My gaze bounced back and forth between the road and Eugene. He was expressionless, almost numb. But I could feel the pain radiating off him.

"It's been me and Harry ever since. Moving from place to place. Until we found Sojourner."

"Sojourner found us. We were led there." Harry spoke for the first time. He turned in his seat the other way. Then he closed his eyes and went to sleep.

"Sojourner found me, too." I meant it.

"He thinks the Capewoods led us there," Eugene said in a hushed voice. Like if he spoke too loud, it would give the woods more power.

I squinted, puzzled.

"We hitched a ride, but Harry had to go to the bathroom. Any other time we would've waited for a busy road so we could catch another ride, but we had the driver stop on Bailey at the edge of the Capewoods. Harry walked right on up. It was scary as hell, and that was even before we'd heard anything about the place being haunted. Then he saw something in the distance: the old broken-down church. We cut through the trees to get a closer look. Halfway through, I wanted to turn back, but it was like we couldn't. We passed the church and kept going. Next thing you know, we heard music and followed it to Sojourner. Funny thing is, no one was playing when we got there."

I wanted to ask more, but Eugene closed his eyes. I wondered what was hidden behind his lids or what sounds he followed.

As the drive went on, the car was jolting and jerking. I looked at Eugene to see if he'd noticed. Eugene was biting his fingernails, giving me enough of a look to share that he was nervous too. Harry was still out like a light.

"Something's wrong," I whispered. A burning smell crept into the car.

I'd had car trouble in the past, but Dad or Robert had always been there to fix it.

Before I could brush off my fear, a grinding, snapping sound hit, and smoke billowed out of the hood.

"My man, what's happening?" Eugene said.

Harry sat up quick, shaken alert by Eugene's tone.

I gripped the wheel and pulled to the side of the road, then hopped out and popped the hood. A passing car slowed and then sped off when Eugene stepped out. The kids in the back had hands to the glass, staring. My stomach turned.

"You think those guys did something to our car while we were meeting?" Harry asked.

Eugene and I looked at each other. Anything was possible.

We checked the car out, Harry standing in the back. With each moment I could feel the afternoon beginning to cool. The sun was going down. Tick. Tock.

"That supposed to be dangling like that?" Harry said, pointing to a red cord.

"Damn," I said. "They damaged the spark plugs."

I tried turning the car on again, questioning if it would work just long enough to get us home, but it revved and ground and took large jolts forward before stopping. I plopped my head on the steering wheel, thinking. I opened the *Green Book* again; there was one home listed that would take travelers, but that was ten miles away, maybe more. There was a grocery store close by, but it wouldn't have what we needed.

"I got to go on foot to find help," I said.

"We going with you," Eugene said.

I shook my head. "It could be dangerous. I can go out to a gas station, pick up a replacement, come back here and hope it works."

"What're we supposed to do?" Harry said.

I watched another car pass by. "Stay in the back seat, lie low," I said.

"For how long we supposed to do that?" Harry threw his hands up.

"Come on, Harry. We ain't got a choice." Eugene's voice was firm.

Harry sulked all the way to the back seat.

"You gonna be okay?" Eugene asked.

"I'm gonna be okay. I hate to leave you, but it's better I go alone."

"Yeah. I know. Hurry up, though." We both looked at the sky: time was running short before sundown.

We pushed the car farther through the grass behind a tree, so it would be partly hidden from oncoming cars, hopefully hiding the back seat more, only letting the front peek out for curious onlookers.

Before Harry and Eugene ducked away in the back seat, I looked into Harry's shaky eyes, then Eugene's.

"I'll be back. I promise." I gave them both a handshake; then Eugene tugged me tight into a hug.

"You better," Eugene said.

I swallowed the lump in my throat, then took off on foot.

The air swarmed around me, thick and heavy, bugs smacking on my skin. After a mile I could feel my lungs tightening and a twinge in my calf. But I didn't stop running, heading straight for a sign that would mark the closest major stop. I pushed forward with tired legs, thinking about Eugene and Harry alone on the side of the road. Thinking about what my dad would say if Alex called, wondering where I was. Then I ran as fast as I could until I could see a sign ahead on the highway.

My chest tightened. A large sign for the county entrance read:

> ## WHITES ONLY
> ### WITHIN CITY LIMITS
> ### AFTER DARK

I stood, feeling like I was going to throw up, as I stared at the sign. From a distance I could hear a car approaching, slowing down. My heart raced.

"Need help?" a white woman called out her window. "Saw an abandoned car back there a few miles. That yours?"

I nodded, uncertain what I should do.

My body ached from the run, and my mind reeled in worry at what would happen if Eugene and Harry were found, distinctly hearing my father's words that towns that made an effort to put up a sign were often Klan towns. Police would enforce a sundown law. It also meant that anyone Black caught after sunset . . . anything could happen to them. Being arrested was the least concerning. I'd heard all his traveling stories. It was a way my father made sure that I understood how important his work for the *Green Book* was. There'd be times I would be tired after a week of traveling. I'd want to hurry up and knock off things on my father's list. But he always said lives depended on a quality job.

"I could give you a ride. There's a gas station not too far

from here." She smiled. Her child in the back seat played with a toy airplane.

I didn't know what to say. I needed a ride. But if anyone found out I was Black, riding in her car, it could be disastrous for me. Eugene's words echoed in my mind: *Nobody comes back for us.* I looked at the sundown sign, then down the road. I couldn't see Robert's car from this far, but I knew Eugene was a few miles away, alone with Harry. And they needed me to be fast.

"Yes, ma'am. Car got stuck; need to buy some more spark plugs." I stepped closer to the car, entering after one more glance.

The woman was friendly, chattering on, asking me questions. I tried not to be nervous, but I couldn't help it. I answered questions about Heritage and living in Pennsylvania.

"I've seen those ads for Levittown. Sounds like a nice place," she said. "I'm Carol, by the way. My son is Mikey."

"Calvin," I said. "Nice to meet you. Thanks for stopping."

"I could probably give you a ride back if you like. Got a nephew about your age—I'd hate for him to be out here alone."

"Thanks, ma'am."

"It's dangerous out here at night. But I guess you don't have to worry about that much in Levittown. It's a shame here in Virginia."

I felt my blood turn cold. There was no way I could let her drop me off and see Eugene or Harry. She pulled up to the service station, and I could finally breathe again. The little boy started fussing.

"Thanks so much for the ride—I really appreciate it. I can find a way back. Your boy looks like he needs to get home."

"You sure?"

"Yes, ma'am."

"So polite. Well, okay, I guess I better get supper ready for him. Good luck to you."

I rushed to the service station and asked for spark plugs. I took the one out of my pocket for the right size.

"What happened here?" The attendant examined the plug and matched it up with ones they had.

"Buddy tried to play a joke on me."

"Joke? They ripped these clean through—that'd ruin your car. What kind of buddy is that?"

"Well, I guess not a buddy. How much?"

"That'd be a dollar."

I handed him a dollar and clutched the spark plugs.

"How far is your car?"

I hesitated. It was miles away, and it was already getting dark. Even if I were to run, it would take at least an hour for me to make it back, putting it close to seven p.m.

"It's about five miles back, near the Stop 'N' Shop." I shared the name of the first store I'd seen off the side of the highway.

"Albert, you give this young man a ride to the Stop 'N' Shop?"

I looked out at the tall white guy named Albert, who stood by his truck. I didn't want him anywhere near Eugene or Harry. But I felt I'd be too suspicious turning down a ride, so I agreed.

Albert was quiet; he didn't ask all the questions that Carol had earlier. He pulled in front of the Stop 'N' Shop, and I left with a "Thank you, sir." Then I watched Albert drive off. As soon as he was out of view, I took off running, two miles back to the car.

I didn't know how I did it, but I ran the whole way. My stomach twisted hungry, but I knew that although I was tired, I probably wasn't as scared as Harry and Eugene were, and that drove me the last mile. When I passed the sundown sign, I almost collapsed.

A police car.

Harry and Eugene sat by the side of the car. I dug deep and ran, only slowing as I got closer to the officer. He had his hand on his baton.

"You their friend?"

"Yes, sir."

"What are you all out here for?"

"Sir." I looked at Eugene. I knew it'd be dangerous if I conflicted with their stories. I hoped they'd stuck with the truth, except the part about me being Black. I went for our cover. "We play in a jazz band. We were heading back home when our car broke down."

"Where's home?"

"P-Pennsylvania," I stuttered out, hopefully confirming Eugene and Harry's story. "I got what we needed." I handed over the spark plugs.

The officer took the bag of spark plugs.

"Get up." He gestured to Eugene and Harry. "In the back of my patrol car."

"Sir," I said. "We didn't do nothing wrong." I looked at Eugene, then Harry. Harry's eyes were puffy from crying. Eugene kept his head down. I calmed my voice so I wouldn't cause a scene.

"Get up, boys." The officer pointed to Eugene and Harry.

They got up slowly, keeping their hands in sight.

"Back of the car." The officer barked louder, and I jumped.

I followed. "Please don't take them. I'll make sure they get out of here as soon as we fix the car."

"You know what time it is?"

I shook my head, afraid to answer.

"Sundown." And the officer kicked me in the knee. I fell to the ground. "No coloreds past sundown. Get up," he barked. "In the car with them."

I wobbled on shaky legs.

"I said, get." The officer swung his baton across my face.

I felt an explosion go off in my head, pitch black, then sparks of light with double vision. Red crossed my eyes. Eugene pulled me up and dragged me to the car.

"Walk straight, Negro," the officer said.

The blood coursed through my head and intensified the disorienting sensation. I could almost taste the metallic tang of fear as I felt blood trickling down my neck from the forceful blow.

"Think you can travel on these roads, you got another thing coming. I know what you are, and you not fooling anyone."

Fear consumed every fiber of my being, sending a chill down my spine. I could feel my heart race, pounding in my chest like a drum. The officer shoved us in the back of the car one by one. Harry yelped. I held my head like if I let go of it, it would split in half. Eugene propped me up so I'd sit straight as the officer lectured me.

"Sir, we could be out of your way if you just let us go," Eugene said low, shaky.

"Let you go, but that would mean you'd be driving another twenty-three miles through my county at sunset. We have families that live out here. If I let you go, what's to say you won't go out and rob somebody."

"We'd never—"

"Don't interrupt me. You going to stay in a cell until morning. Then you can get on out of here. And not a minute before."

I blew out a breath of relief. I was hurt, and he knew I was passing. But I would take a trip to the station with Harry and Eugene over the alternatives. As the officer drove, my head whipped left to right. I was still discombobulated but wanted to confirm that he would take us where he promised. We arrived at a small police station, manned by a front-desk attendant and two officers. I shut my eyes while Eugene kept me up and guided me to a cell. We weren't booked, but our names were taken, and we shared the cell.

In the morning, we were starving and thirsty, but when the officer dropped us off, we fixed the car and I drove the speed limit, with an officer escort the entire twenty-three miles.

CHAPTER 28

THE SILHOUETTE OF THE POLICE CAR DISAPPEARED WHEN WE CROSSED out of the county. But that didn't ease my worries. Eugene and Harry sat silent. The quiet left waves of an undercurrent—fear—unsaid. Their eyes were peeled on the road. Cars passing left a familiar dread, like caught breath pulling the oxygen from the car, then bursts of relief when drivers passed us. In the back there were no whispers. No chatter. A ghostly stillness.

We arrived at Sojourner, and I parked the car just in front of the stairs to the porch. My cramped legs protested and arms screamed out for me to shake off the tense hold I'd kept the entire drive home.

"You coming inside?" Eugene's voice was hollow. Obligatory.

"Gotta head to Alex's first and get my cover before going home. So I can explain this." I pointed to the bruise, now a deeper red, growing on my cheekbone, hot and tender. I winced as the pain came back to my body.

"Ideally, this week, before Thanksgiving, Calvin," Eugene said. "If we don't get the paperwork for everyone turned in by December, we'll have to wait until next fall to start. Come by Monday and let's finalize the plan."

Before I could say goodbye, Eugene was already up the stairs, leaving Harry standing with the car door open. It was understood: there would be no changing my mind. Not if I ever wanted to show my face at Sojourner again.

"You be safe, Harry."

Harry dropped his shoulders, nodding. Then followed Eugene.

With everything going on, I'd never made that check-in call to my parents. I'd also thrown Alex off by ditching the dance early. I needed to make sure that Alex hadn't blown my cover by calling or looking for me. I'd rather know what I was walking into before I headed home.

I didn't like lying to my parents. Somehow going to Alex's house made me feel like I wasn't all the way deceitful. If they asked about him, I could say I'd just left his house, and ignore everything else. But that wouldn't help in explaining my bruised body. Using another fight as an excuse wouldn't go over easy. Not after the last time I helped Lily.

"Where you been?" Ben hollered, approaching me as I arrived at Alex's.

"Working." I waved at Alex and his parents as they watched us.

"You left the dance without a word." Ben put his hands up.

The worried look in Alex's eyes leaped off him. His parents watched us through the window with curious looks.

"Did you tell your parents?" My voice cracked.

"I didn't tell them," Alex said. "They're watching because Ben rushed outside to greet you. He was worried you hated him."

"Was not." Ben's cheeks turned red. "I'm sorry I didn't tell you about Mary. I thought you just needed a nudge."

"I told you it was a bad idea," Alex said. "Calvin doesn't like Mary."

Relief poured over me. They thought I hadn't called them because I was mad at them.

"Were you in a fight?" Ben said.

Alex squinted as he came closer to me. "That looks bad."

"Got into it with some older kids who jumped me in the parking lot." I looked away.

"You should've called us," Ben said.

"Yeah, I was working, just got off," I said.

"Really, because we went by Vernon Realty," Ben said. "They said you weren't there."

"I . . ." I took a quick breath, searching for a response.

"So we swung by your house."

"You didn't." I rushed to Ben. I could feel my face distorting. This would be a disaster.

"I knew it." Ben busted out a laugh. "You should have seen the look on your face." Ben pointed to me, then hit Alex's shoulder; Alex laughed out of obligation. That is until Ben snorted so hard he almost choked on his own spit. Then Alex belted out a real laugh. I forced a few chuckles.

"I told him that going to your house was probably a bad idea," Alex said.

"Thanks. That would have been bad." If he only knew how bad.

"So, really, where have you been?" Alex said, leading me down the wide street of his neighborhood that looked exactly like mine.

I didn't answer. I hadn't thought about what I'd say coming here. I went out of town and didn't tell my parents? To do what?

"I'm not letting you get away without telling us," Ben said.

"He's not," Alex said. "I made him promise to stay away from your parents and just ask you."

"I was hanging out with friends."

"I knew it. I knew it," Ben said. "Got rid of the old girlfriend and picked up a new secret one."

Ben seemed so satisfied that I couldn't help but agree.

"Yeah. Sorry. My parents are super strict."

"Anybody we know from school?" Ben said. Before I could even answer, Ben rolled off a list of names. "Shelly. I bet it's Shelly Pritchard. Mary's sworn enemy. You sly dog."

I bit back a protest, holding my face together. I had to think quickly.

"No. No one you know."

"Does she live around here?"

"Not in Levittown."

"Well, where, then?" Ben said.

I looked to Alex to be saved, trying to remember exactly what I'd told him about my "out-of-town girlfriend." The only girl who kept crawling into my mind was Lily. I tried to push her image away so it wouldn't slip, but I caught Ben's eyes and it was like I telegraphed it to him.

"Wait a minute. Don't tell me you have been necking with Lily Baker. I knew it from the moment you were fumbling over her at the music store and dashed out without talking to us." Ben laughed hard, hitting my shoulders, like it was another one of his jokes.

I wanted a fit of laughs to creep from my throat, but all the veins in my neck held it in. Unable to deny Lily.

"What?" Ben snapped. "No. No. Tell me I'm wrong."

I couldn't answer. I couldn't let my loyalty sway from Lily.

"Bwahahahahaha. You are in love with a colored girl!"

"Stop, Ben," Alex said.

"You never have a crush on anyone at school. What kind of new boy doesn't like Mary Freemen or Shelly Pritchard? Mary has been after you every day, but you won't even look her in the eye."

I felt a frog in my throat, knowing I needed to speak, but not enough to make me deny Lily any attention. She was the most beautiful girl I'd ever met, and she hadn't escaped my mind since the first time I saw her.

"Gotcha!" I said.

Alex let out a smile.

I blinked hard before saying, "I was supposed to meet my girlfriend from Chicago. I was going to ask you all for a ride to the bus station, but then Mary came along and I couldn't ditch."

"That when you got jumped?" Alex pointed to my head.

I touched my head, the pounding building as I tried to keep my story straight. "Got into a bit of trouble leaving the dance. Nothing I couldn't handle."

"Maybe it was the same guys that stole my bike?" Ben said. "Were they on bikes?"

"No." I paused. "They were driving, then jumped out."

"So no real secret girlfriend?"

"No." I chuckled. "Felt silly still hanging on to my old girlfriend."

"That all?" Ben said. "Why didn't you say so?"

I swallowed hard, hating myself for all the lies.

When Alex dropped me off, my parents were so excited to hear I'd had fun at the dance and with Ben and Alex the rest of the weekend that they didn't ask too many follow-up questions I couldn't answer. They were just happy I was fitting in. Even my injuries were easy to explain—I floated a lie about flag football and Ben playing too hard. The way my father looked at me, I could tell he'd be willing to believe anything I said. Because believing it meant that I was still safe. That the choice he'd made to move us was the right one. Bruises and all.

I let him believe that lie too.

CHAPTER 29

AFTER SCHOOL ON MONDAY I HEADED STRAIGHT TO SOJOURNER. KEEP-
ing my promise to Harry and Eugene that our plan to pick up
school registration forms was still in play before Thanksgiving
break so we could get them in by the December fifteenth dead-
line to start the next term.

This time when I arrived at Sojourner, Robert greeted me
on the steps with his arms crossed.

He was a spitting image of our father when he was disappointed. I approached slowly, preparing for a tongue-lashing.

"This how you choose to rebel against Dad?" Robert said.

"What?" I answered innocently.

"What? You know how dangerous it is taking them out of
town like that. And to Virginia? You should've told me."

I thought of the police car. How my body had trembled at
the sight of the officer. I'd hoped to keep the trip to Virginia a
secret, but I should've known better. Eugene and Harry stood

behind my brother. Harry looked down, and I knew he was the rat.

"You said you were okay with us hanging out together." I avoided my brother's eyes.

"Yeah. At the school. At the barn. Hell, any location. As long as it's in Pennsylvania."

I'd finally felt like I could survive in Pennsylvania, and the trip had changed everything. It was dangerous for them to be seen with me. Dangerous for me to be found out.

"But I'm not doing anything different than you did in Chicago. And you know I can't be seen with them anywhere in town." I stared at my brother with weak excuses.

"Damn it, Calvin. Don't mean you can go to Virginia. And I learned my lesson. We all know what happened to Charlotte. That's why you're here in Levittown now." Robert paced in front of me, kicking up dirt and brushing his hair back with his fingers. His hands were shaking. "Harry's only fourteen."

"I was thirteen when I started traveling with you and Dad."

"It's not the same."

"How? We hardly went as far. And we used safe routes from the *Green Book*."

"Oh yeah? How safe was it?" Robert threw his hand up. "Hell. You know it's not the same—we could pass."

"You can't pass," I yelled.

"I'm damn near translucent compared to Eugene and Harry. They're my kids, my responsibility. You might be able to get away with certain things, but they can't. If folks see you, they don't know what you are, but for them . . . it's dangerous."

He wasn't going to let up. And he was right. But I kept

pressing on, because to admit he was right would mean admitting I had risked my friends' lives.

"We're supposed to be family."

"No. You have the family. Harry, Eugene, they're my family—everyone at Sojourner. I gotta look out for them."

"What about me?" I pleaded.

"Go home," Robert said. "Leave my boys alone."

"We got a right to go to Heritage too," Eugene said. "A better education can set Harry up for college. You know what that would mean for us?" Eugene pulled out his pocket, and only cotton came out. "I can't live here forever. I'm eighteen. I get that it's a favor to keep me longer, but next year I'm on my own, with Harry still here. If I go, you know he's going to follow me."

"What kind of caretaker I look like letting my students run around trying to get into a school that'll start a riot? You want a better chance, I'll enroll you in a different school. Just not Heritage."

"It's too late," Eugene said. "We already have people lined up ready for Heritage as soon as we get the registration paperwork. We've been through a lot worse before we came here. I'd like you to be cool with this, but if you can't be, I'm not asking."

Robert's jaw tensed. He looked back at me, shaking his head.

"Fine. But don't say I didn't warn you. Something happens to you, it won't be on my conscience. That's on y'all."

Harry hesitated to move.

"Go on. Hurry up. And as long as you live here, I want to know everywhere you going and where you stopping," Robert said.

"Thought it wasn't on your conscience?" Harry said.

Eugene shot Harry a look. "All right. Deal."

Robert and Eugene shook hands. Then I followed Eugene to the barn to discuss our plan to get the registration paperwork. The guilt flip-flopped in my stomach.

"You sure we should do this? Maybe my brother is right." I hated that Robert's words were starting to take over my thinking. But so much of what he'd said was true.

"Your brother is too safe," Eugene said. "He's got it easy."

"You don't know what my brother's been through." I paused. "What my family's been through."

"We've all had it hard," Eugene said.

Robert must've never told them about our life before.

"My brother was an organizer in Chicago. He's faced police, mobs of people, organizing hundreds of people to protect our homes there."

"Robert?" Eugene said. "I don't believe it."

"He'd have underground meetings, getting the local newspaper and the *Defender* to write up stories. Robert was like that—he'd write letters to the editor, and he could draw people like a magnet. Everyone listened to him."

"Well then, he should help us," Harry said.

"No, you don't get it. They . . . they went after him. Our sister was killed. His twin."

I could see the flames.

"I didn't know," Eugene said. "I'm sorry."

"I'll help you get the paperwork for registering you for school," I said. "Just not today, okay?"

"I'll meet you tomorrow, then," Harry said.

I flicked my eyes at him.

"Be the handoff for the paperwork."

"It's not a bad idea," Eugene said. "But we need a lot of applications."

As he spoke, I could vividly picture the repeated trips I might have to make for the paperwork. I knew deep down that I only had it in me to do it once. Besides, I'd definitely draw suspicion. A thought sparked in my mind, a clever work-around. "What if I said I needed a stack for Mr. Vernon for all the new home buyers. That way it wouldn't tie directly to me, and I wouldn't have to keep going in."

"That's a good idea," Eugene said. "Give me half, then take the rest to Vernon Realty."

Robert had reminded me what we had to lose. How Eugene and Harry always had to look out for themselves. If I was their friend, I needed to do that too, for them. I had Thurgood Marshall's card. If I could get more files from Vernon Realty, maybe I could do something. Put the spotlight on Mr. Vernon's plans so he wouldn't get away with hurting anyone else.

"Are you in or what?" Eugene said.

"I'll do it tomorrow."

I pulled myself up from the ground. Ran out like the flames from the past were chasing me home.

CHAPTER 30

HOPE ORBITED AROUND ME AS I LEFT SCHOOL THE FOLLOWING DAY. But there was something about taking those same steps downtown, without trailing behind Lily, that made me think of only her. My heartbeat sped up at every corner in hopes she'd be waiting with a shy smile she couldn't hold back.

I was thinking so much about her that I mindlessly veered away from downtown and toward Lily's route home. Soon Harry would arrive, which I knew was just their way of making sure I didn't chicken out. At the dance, I'd made a promise to Lily that I'd see her and tell her everything. The truth was, my relationship with Lily felt vulnerable. I was worried she'd forget me. Forget that kiss under the darkened cover of the back of her house. Our moments at the dance and escaping outside. How her body just melted into mine. I didn't want that to be a moment. I needed her to know me, again. And maybe just a little part of me was delaying going to the school board office to take the paper-work.

I went down Bailey Road and cut along the trail that led to the grass and wooden stumps where Lily and I had met before. I sat waiting for her, the wind blowing the grass back and forth. Riding near the woods, I'd heard the crackling. The way the trees would breathe. I'd been afraid before, but knowing I'd see Lily, that she had no fear of the woods, I ignored it.

Lily appeared, riding on her bike with her skirt tucked so it wouldn't fly up. Her hair danced in the wind with a scarf tied around it to keep it together. She hopped off, nervously look-ing behind her before cutting to the trail, where she finally caught eyes with me. I ran to her, stopping short a few feet to give her space. My toothy grin showing I was wide open for Lily Baker. She brushed her scarf off and pressed down her hair.

"Thought you wouldn't show," I said.

"You're early."

"So are you." I grinned.

"I was worried." Lily touched my hand. "I'm glad you're back. What happened?"

"Come." I ran ahead to the stump, draping my jacket over it so Lily could sit. She joined me, our legs pressed next to each other. Lily slid her hand in mine and goose bumps ran up my neck.

I could smell her, like clean linen. I stared at her, wanting to say something, anything, everything. A burst of courage must have overtaken me because I kissed her instead. She didn't hesitate, meeting my lips, then pushed back as she took a long deep breath in.

"Thought you came to talk about your road trip," Lily said.

"I . . . yes . . . I did. I'm sorry. I missed you." I could feel my cheeks flash hot with embarrassment. "I can't stay long. I've got to take care of something."

Lily leaned in and kissed my cheek.

"When can I see you?" I said. "I don't like not knowing. Every day I walk through the halls, hoping to see you."

"I wanted to keep going to Heritage, but my parents . . . They got scared."

"We have a plan, though, that could change all that." I caught her up on the CORE meeting in Virginia and what fell out after.

"It doesn't matter. We might have to move."

"Are you still being harassed at home?"

"They quieted down for a while, but every time we let our guard down, they seem to come back. Someone driving by cursing. Or dumping trash on our lawn so we get fined."

"I'm sorry. There must be another way."

"I bet Eugene's just waiting on saying he told me so." She looked away.

The question floated in my head as Lily looked up at me with hopeful eyes.

"Do you still have feelings for him?" I wanted a straight answer, and I couldn't ask Eugene. Couldn't risk him telling me he did, because then I'd have to choose our friendship or Lily.

"It's complicated. Sojourner is so small, so it never seemed like we should . . . Then we were going to, but he got mad when I was thinking about going to Heritage."

"Mad? But he's doing all this to get more students at Heritage."

"He is, but his way. My whole life has been about what I can't do. My mom was always talking about me working at the same restaurant as her when I graduate high school. College not even a question."

"Going to Heritage was about changing that?"

"I just got tired of people telling me what my future is. And Eugene, his meetings, it was always about what he wanted. Always planning with no action. I guess I just got tired of talking about it. So I signed up. I mean, little old me. What was I gonna do? God, that was so stupid."

"It was brave."

We met eyes, and I took Lily's hand again.

"When I went to the office your first day, I thought they'd discovered who I was. I never thought it would be you. That day, you held your head high. I haven't done that since I started. I'm an imposter. You know who you are."

"If you had a choice, would you still pass?"

"No." I didn't have to think about that.

"Then stop blaming yourself. You had no choice."

"Didn't I, though? I could have stopped it somehow, but now it's too late. So I'm stuck with all these feelings on the inside about who I really am. Who I still want to be. I'm split between two worlds, and it hurts so bad. Maybe I should stop drifting between lives, like my parents. Pretend I'm white, all the time." I looked up at Lily.

Her eyes watered like she felt sorry for me, and that wasn't what I wanted. I touched her chin, so she knew I meant what I was about to say. "But then I wouldn't be able to see you."

Lily kissed me. It took me by surprise. I laughed between kisses. Like a giddy excitement bubbling inside me. We wrapped our arms together and lay on the ground. Kissing.

"Come with me," Lily said with hushed breath.

She led me to the edge of the Capewoods. My heart pounding. Afraid. In love. My insides twisted until I stepped closer and let the trees cover us. Lily urged me on to follow her further in, but I couldn't get my feet to move. We kissed, holding each other, pawing at each other. Until it got too difficult to see clearly. Lily pressed her hands on my chest.

"Just because we can't find a place to be public with each other doesn't mean I'll want to hide the whole time. I'm worth being seen with."

"I never—"

"I'm just saying." Lily kissed my lips, soft, and I settled. "I missed you too. You're not like anyone I know."

I creased my brow, trying to understand what she meant.

"And I don't mean because you look white." Lily laughed as she watched me try to make sense of it. "I mean, you don't look white to me. Your life's been hard. I guess I just want to get to know you more."

"I want to get to know you, too. I'd want my parents to meet you even. Well, at least my mom, if she knew about you, she'd want to meet you. I think she already knew after I got into the fight with Darren."

"I'd want you to meet my parents too. Maybe after some time . . ."

"There's a drive-in theater not far from here. On Sundays they play a show we could watch in a car. I'd like to take you." If we were in a car, we could hide in the darkness.

"I'd like that."

We pressed farther into the woods. Her touch was the first time I'd ever been like this before. We were tentative, holding each other. Like we'd never see each other again and we just couldn't stop.

We lay on a patch of grass at the edge of the woods in each other's arms. Until Lily sat straight up.

"It's late. My parents are going to kill me."

"Wait." I pulled her gently back down. Her parting from me felt like I was losing a limb. Still dizzy from the feeling of her next to me.

"Didn't you have somewhere to be too?"

I sat up straight. "Shoot. The paperwork. I told Harry I'd be there over an hour ago—he's waiting downtown for me. I have to make it there before five p.m. The office is almost closing."

"Of course. Harry'll never let you forget it."

"I know. He'd weasel his way to a good year in favors before we were even."

We sat up, putting our clothes in order. I reached over and pulled some grass from her hair, then touched my hands to her cheeks.

"You know I've never—"

"I've never either." We both paused without saying more. I met her lips with mine, letting our kisses tell each other our secrets before we pulled apart to leave the woods.

We held hands until the sun touched our skin, the daylight taking away our connection. Lily propped up her bike as we walked together, not wanting to let go of the close moment we'd just shared. We walked through the trail and off Port Lane. Even knowing it was getting dangerous, we no longer cared who saw us.

A car approached, but it was moving so fast I couldn't help but give Lily a deep kiss goodbye because I didn't know when I'd see her next. She hesitated but let our skin touch one more time before she hopped onto her bike and began pedaling away. I rode on shaky legs in the other direction, in love with Lily's smile. Her lips. Her laugh.

Lost in thought, I didn't notice that the car had parked on the side of the road. Until I recognized two people in the car, gawking at me.

Alex was on the driver's side, Ben in the passenger seat.

My heart raced, dizziness taking over as I tried to come up with answers. Excuses.

Their windows were rolled down, mouths wide open. I didn't know what to do. They had only stopped for one reason. Because they'd seen me with Lily—kissing.

If I could have turned back around without looking guiltier, I would have. But I was forced to run right into them. They hopped out of the car to meet me.

Ben's face twisted before he spoke. "Are you out of your mind? Is this what you have been doing?"

I couldn't answer. I'd been stupid to think I'd get away with seeing Lily in public.

"I don't want to talk about it," I said, and moved to pass them, but Ben pulled my arm back.

"You have to talk about it. You can't use Alex just so you can see your secret girlfriend," Ben said.

"Just because you want to follow Levittown rules doesn't mean I have to. I can be with anyone I want. Black or white."

"I have no issues with her kind," Ben said. "But isn't this the reason they want to keep schools segregated? So stuff like this doesn't happen?"

"Ben," Alex said, "leave him alone. Let's talk about this another time."

"No. We're going to talk about this right now."

"I don't need this," I yelled, thrashing my hand around.

"You don't have a choice. You're lucky it was Alex driving and not somebody else. This is crazy, Calvin." Ben's round face was bright red.

"What's wrong with me seeing her?" I wanted to know what my friends really thought.

"It's . . . it's not natural. She's Black. You're white. It would never work."

"Have you really been seeing her and saying you're with me?" Alex's voice was shaky.

"She's just like you and me."

"Hey," Ben said. "I get it. But what happens if you have kids?"

"Who cares." I gritted my teeth. "Besides, it wouldn't matter if we had kids. She and I . . . we're the same."

Alex and Ben got quiet.

"What the hell do you mean, you are the same?" Ben said, his mouth curled in disgust.

His contorted face was the last straw. All I could think about was my classmates dancing around making jokes about Africa, and how I'd said nothing. How they'd mocked the death of Bobo. How the officer had taken me in. All the rage and secrets boiled over inside me, and I erupted. "I'm Black too. You spent all this time with me, and you didn't even know. And your life didn't get ruined, now, did it?"

"You're lying," Ben said.

"I've got somewhere more important to be." I bumped Ben's shoulder as I walked away from him, done with the conversation. My eyes stung from holding my anger in. My tears. I didn't care anymore what Ben and Alex thought. Harry was probably long gone by now, but I was determined more than ever to get those registration forms. I'd burned up my friendship with Ben and Alex. Maybe that had been my plan all along. To get the guts to finally do it, where I had no choice and wouldn't have to lie about seeing Lily. I'd surely dreamed about this. Going to Sojourner for school, Robert and my parents forced to go along. I'd mapped it all out. This kept running in my mind until I got shoved in the back.

"Listen to me when I'm talking to you," Ben yelled. "Are you saying you're Black? Are you Black, Calvin? How?"

"Leave him alone." Alex's voice was shaky but firm.

"You know what'll happen to me and Alex if people find out and thought we knew this whole time?"

"What? Like all the friends you have now? Everyone thinks you're a joke."

Ben lunged at me, arms around my neck, and shoved me to the ground. He pushed me, and we tumbled along the side of the road, onto the grass. Alex yelled for us to stop. But we kept punching each other until Ben was so winded, he fell in a heap on the ground.

I didn't realize why Ben had stopped until I looked at Alex, who was red-faced, yelling. Pleading for us to stop.

"You can't come here and ruin everything for us," Ben said. "Alex doesn't need more problems. Do you know how long it took for him to be accepted after they tried to get his family to leave?"

We stood, staring at each other, which gave me a moment to catch my breath. As my adrenaline steadied, the weight of what had just happened sank in. I flung my hands to my head. *No. No. No. What did I just do?* I whipped my head to Ben and Alex, willing us back in time to no avail. I had let my guard down. Let the anger take over because I felt so guilty about hiding Lily from the world, about having to choose sides. I'd outed myself to the only friends I had at Heritage. I felt the hot drip of tears coming down my face. "What are you gonna do?" I cried out. "You gonna tell on me? Have my family disappear too?"

I rushed to Ben, who flinched at my approach. I held on to his shirt, desperate, pleading. "Please. Don't say anything. You know what they'll do to me. To my family." I shook him gently, begging as my fingers gripped his shirt.

"I'm not going to tell anyone," Ben said.

A small, desperate smile of relief hit me, until I noticed Ben's lips curled.

"What do you think they'd do to us if they knew we were friends? Stay away from us, you hear? We're no longer friends." Ben shoved me back.

"Ben," Alex said. "Let's take a moment to figure this out."

"Does your family need this, Alex?" Ben said. "'Cause my family sure don't. Do you realize what could happen to us if they thought we knew all this time?"

I needed to make sure Ben was more scared of me than of what other people would think. I needed me to be the reason he stayed silent. I lunged at him, tugging at his collar.

"You tell anyone . . . You tell anyone and I'll . . . I'll kill you. I'll tell them you knew all along." I shook Ben. His face was red, eyes big.

Ben tugged my hands and pushed me off. "We're not going to tell anyone. But we are no longer friends. This is it. And if you knew what was good for you, you'd quit meeting her where you're going to get caught. For all of our sakes. Come on, Alex, let's go."

I looked to Alex, who had tears in his eyes as Ben walked to the car.

"He can't say anything," I said. "He can't tell anyone."

"He won't," Alex said, then joined Ben in the car.

I watched them pull away. My body shaking. Tears streamed down my face as I rode past the entrance to downtown and headed home, unable to face Harry. I would just have to get the forms tomorrow.

CHAPTER 31

THROUGHOUT THE EVENING THE PHONE RANG. I KNEW IT WAS EUGENE or Harry. I couldn't answer. Not because I didn't want to, but because I didn't have a choice. When I circled the phone, cautious eyes landed on me before Dad answered. A click of silence met him on the other end.

The next morning, I left for school like normal. But I had no intention of going there. At least not at first. I needed time to think about how I'd left things with Alex and Ben. I couldn't trust them. Secrets like this couldn't stay dormant. Not for long. And not with Ben's big mouth. It was only a matter of time. I also owed Harry an explanation, one that could only be remedied with paperwork in hand. They'd be angry with me for cutting it so close. If we wanted our plan to work, we'd have to have the forms slowly trickle in over the first two weeks of December.

As I made my way downtown, fear crept into my body.

The kind that rings alarm bells but is rarely listened to. It's the prickle running down your skin. The shortness of breath. Signals that ancestors and angels from beyond send to try to warn you. But there was no time to delay: Thanksgiving was tomorrow, and if I didn't pick up the forms today, I'd have to wait until Monday.

When I arrived downtown at the school board office, I found a small crowd of men standing outside the building, lined up with bats. Mr. Vernon was planted at the top of the steps with a stack of papers in his hands. I choked out a yelp, covering my mouth.

Behind a bush I squatted to listen, hoping they hadn't spotted me racing around the building. Their mumblings became crystal clear—they had discovered our plan. I said a silent prayer of thanks that I hadn't yet mentioned to Mr. Vernon that I was picking up school registration forms for his office.

I jumped on my bike and raced toward the parkway, then down Bailey Road until the turn for Port Lane to Sojourner, my mind whirring with whatever I must've missed.

I could see the top of Sojourner through the trees. The closer I got, the heavier my stomach felt, weighed down by having to explain to Harry and Eugene why I hadn't shown up yesterday to get the transfer forms.

And how it might be impossible now.

Before I could reach the door, Eugene stormed out. He thumped his finger at me, pounding three rapid digs into my chest.

"Where you been?"

"I'm sorry. I couldn't get to it." I looked away. "It was too late."

"You mean because you were with Lily," Eugene spat out.

My head turned, mouth open. Not sure what to say. Were Alex and Ben not the only ones who saw us? Then I looked at the Capewoods. Had Eugene cut through from Sojourner? My stomach sickened at the thought of Lily and me being watched in the grass.

"I was heading there, after."

"You were too late, and now Harry's too scared to come home without the paperwork." Eugene looked past me like he was looking for Harry to pop up.

"Harry's not here? Where is he, then?" I watched Eugene, realizing he wasn't as much angry as he was terrified. "I didn't see him yesterday. I was caught by some kids at school after I left Lily. They held me up, and it was too late to go to the office."

Eugene gripped his hands on my shoulders and pulled me by my collar. "Harry didn't come home last night."

My jaw dropped.

"Harry?" Robert called from inside. Then he grew quiet when he stepped outside and saw me tangled up with Eugene. "Where is he?" Robert's voice shook.

"I don't know," I cried. "I don't know. I didn't see him."

"We been looking for him all night. Tried calling you at the house. Why didn't you answer?" Robert said.

"I swear I didn't see Harry. I would've gone. . . . Alex and Ben caught me on Port Lane with Lily. We got into it. . . ."

"You mean your friends."

"It wasn't like that. They know. . . . They know who I am," I said.

I teared up, looking at Robert. Robert took Eugene's hands, which were still holding on to me, and made him let go. Then he put his arms around Eugene.

"I'm sorry," I said. "Dad wouldn't let me near the phone. I couldn't risk him finding out. I didn't know Harry was in trouble. I swear."

"He'll be home," Robert said. "You know he ain't never want to let you down. Probably didn't want to come empty-handed and is waiting out downtown, hoping to scope out Calvin. We'll find him. Harry's a big boy."

Eugene nodded. I wanted to agree. I wanted to say I'd check it out and bring back Harry. But something told me that wouldn't be happening.

"I went by the school board office this morning to get the registration forms." I paused, not knowing how to tell them it might be even worse.

"And?" Eugene said.

"I went in early to grab them so I could meet you here. But Mr. Vernon, my boss, he was there with a group of men. The same ones I saw in school the day Lily started. Mr. Vernon had a stack of papers in his hand."

"What does that have to do with anything?"

"The rest had bats. All lined up in front of the office."

"Do you think they found out?" Eugene asked.

"I don't know. I thought maybe Alex and Ben had said something about me, but they didn't know about the plan to enroll everyone at Sojourner. Just that I was passing."

"How could you be so stupid? You can't trust them," Eugene said.

"Come on." Robert's voice rose for the first time. "Mom and Dad are in just as much danger. Why did you say anything?"

"I didn't have a choice." It had been a mistake. I'd gotten caught up in the moment. Something that Lily had said. I'd just wanted to be with her. Now my family was at risk.

"What about the men—do they know who was involved? That it was kids from Sojourner?"

"There's nothing that would get them to suspect anything. . . ." My voice trailed off. Someone had to have tipped them off.

"What is it? What did you do?" Eugene tugged at my arm.

"Maybe they caught wind that I was looking through Mr. Vernon's files. But he would have asked me about the files if he'd found them missing. Me and . . ." I thought of Barbara, how she'd been fired. If he thought files were missing, he'd suspect Barbara, not me.

"It's only a matter of time before he notices," Robert said. "What were you thinking?"

"We needed evidence of any illegal activity Mr. Vernon was involved in. That's why we went to Virginia—to get a plan together for what to do with the information we had."

"You are in over your head." Robert paced. "If they found out those files are missing, then who knows what they'll do to Harry."

"They won't put two and two together."

"They better not," Eugene said. "You need to return those files."

"But what if there's something in there that could help us?"

"We need Harry back. Tell me you'll return those files." Eugene grabbed at my shirt.

"We just have to hold on tight. I bet you're right about Harry. Bet he's just waiting for me. We can look for him. I can go to school. If I hear something, I'll return the files before Mr. Vernon finds out they're missing."

"No," Robert said. "Stay here. Let's spread out. Going to school might be—"

"I don't have a choice," I said. "I've got to find out if Ben or Alex knows anything about Harry. Maybe that would get me more information about what Mr. Vernon was doing at the school board office."

"I don't like it," Robert said.

"He doesn't have a choice," Eugene said.

By the time I got to school, it was fourth period. Alex was my only hope for answers. Ben would be no help.

I jumped out of class after the bell and ran down the hall to cut off Alex before he got to his locker. When he saw me, Alex's face drained. He looked like he was about to backtrack and go the other way. I wouldn't let that happen.

"I need to talk to you."

"I don't think we should be seen together," Alex said in a hushed tone. "Ben will be pissed."

"I need to know. . . . Did you . . . did you say anything?"

Alex signaled for me to follow him through the side doors. Then we met up in the boys' bathroom.

"Of course I didn't say anything. How could I? But Ben—"

"He didn't, did he?" my voice barked.

"No. He didn't. But you know Ben. He won't be able to control himself for too long. Not if you keep talking to us."

I wiped my forehead in relief. "So y'all didn't say anything to anyone?"

"No. We didn't say anything. I made him promise."

I nodded, then put my hands in my pockets. "Does this change things with us?"

"I don't care. . . ."

"But this isn't the kind of place that would let us stay friends."

"I'm sorry, Calvin. If things were different out here, I would, but my family . . ."

"I get it." I swallowed back the tightness in my throat. "My family could be in danger if they find out. Promise me you won't say anything. That you won't let Ben, either." I took Alex's shoulders and held them snug, so he'd know I was serious.

"I'll never say anything." Alex walked to the door, then stopped. "I wish things could be different."

We left the bathroom separately. My feeling of relief quickly disappeared. If Alex hadn't said anything and Ben hadn't either, then what was going on at the school board office? And what had happened to Harry?

CHAPTER 32

THAT MONDAY AFTER THANKSGIVING WE STILL HAD NO WORD FROM Harry. Over the weekend I'd kept my shift at work, but it felt like Mr. Vernon was watching me like a hawk. And if he stepped away, Sharon wouldn't let me out of her sight. There was something going on, but it was left unsaid. The files were heavy on my mind, tucked away in my bag, waiting to be returned.

Even Lily was hard to reach. I called her incessantly when I could sneak away, begging to see her. Finally, she agreed. This time not off Port Lane but at Sojourner. At first I thought it was a trick, that Eugene would be waiting there for me. But when I arrived, Lily stood in the doorway of the barn. She disappeared inside. I followed, my chest beating hard.

Lily was wrapped up in her coat; the temperature had dropped into the thirties. Weather out here was different from in Chicago. Back there, we were always pressed into homes on top of each other, and buildings connected. So even when the Midwestern wind whipped against your skin, you could always find a shelter to block the blast. But in Pennsylvania, the chill was cold to the bone. I could feel a snow coming on, and it terrified me. If Harry was out there somewhere . . . I couldn't bear to think about it.

"You came." I met Lily, a pull inside me making me forget all my worries and desperately want to be near her again. Breathe the same air. I locked my hands in hers, hoping she'd receive me.

"Have you heard anything?" Lily squeezed my hands, and my chest opened up again.

I shook my head, ashamed. Wanting to know more, to have answers. But I had none.

"I should've been more forceful for you to see Harry right away that day. I would've waited for you to come back." Lily laid her head against my chest, her lips resting near my neck. I turned to kiss them softly. Wanting more, but her eyes were welling.

"I'm sorry," I whispered. "When you left, there was still time. But Alex and Ben saw us near the woods walking together. . . ."

"I know," she finally said. "Eugene said Alex and Ben know you're passing. Have they told anyone?"

I shook my head. "I don't think so."

"And they know . . . about us."

"I'm sorry."

"It shouldn't have to be like this. I don't want it to be like this."

"I know." I held her tighter.

"Calvin, where could Harry be? Do you think Mr. Vernon knows about you? About what Harry was meeting you for?"

I couldn't let Mr. Vernon get away with scaring off Harry. Or worse.

"I don't know how he would. Maybe Harry went in and tried to get the forms himself? I'll find him."

Lily looked at me, her mouth twitching. "I can't see you anymore."

"What? No! Don't worry, Ben and Alex won't say anything."

"It's not about that. I can't. I'm not going to hide."

"You don't have to hide."

"I do, Calvin. What if we're caught again? And now Harry has gone missing."

I bit my tongue, holding back my anger. Whatever happened to Harry was my fault. My heart ached as Lily stood up.

"I'll find Harry," I pleaded. "I'll fix things."

"Do that, Calvin. I hope you do that." Lily wrapped her scarf around her neck and pulled her coat tight as she walked away. I couldn't tell if Lily meant that would make us closer or if we were already over.

I knew better than to show up at Alex's house uninvited, but with no other options, I had to see him. I knocked on the door and stepped back when Alex's father answered. I watched his surprise, trying to read between the lines, figure out if Alex had told his father.

"Is Alex here?"

"He's in his room. Is he expecting you?"

"No. I'm sorry. I was in the neighborhood." I shivered at the unexpected brisk cold air stripping my skin. I'd left the house without much to keep me warm as I rode out to Sojourner. My hot clammy skin had cooled, and I felt the ice in my bones.

"Okay, he can't have visitors too long; he's preparing for a big test coming up."

I grimaced. I hadn't started studying. My interest in school faded with each day.

"Yes. It's about the test," I lied. "I would've called, but I was in the neighborhood already."

"Sure. Son, get inside quickly; it's freezing." I followed him in. "Alex, Calvin's here."

Alex made his way to the hallway. His eyes widened as he studied me and then his father.

"Ten minutes," his dad warned.

Alex nodded, and I followed him to his room.

"What are you doing here?" Alex said when he closed the door.

"I'm sorry. I won't stay long. I just—"

"I wouldn't say anything. I told you that. But it's not a good idea for us to be seen with each other."

"What do you know about a boy who's gone missing?"

"Someone from school?"

"No. A Black boy. Fourteen."

Alex scratched his head, shaking no. I had hoped he'd know, that word had gotten out. But Alex looked genuinely confused.

"What about around the neighborhood? Any more meetings about fighting integration?"

"Shhhh." Alex flicked his finger to his mouth and waved me closer to the window, away from the bedroom door. "Were you a part of that?"

"No. Wait. What? I saw Mr. Vernon and some other men at the school board office."

"I heard"—Alex looked toward the door—"Mr. Vernon got the heads-up that more people planned to integrate."

"Where did you hear that?"

"A neighbor came by. My dad doesn't go to the meetings, not since the Sampsons."

"What else?"

"That's it—I don't know any more. I didn't hear anything about a missing boy. Who is it?"

"A friend. My friend. It's my fault. I was supposed to meet him, but that day you stopped me on the state parkway, I went home instead. He's been missing ever since."

"I'm sorry. . . . I'm sure he'll turn up."

"I don't think so." My eyes blurred "He's gone. He . . . Could you find out more? I can't ask anyone else." I tugged on Alex's shirt.

Alex's eyes looked scared. Like he wanted to say no. But his mouth said, "Yes. I'll try. I . . . You have to go, though."

I nodded. Then I headed down the hallway to the front door.

"You're not walking, are you?" Alex's father said.

"I'll be fine. I got my bike. . . . Thank you, Alex. For helping me with the test," I said before rushing out the door. Snowflakes drifted down on top of my head.

CHAPTER 33

A BLIZZARD CAME THROUGH OVER THE NEXT FEW DAYS. I WAS BLINDED by the brightness of my room. My window was dusted with snow. I jumped up to look outside. A white sheen went as far as I could see. Each flake another hairline lash on my skin, a prickling reminder that Harry wouldn't be found. No search party to look for him. Outside, the rows of houses had white rooftops. The streets were so packed with snow I couldn't tell where the grass met the road. All untouched like an innocent morning. But it was dreadful. The piles of snow mounting over sidewalks, and on my dad's car, solidified that I'd be stuck here. No way to return the files to Vernon Realty like I'd promised.

Trapped inside my home, I paced and plotted ways to jump on the phone. Outside was a quiet and serene picture fooling us all that everything was as it should be. As if nothing bad had ever happened. As if my friend weren't missing.

School was closed. Stores shut down. There would be no reason for Harry to be away from Sojourner. Each day I hoped for good news as I snuck the phone into the corner with the long cord to dial Robert. Lily. What made it worse was that my parents were practically on top of me wherever I went. It was like they knew I'd done something wrong. They just hadn't figured out what.

The only thing giving me hope that I'd be able to leave as soon as the roads cleared was how Dad seemed to be itching to get out just as much as me.

I watched the kids from my neighborhood make their way outside. Sledding and letting their dogs run loose. The blizzard had gone and just left snow. After the fourth day, drivers began testing the road, taking chances. When the temperature finally rose above freezing on Saturday, the melting began as the sun popped out. I was ready to return to Vernon Realty and finish what I'd promised.

Mom packed lunches for us as she listened to the radio. Worry filled her face about Dad and me heading to work as she looked out at the roads, but she wasn't going to convince Dad otherwise. Or me.

When we arrived downtown, the parking lot was bustling, with everyone who had cabin fever out and about. I wished I'd been able to go downtown when everything was shut down because of the snow, so I could've been alone, walking through streets without having to look over my shoulder.

"Meet me here at five," Dad said. "Let's not worry your mother more; we'll get on the road before it freezes again."

I nodded, then watched him walk to his office two blocks away before I crossed the sidewalk to enter Vernon Realty, my backpack filled with Vernon files tugged tight to me.

The bell rang above me. I expected it to be a quiet morning, but there was a murmur that reverberated from the back to the doors. My gaze darted to the back room at the echo of voices bouncing off the high walls.

A group of men had gathered, but this time with their sons by their side.

I walked to join them, legs shaking with each step. They were planning something. I could feel it in the air. The way the silence from the snow had shut everything in, and as soon as it was released, this wicked energy had escaped. The storm inside men's hate rushed for a place to go. I worried where it would land—I worried for Sojourner.

"Mr. Vernon." I approached him. "What's going on?"

"Break-in. My files were stolen." Mr. Vernon paced back and forth.

I clutched my bag, watching the men with their bats in hand. I stepped closer to the file cabinet. My mouth dropped open as Mr. Vernon hovered near the usually locked drawer, now jammed open. Empty. The files were a weight that would sink me. I'd stolen some. . . . Where were the rest?

I glanced past his shoulder and noted the shattered back-door glass. I swallowed hard. Maybe Harry had done this? Or Eugene, thinking that somehow he could fix things, threaten someone to tell him where Harry was? Eugene couldn't wait for the snow to melt; time was running out for Harry. We all knew it. My face drained at the thought of being caught. I flung my bag down under Sharon's desk.

Someone tugged my arm, and I turned back to see Alex.

"You should get out of here," Alex said in a hushed voice.

I stepped back, surprised. "What are you doing here?"

"I came with my dad. He's trying to get them to calm down."

"You didn't tell him—"

"No," Alex said. "But if my dad finds out . . ." His voice was grating now.

"Don't say it," I barked. Alex flinched.

"Was it you?" Alex pulled me toward the broken window by the back door.

"No. Of course not. Why would I break in when I work here?" I looked desperately at Alex for answers.

"Please go," he said.

"What are they going to do?"

"They think the break-in was tied to Bobby Simms, who's been leading the charge against the housing setup in Vernon Realty. They're going to find Bobby."

There would be a lot more than talking going on. I watched the men gather their things, soon to be on the road. I propped up in front of the desk and called Sojourner. No answer.

"I have to go." I slammed the phone down and ran out the front door with my bag clutched in my hand.

I raced down the street, bumping into people and making my way to my father's office. In the window I could see him occupied with a customer at his desk. My breath was ragged as I made my way inside, avoiding being seen. Then I tugged at my father's coat, hanging by the door, and searched his pockets for his car keys. They dangled in my fingers. Before I could change my mind, I left.

CHAPTER 34

THE ENGINE OF MY FATHER'S CAR REVVED GETTING INTO GEAR AS I pushed through the piled-up snow that crunched and rocked the car. I left the parking lot, sliding through a stop sign, and another, chasing away the fear that the car would lose momentum on roads with half-melted snow and black ice. Nothing was going to stop me from warning everyone at Sojourner.

I'd made it only a few miles, driving erratically, before the siren of a police car trailed me with a signature wail I'd almost forgotten after living in Levittown so long. I prayed the officer was headed elsewhere. He continued to tail me close, and I reluctantly pulled over. My heart was beating fast as the memories of my last encounter with the police rocketed into my mind.

The officer approached my window. I rolled it down, and the chilly air slapped me in the face.

"Hello, Officer." My teeth chattered from the whip of cold and fear zipping through me.

"Son, these roads are pretty dangerous. Out to start some trouble?"

"No, sir." I shook my head hard. "Finishing up one more errand. Been a bit stir-crazy in the house, not having supplies."

"Let me see your driver's license."

I handed it over, hoping that my father hadn't called in his car as stolen. The officer went back to his car with my information. At first things seemed normal, but then the officer began shaking his head and took off running to me.

I braced myself for another assault. Instead the officer had a distressed look on his face.

"Your lucky day." He flicked the driver's license at me. "Gotta run. Seems like a change of plans. Stay inside today."

"Why?" The way his voice lingered, I knew there was more.

"A bit of trouble. On the west side."

"I . . ." I needed to know more but didn't have a reason to ask. "I was supposed to pick up my mother's help today." The word *help* felt dry on my tongue. A word I'd dreaded to use as an excuse to go to the west side.

"Well, stay off Pleasant Street. A mob is building, and things are getting a bit rowdy there."

Lily lived on Pleasant Street. A flash of Trumbull Park scraped my mind. I swore I could hear the *boom boom boom* of small bombs that sounded like firecrackers.

I nodded, but inside I was drowning.

The officer sped past me, and when he turned the corner, I followed.

As I got closer to Lily's neighborhood, my heart beat so fast, I could hardly catch my breath. Instead of turning left where I could see police officers beginning to circle the crowd, I went to the back road Lily had shown me.

I drove over the gravel, the snow slowly melting. The road was blocked with trucks parked and getting ready to build the next lot. I parked, then hopped out and ran until I found Lily's home. It wasn't hard to find—I could hear the chants, the breaking of glass as people threw rocks at windows in the front of the house. The back was easier to navigate, because the homes were closer together than in my neighborhood. I came from behind the house, ducked down low, and knocked quietly at the back door.

Small hands were pressed against the window. Lily's sister. Her eyes bugged out when she saw me. Of course if her family saw me, they'd be afraid.

I mouthed, *Please get Lily. I'm a friend.* I gave her my kindest smile.

She peeked her head closer, then closed the curtains before I heard her feet patter off.

I wanted to knock louder, but then I'd draw attention from the front of the house or terrify her family even more. I didn't have to worry long: Lily appeared in the window, behind her her mother and little sister, who squeezed her way to the front. Lily opened the door a crack.

"What are you doing here, Calvin?" she whispered. "It's dangerous."

"I came to get you. I have my car." I pointed down the road.

Lily looked at her mother, then her sister. "I can't leave them."

"Of course not—they can come with us. But we'll have to hurry. There're more people coming from town."

"Who are you?" Lily's mom grimaced, tightening her hold on her daughters.

"Mama, this is . . . Calvin."

Lily's mom's face warmed a bit, the grip on her youngest daughter releasing.

"You should get out of here," Lily said.

"No, I won't. I've been through this before. I wish we'd left. I wish my father had made us go." My eyes watered, the ghost of Charlotte coming to me in flashes. I could feel the cold prickle my skin. The scent of honey and ginger, like the candies Charlotte sucked on to help her asthma. When I looked at Lily's family, I saw my mother, my father, all stuck in the house, not wanting to leave because we couldn't find Charlotte. It was how my mother had burned her neck. A mark she now covered with scarves. I thought of my mother staring out the window like she was waiting for Charlotte to appear, somehow, some way. Dreaming that she hadn't been swept away in the fire. I had held that dream too. That maybe my sister would show up, whispering how silly we all were to think she was gone.

"Please." I reached for Lily's mother's hand. "Come. You can stay at my house. Call your husband from there. Let him know you're safe."

"My husband. He's out of town. If we're gone—"

"You can call him from my house. Let him know you're safe," I repeated.

Another boom went off, shaking the house. I could hear more cars driving up in the distance. The crowd getting louder.

"We've got to go now."

Lily's mother nodded, then closed the door behind her. A few minutes later they held small bags in their hands, and I led them down the back road, our feet crunching over snow.

I didn't dare look behind us, for fear of a trail of people following me. I unlocked the car door and waited for Lily's family to pile into the back seat. Lily went to sit in the passenger seat, but I directed her to the back, throwing a blanket over them to duck under and hide if necessary. I reversed until I could turn around. Then watched an onslaught of cars coming toward Lily's house. There were trucks of men and boys standing in the back with bats and sticks. The roar of their voices shook the glass and rang inside the car until we were finally far enough away to breathe.

The car was silent the rest of the ride. My mind raced, planning what I'd say to my mother. She couldn't deny me. Not a mother and her children. No, I knew she would help.

When we arrived, I opened the back door for Lily and her family. They had the blanket wrapped over their shoulders and bags in their hands. My mother had a glazed look in her eye, like she was seeing a ghost. Then she shook it off when she realized we were real.

I felt hairs prickle on the back of my neck. When I turned around, Mary stood outside, mouth gaping open. I placed my finger to my lips, begging her for silence. Mary didn't speak; her cold eyes said enough.

"Come in. Come in." Mom's voice shook as she rushed us inside. She shut the door quickly behind us. I bristled at the thought of Mary, a worry for later.

"Calvin, what is going on?" Mom said.

I couldn't speak. I just looked at Lily with tears in my eyes.

"This is Lily," I said. "The girl from school."

Mom reached for her hand. "Nice to meet you, Lily."

"This is my mother, Darla. My sister, Vera," Lily said.

"Nice to meet you." Mom smiled, touching Vera's hand. "I have a sister named Vera."

"Mom, can you watch them? Keep them safe. Their house is . . . There's a mob in front of it."

Mom drew in a hard breath. "Yes. Yes of course. You can stay as long as you need to."

Mom rushed to the front window and closed the blinds. I ran to the phone and dialed Robert's number.

"I'm sorry, Mom. They might be headed to Sojourner next. I have to warn Robert."

"What's wrong with Robert?" Mom reached to my shoulders to shake me. "What did he do?"

"He's fine—Robert didn't do anything wrong. It was me. It was . . . It's too long a story. But I can't reach him. I have to go. Keep calling. Tell him he has to get everyone to leave before a mob arrives." I searched the desk for something to write Robert's number on for Mom so she could keep trying to reach him.

"I have his number." Mom pushed the paper back to me. "You think I don't know how to reach my son?"

I gulped before I flung my backpack toward her. "Keep this safe. If anything happens to me, send the files to the man on the business card." I prayed that once she saw Thurgood Marshall's name, she'd know what to do.

"You can't go alone." Mom reached out to stop me.

"I'll go with you," Lily said.

"No," I said. "It's too dangerous."

"Your father," Mom said. "Where is he? Is he okay?"

"Yes, he's fine. He's . . ." I looked outside to his car, realizing he'd be stranded downtown.

"You can't leave him."

"It'll be too late. I'll take his car back, then run to Sojourner. It's not far, and Robert has a car."

"That's not safe," Lily said.

"Take your father with you," my mom insisted.

"I'll be fine. I won't be long." I hugged my mother and took one last look at Lily, then left before I could be convinced otherwise.

Downtown, I dropped my father's car off, keys inside it. I didn't stop to get him. I couldn't take the risk that he'd stop me, so I left on foot, running for my life.

CHAPTER 35

WITH EACH POUNDING STEP, I KNEW THAT CUTTING THROUGH THE Capewoods would shave my arrival time down. I still wasn't ready to test the lore of the haunted place, but I was the only thing between the mob and my friends' safety. A car veered fast alongside me, and I dipped below tree branches to see car after car moving quickly.

I finally accepted that the woods were my only option. I hoped that once my feet touched the ground, I'd be lost in a dark thicket of trees and brush. Trees that would engulf me and hide me from the road so I could get to Sojourner before a mob could arrive.

As I ran through the Capewoods, a howling scream caught up to me, and I covered my ears to drown out what sounded like the dead. I felt wind whipping at me like I was being chased. I feared I wouldn't make it to Sojourner before the woods had their way with me. I passed the abandoned church, smack-dab in the middle of the Capewoods. I was tempted to stop and let the sounds pass, but I'd come too far, and Robert was close. So I ran through the rest of the woods and out the other side, where Sojourner stood tall. I headed to the doors, relief setting in that there wasn't a mob there yet.

I entered Sojourner, yelling, "They're coming. We've got to leave. Everyone."

James popped out of the kitchen. "Calvin! Calvin, what's wrong?"

"Where is Robert?" I shook his shoulders lightly, desperation in my eyes.

"Robert's upstairs."

Footsteps came down the stairs, shouts and calls echoing through the house.

"What the hell is going on?" Robert said.

"Why didn't you answer the phone? We have to get out of here. They're coming."

"Calm down. The phone's been off since the snow," Robert said. "Who is coming?"

"Someone broke into Vernon Realty and took more papers from the files I've been pulling. I don't know what was taken, but they already know about the attempt at integration." I rested my hands on my knees, trying to catch my breath. "Mr. Vernon called a group of people, and they're going after Bobby Simms to find out what he knows. They'll beat the truth out of him. And then they'll be headed here. There's already a big group at Lily's. I got her and her family out."

"We have to get out of here!" Robert yelled upstairs.

Robert's students filed downstairs, terrified. Eugene stood at the top of the third flight, looking down at me, then made his way slowly. He didn't have to say it. He had broken into Vernon Realty.

"Is this everyone?"

"Yes, everyone else is gone because of Thanksgiving and then the snow." Robert pointed to the four students beside Eugene. "We have to go. It might take a few trips to get everyone out." I looked out the window. I could see a car in the distance turning down Port Lane. We had maybe three minutes.

"The woods." I pointed to the Capewoods.

"No. It's too late. We wouldn't have anywhere else to go." Robert said. "If we head in there, they'll follow. We can't stay outside that long; we'll freeze."

"The tunnel entry in the barn," Eugene said.

I whipped my head at Eugene, confused.

"Let's go." Robert led everyone to the barn. James and Eugene pulled up crates and a table. Below was a hatch they heaved open. Hidden in the floor was the entrance to a tunnel. Barbara's description of the Capewoods sank in.

"Come on, hurry," Robert said.

I couldn't believe it was true. That an Underground Railroad tunnel lay below this area. I realized that must've been what Lily had meant when she'd shared that she wasn't scared of the Capewoods. Maybe the sounds people heard in the woods were only wind running through the tunnels. The woods had been a place to hide when slave catchers were searching up North on this land. And anyone who was hurt then—they were ancestors. They wouldn't harm us.

James moved a flat piece of wood that covered up the entrance, then went below to help everyone else come down safely. Eugene and I watched them all go in, Robert next. He reached his hand up for me to join.

"No." I turned to Eugene. "I'll take care of this."

"I'm not going if you're staying."

"I know them. Besides, how will you close this?"

"Don't worry about me," Eugene said.

"Eugene, we don't have time. What if the mob from Lily's house comes here?"

"Then I'll hide in the barn in case you need me." Eugene stuck his hand out. "I won't let you do this alone."

"They won't find us," Robert called from below. "We have to go."

"What if they come in the barn and find this hideaway?" I said.

"This leads to the church," Robert said. "We'll run out and through the woods if we have to."

A yell from outside caught our attention. Flames danced across my eyes. The smell of smoke that had followed me from Chicago, lingering. I couldn't let another home be ruined. "Go." I shoved Eugene closer to the tunnel entrance below.

"I'm not going," Eugene said.

"I'll come back when it's safe!" I yelled down to Robert. "Wait for Eugene." Then I begged Eugene, "Go. I can do this."

"But Harry."

"They won't tell you where Harry is if they have him," I said. "You have to trust me."

"Be safe," Eugene said, grabbing my ears with his hands. "Don't make me regret it."

"Check the house." Shouts from outside the barn jerked me into action as Eugene scurried into the tunnel. His feet slammed against the wooden steps before he plunged down, dust kicking up and floating to me. I took one last look down, a handful of eyes staring up at me as I put the floorboard back in place, layering a mat over the hatch to cover it from view. I wiped my forehead so the sweat, the fear, wouldn't show. And stepped outside the barn.

CHAPTER 36

WHEN I OPENED THE BARN DOOR, THERE WASN'T A MOB. BEN STOOD IN front of his dad's car, Darren and Alex by his side. I clenched my fists at the violation of them being here. Shivers ran through me as I cautiously stepped closer.

"What are you doing here?" Darren yelled to me.

I paused. "Mr. Vernon sent me," I said. I watched him only slightly back down. "I came by to check it out."

"Anyone here?" Ben looked toward the Capewoods, like he was searching for something.

"No one inside. I—I searched already," I stuttered out. My eyes became fixed on a bat in Darren's hand.

Ben looked at Alex, who kept his head down.

"What about in there?" Darren said, suspiciously eyeing the barn behind me.

"Empty." I avoided Darren's eyes.

"I know they live here," Darren said.

"Who?"

"The people who broke into Mr. Vernon's office. The ones trying to ruin our town. Fill up our school with thugs." Darren's voice was darker than before. The mob mentality was rubbing off on him—a spark that could catch flame easily.

"Well, whoever they are, they're gone," I said. Then I paused. "Why'd you think to come here?"

"Mary called me. She was pretty shaken up," Darren said.

I lowered my head. Mary. *What else did she tell him?*

"She's pretty convinced you're in close with Lily," Ben said, his voice cracking. He hadn't told Darren yet.

"And I believe her," Darren said.

"How would Mary know that?" I said. "I don't like bullies, that's all. Besides, Mr. Vernon said to lie low. Everything you've done puts things at risk."

"It's cold," Ben said. "Check the barn and the house, and I'll stand watch."

Darren jogged over to the barn. I was still except for my fists balled up, ready to fight Darren if I had to.

"We didn't say anything," Alex said low.

Ben gave him a glare. "It won't be long before people find out. You should just help us; then everything can go back to normal."

I shook my head. "Help you do what?" I forced a chuckle. "Let's get out of here."

"Not till this is fixed." Ben paused. "You have anything to do with breaking into Mr. Vernon's, and all that mess with the school registration paperwork?"

"No," I said. "I told you. Mr. Vernon sent me here."

"So you're here to help, then?" Ben said, relieved. Then he

looked to the Capewoods again. "I'm checking the woods out. Stay here."

I pulled his arm, holding him back, giving my friends time to escape if Darren forced them through the other end of the tunnel.

"Let's just go," Alex said. "I don't want any trouble."

"Yeah." I looked at Alex for help.

"I don't either," Ben said. "I just want things to go back to how they were, but I don't know if they can."

"Things can if you let it go," I said. "We don't have to follow their rules."

Ben shook his head. "Glad you're here, Calvin. Lily doesn't go to our school anymore. And once we help Mr. Vernon, we can be back to normal again. I've thought about it. You're just like me. Just as white as me. That drop-of-blood rule is dumb. You're white, Calvin. You can be white."

I nodded. Tears welled in my eyes, and I blinked them away, faking my agreement so he'd leave.

"No one's there." Darren pushed his way out of the barn. "We need to leave them a message. Let's burn it down." Darren pointed to Sojourner.

"What?" I screeched. "Are you out of your mind? You don't even know who lives here!"

"Yeah, I do. We've seen them." Darren looked to Ben. I scanned between both of them, wondering exactly what he meant.

"That's ridiculous," I said. "Just calm down. Let's go. No one's here, okay?"

"Let's go," Alex said.

I stepped toward Ben's dad's car to sit in the back. My gaze stopped at the trunk, which wasn't fully closed. Bronze metal sticking out. I ran my hands along the car, unraveling some twine hitching the trunk closed. My hands were tingling. Afraid to touch Harry's bike. Ben had been here before. I wanted to choke him.

"When"—my thoughts swirled in my head, and I struggled to get them out without yelling—"did you get it back?"

"Last week," Ben said.

"Where did you find it?" My voice rose, and a strange throttling sound came through. I flicked my eyes to the barn; if Eugene knew they had Harry's bike, he would explode. I forced the bike deeper into the trunk. Before I could pull my thoughts together, Darren yelled.

"Look!" Darren pointed to the Capewoods. "That's where they are."

I stepped forward, watching as someone stopped in the woods, staring at us. *No. No. Why wouldn't they wait?*

Then I saw a flash, and the person ran back deeper into the trees.

I almost collapsed.

Lily. It couldn't be. I looked at Alex, who touched my arm to hold me back.

"Help me," I pleaded. "Make them stop."

"I was trying to," Alex added quietly. "That's why I came. I wouldn't be here to do this."

"Help her get away," I said. "It's Lily."

Alex nodded as Ben took off running behind Darren. My skin prickled as Lily's scream echoed through the Capewoods.

CHAPTER 37

AS I ENTERED THE WOODS, A PAIN HIT MY CHEST. LILY HAD COME, BUT what would be the reason she'd risk going alone? Then a sickening feeling overtook me: this was only going to get worse. The sky was hidden by the trees; it was dark, and the cold air mixed with the ground caused a fog to rise.

Wailing noises floated through the woods as my feet whipped over snow, through dead grass and fallen branches. It was like the woods were springing awake. Prickles ran up my spine.

I pointed for Alex to follow, but I couldn't see him through the mysterious fog and the trees that appeared to be moving, ripping from their roots. I blinked hard to shake the image.

A scream broke through the air again, ricocheting through the forest. I swore it was Lily. But I could still hear Darren yelling; he hadn't found her. So why had Lily screamed? With everything swirling and changing in front of me, I didn't know if I should go left or right, so I shut my eyes and stood still, searching for a direction to follow.

Dread wrenched my insides.

I opened my eyes and shut the noises out. I could see clear as day again.

Ben weaved through the fog, running in the opposite direction from Darren. My feet now numb, I stepped toward a trail of what I suspected were Lily's footprints.

And it was like a solution appeared in front of me, clear as could be. The abandoned church was ahead. I thrashed through the woods, cutting my face and arms on branches as I made my way. I clawed myself inside, hoping superstitions about the hallowed ground would stop whatever was chasing me and I would find Lily safe inside, escaped to the tunnels.

"Lily. Lily," I whispered over and over again.

The church was small, maybe eight hundred square feet in total. I looked in every crevice, searching the floorboards for the tunnel exit that Robert had mentioned. At the very back of the church was a closet that had to lead to the tunnel. I ran my hands across the grooves of the floor where the carpet was pulled back. A hidden door with a latch. The edges looked disrupted, fresh dust wiped away from the floorboard. Desperation helped me lift the hatch with a heave.

I pulled and shoved the handle until it popped. A cracking noise reverberated in the tiny room. I reached for a small ladder plastered to the wall. When I put my weight down, I had to quickly lift my foot at a snapping sound. The old wood was clearly unstable. I shut my eyes and took a chance, plunging to the ground below.

The landing was hard, but the fall shorter than I'd expected. Tentatively I stepped forward, squinting as I felt along the wall.

I heard a croak. "Who's there?"

"Lily, is that you? It's Calvin."

"Help." Another whisper. I waited until my eyes adjusted. A clicking noise came, followed by a faint glow from a flickering flashlight.

I touched my trembling hand over my chest. "Harry. My God. What are you doing down here?"

I rushed to him, slumped in the corner along a caved-in wall. The ceiling had collapsed, cutting off the tunnel to the barn. He looked like he'd lost ten pounds. He had a thermos of water and food wrappers strewn around him.

"Trapped." His voice was raspy and weak.

"Hush. Save your voice." I was in shock. Harry had been hiding in the tunnel. Eugene was going to kill him as soon as I saved him. Then I gasped with worry, turning away so he would miss my concern. If the tunnel were collapsing here, there was no certainty that the almost three-hundred-year-old tunnel would be stable anywhere. For us, or for everyone on the other side of the collapse.

"Did you come to help me?"

"Yes. But you have to be quiet. They're searching the woods for Lily. It's . . . a long story."

"Who?"

"Wait. Just wait." I couldn't tell Harry after all this time underground that outside was worse. So much worse.

"I have no choice." Harry pointed to his ankle.

I grimaced; it was swollen. Probably broken.

"I got the papers."

"What?"

"The papers." Harry pointed to his bag. Crunched up inside were registration forms for the school.

"How did you . . . ? Never mind. Harry. God, Harry, it's so good to see you. How long have you been down here?"

"Since we were supposed to meet downtown. I raced down here to hide."

"But the water and food?"

"I go down here sometimes, exploring the tunnel. I wanted to see where people hide in the woods when they disappear, to prove they're not ghosts," Harry coughed out.

"Did you find anyone hiding?" I had to ask with a broken chuckle.

"There are ghosts." Harry coughed again. "Definitely ghosts." His eyes closed, heavy, and I shook him.

"I have to leave you here. I'll be back."

"No!" Harry cried. "Don't leave me here with them. They're so scared and lonely here. Like an echo from the past."

I looked around, seeing nothing. He must be delirious.

My eyes teared up. Harry had been here so long, who knew what he thought he'd seen and heard. I touched Harry's face, wiping away dirt and grime. Brushing off my own thoughts about what was really out here in the Capewoods.

"Harry, I'll be back. I'll bring Eugene, but I have to wait until it's safe. Do you trust me?"

"Don't lock the door." Harry reached for me. "He locked me in here, took my bike."

I could feel rage toward Ben work its way inside me. I looked at Harry. "Be brave. Just a little longer."

"Okay." Harry gave a weak, tired smile.

I held back tears, and my throat swelled. That hopeful smile and crack in his voice let me know he hadn't been broken yet. But he couldn't stay down there much longer.

I climbed up from the tunnel and out into the church, but not before double-checking that the latch was released so if something happened, if for some reason I couldn't make it back there, maybe Harry could get out. His foot looked infected, though; I knew time was running out.

When I stepped outside the church, the fog was still cleared, but somehow just for me. I watched Darren walk aimlessly, lost, dipping in and out of pockets of trees tentatively. My relief only lasted a split second, though, because Lily was trapped behind a tree. If she ran, Darren would spot her.

Lily stood in place, gripping the tree with her back to it. As Darren got closer, I sprinted toward her, but she was too far away, so I yelled. Except that the sound traveled before my voice escaped from my mouth. Like an echo, I yelled her name and the woods repeated it. Or at least I thought they did, until I realized Eugene was yelling too. Eugene was cutting through the trees from the barn, racing toward her.

Lily zigzagged to avoid Darren's grasp until he trapped her. Her scream was like blood running through my ears. I pumped my arms to move as fast as I could. Darren slammed her to the ground.

Eugene reached Darren first, trampling him. They fought and tumbled around.

Darren's punches were followed by slurs before he wrapped his arm around Eugene, choking him.

"Stop! You'll kill him!" I jabbed at Darren, punching and punching the back of his neck. "You'll kill him!"

Darren didn't loosen his grip. I punched harder until he eased up on Eugene, who was able to scramble away and catch his breath.

But I wasn't a match for Darren. He shoved me off him, knocking me to the ground. I slipped through snow, so dizzy my body didn't respond.

"I'm gonna kill you," Darren yelled at Eugene, and flicked a knife out from his pocket.

"I know you," Eugene said. "You were here before. I saw you run through the woods. The day my brother went missing."

It was Darren, not Ben, who'd locked Harry in. Or maybe both of them had done it. I seethed.

Darren froze. He couldn't deny the guilty look on his face.

"I'm going to kill *you*," Eugene said. "What'd you do to him?" Eugene stepped closer, more distraught than angry. Darren took advantage, charging toward him. And before I knew it, he'd sliced his knife across Eugene's side.

"Your little brother fought harder than you," Darren said.

"Aaaaaah!" Eugene threw all his body weight into Darren's chest. I watched in horror as Darren slipped on the snow and fell back on his head. We all stopped in place at the sound of a crack.

Eugene gritted his teeth, touching his stomach. His face pained, he rocked back and forth as he held his hand over the blood seeping out. I raced to cover his side, using pressure to stop the bleeding. Darren still wasn't moving.

"Darren!" I called, before glancing at Lily to see if she was safe. She sat, breathing heavily as she rubbed her hip.

Eugene and I stayed far enough away from Darren in case he jumped up and gave us hell again. Alex emerged from the trees and knelt down before placing his ear to Darren's mouth.

"He's not breathing," Alex said.

"No. No. No." Eugene bent over, touching his wound. "He was after me. He admitted he hurt my brother—you heard him, right?" Blood was smeared all over Eugene's shirt and covered his hands as he tried to stop the bleeding.

I ran to Darren and rolled him slightly, and that was when I saw the blood seeping from his head. A large rock lay beneath him. Without thinking, I pulled at his shirt and shook him.

"Wake up, you son of a bitch," I said. "Wake up!"

"He isn't . . ." Eugene didn't finish his sentence. We all knew what had happened. Darren was dead.

Lily got up from the ground where she was huddled, then made her way to Eugene, touching his hand as he pressed on his wound. "It's not your fault. Eugene. Look at me. It's not your fault."

I couldn't help but think about Bobo. What happened to him would pale in comparison to what the mob would do to us if they found out about Darren.

"We have to hide his body." I stood up, dropping Darren in place.

"What?" Alex said. "How? We can't do that. What about . . ."

Alex trailed off as I stepped closer.

"Where is Ben?" I scanned, surprised he still was nowhere in sight.

"He must've run toward Bailey Road while we covered the woods," Alex said.

"We need to hurry," I said. "Grab his legs."

"Hide his body and then what?" Eugene said. "Your friend is gonna tell on us, and we'll all be dead. I have to say I was alone here. They won't care about what really happened."

"If they find him, I'll take the blame," I said. "If that happens, we need to tell the same story. Lily and Eugene were never here. It was you and me, Alex. He attacked me, and I defended myself."

"We can just tell the truth," Alex said.

"We can't," Eugene said. "The town is out for blood. There won't be an investigation if they find out what happened. They won't care about self-defense, not if it was me or anyone else Black."

"They'll listen," Alex said.

"They won't," I said. "They're piled up in droves at her house."

Lily nodded, now holding on to Eugene.

"We can't trust him," Eugene said. "There's no reason for you to get in trouble too."

"No. We can trust him. Alex won't say anything. If we hurry, we can do this before Ben gets back." I shook Alex's shoulder. "Alex, you'd have to go on trial. Your family would be on trial. Your secrets would come out; they wouldn't trust you, either," I warned.

Alex looked at Eugene and Lily, who were confused by my words. "I . . . How did you know?" Alex said.

"Tell me," I said. I wanted to hear it from him.

"I . . ." Alex looked at Eugene. "I'm Jewish. My family. My mother's side. My dad is Christian. Mr. Vernon knows; he just kept the file quiet because of everything that happened to the Sampsons. Too much for him to be blamed for, letting it happen again under his watch. But if we were to go to trial, I'd be blamed too." Alex looked at Eugene and Lily. "We'd all be blamed."

I stood. I could lie and say it was me, but then it would drag in my family's and Alex's secrets. But if I told the truth, they'd want Eugene. Lily, too.

"We have to bury him," I said. "It's the only way."

Everyone froze.

"We have no choice," I said. "Darren did this to himself. He would have done worse." I picked up Darren's arms and waited for Eugene and Alex to help.

"Lily," Eugene said. "Head to the barn, everyone's in the tunnels, tell them it's time to go quickly before the mob comes."

"Grab water and the first aid supplies from the house," I said, breathing heavy as we carried Darren. "I'll explain later."

Lily hesitated, then looked at Eugene's bloody side before running back to the barn.

"Where are we taking him?" Eugene said.

"To the church. Where Harry is hiding."

CHAPTER 38

"YOU SAW HIM?" EUGENE'S VOICE CRACKED AS I SHARED WHERE HARRY had been hiding.

I nodded.

"I didn't know," Alex said. "I swear."

"Let's hurry." Eugene surged with adrenaline as we dragged Darren's body to the church.

Eugene rushed to the doors and made way for us to drop Darren on the ground.

"You sure we can trust him?" Eugene said, glaring at Alex.

"We don't have a choice," I said quietly.

We both made an audible heave as we dragged Darren's body over the threshold into the church. In the back, at the closet door, was Ben, hunched over.

"Leave him!" I raced toward Ben, gripping his shirt. "You've done enough."

"Stop." Ben's face pleaded. "He won't come to me."

I shook Ben; Eugene hovered over my shoulder.

"Stop this!" Alex yelled. "Just stop—no one else needs to get hurt."

"He won't come. I tried to tell him I'm sorry. I came here to help him." It was then that I noticed the tears on Ben's face. I let him go, shoving him out of the way and looking down onto the floorboard.

"Stay back there," I called to Ben.

I eased down into the tunnel, no longer afraid of the dark. I was afraid of what would happen if we were too late.

"Harry!" Eugene yelled.

"Harry, I'm back," I said.

We were frantic. I waited for him to call out, but when my eyes finally adjusted, I saw that Harry's were shut. I rushed to him.

"He's after me," Harry whispered. He'd dragged himself closer to the part of the tunnel where the ceiling had collapsed, to get away from Ben.

"He's dehydrated. In shock—his ankle is broken." I felt for his body and began moving him with help from Eugene, who'd refused to stay back. We carried Harry through the tunnel and to the exit; Alex and Ben helped lift him onto the church floor. When we got up, I looked to Ben for answers.

"Harry! Harry!" Eugene called while I put my head near his mouth and chest.

"He's still alive. He needs a hospital."

"So does Darren," Ben said, noticing Darren for the first time. He stood frozen, his face morphing into shock. Ben reached for Darren, and I pulled his arm back.

"It's too late for him," I said. "We need to hurry."

Before we could go on, we wrapped Darren's body in old altar linens and drapes from the church; then I jumped into the tunnel so Alex and Ben could lower him down to me. I dragged his body to the end of the caved-in tunnel, trying to ignore Ben's shaky voice asking questions about why we were doing this. I held back the tears, the fear, the fact that this would be a day I'd never be able to erase. I'd never be able to explain why we couldn't just call the police and say it was an accident. Because if we did, there would be no trial. No self-defense. Our trial would be in the woods. End in the woods.

I pushed through everything in me that told me I should do different. When it was done, I sucked in all my sympathy. Darren had left Harry to die.

I closed the hatch behind me, never to return.

CHAPTER 39

WE CARRIED HARRY TO SOJOURNER, YELLING OUT FOR HELP. LILY MET US by the barn with Robert; James and the students huddled behind him. Robert looked ready to fight, but he dropped his fists at the sight of us. Bloody, beaten, and broken. But all of us together: me, Eugene, Harry, Alex, and Ben.

"We have to get Harry and Eugene to the hospital," I said.

"We have things to clean up," Eugene said, glazed-eyed and shaking; I could see him replaying it all in his head.

Robert ran his hands across his face like he was physically trying to remove his concern to stay calm. Robert pointed to his students. "Go inside and pack a small bag. We need to get you kids out of here." I waited until they were inside Sojourner.

"There was an accident." I tried to explain. "I'll fill you in. But first, Harry and Eugene."

Silence took over, and I couldn't help but look away.

"I'll take them," James said. "Think you've got bigger things to manage here."

"Take care of them," Robert said.

"With my life." James hugged Robert; then they helped Harry to Robert's car. I slung Eugene's arm around my shoulders as we hobbled to join them.

"Thank you, Calvin," Eugene said weakly as he crawled into the back seat, nursing his stomach after making sure Harry was secure.

"Hey," I said. "Keep your eyes open back there. You gotta stay awake. For Harry."

Eugene nodded, more alert.

"What's going on? Someone needs to explain." Robert said.

"He should tell us." I stalked my way to Ben. "What did you do!"

"It's not what it looks like. I didn't come here for Darren or Mr. Vernon—I came to get Harry out."

My face scrunched up. "What?"

"Darren saw him with my bike . . . his bike. He wanted to get it back. I just thought he'd play around. But then he chased Harry here through the woods and into the church. Harry ran into the closet; Darren said he disappeared. I thought he was joking, until I looked and he was gone. I thought it was all the haunting people talked about. But then I heard he was still missing. That's when Darren finally told me there was a tunnel and that he'd locked Harry in. I wanted to go back to free him, but the snow came. Today was the first day I could get out."

I stood stunned. Unable to decide whether Ben's story was true.

"Why didn't you say anything?"

"I didn't know what to do. Alex told me you were asking about a missing kid. I knew Darren didn't let him out. I wanted to help. I swear."

"He could've died." Lily's voice cracked.

"Why didn't you tell me?" Alex said. "We could've told Calvin."

"I don't know." Ben began choking up. "What about Darren? What are we going to do?"

"You're going to keep your mouth shut," I said. "Just like you did about Harry."

"We can't do that to him. His family," Ben said.

"We can and we will," Alex said.

"Who is Darren and what is going on?" Robert said.

"It was an accident," Alex said. "Darren was going to hurt Lily, probably try and kill Eugene if he could get away with it."

"Darren stabbed Eugene," I said. "Eugene pushed him back to defend himself, and while they were fighting, Darren tripped and cracked his head. . . ."

"Oh my God." Robert blew out a long breath. "This isn't something you can cover up."

"We will," I said. "And we have to. He's in the tunnels. They won't find him."

"Did anyone else know Darren was coming here?" Robert asked.

"No," Ben said.

"I don't think so," Alex said.

"Anybody asks, he wanted to go to Concord Park. To join the mob. You dropped him on the side of the road and turned around," I said. "Ben, this goes to our graves."

Ben nodded. "I'm sorry. I swear—"

"Our graves." I stuck my hand out; Ben shook. I didn't let go until I was convinced the look in his eye was a promise.

"Get out of here and go home. Don't tell anyone you saw me or that you were here," I said.

Alex nodded. "Come on, Ben. Let's go."

Alex opened the trunk all the way, then helped Ben lift the bike out and place it on the ground. They pulled around and drove away.

"Do you trust him?" Robert said.

"We have to," I said.

Robert ushered the last few of his students to gather their things and find locations to stay the next few days, until things quieted down. Thirty minutes later, a pastor from a church a few miles away picked up the rest of the students.

"Are you hurt?" I touched Lily's hand.

"I'm fine. I . . ."

"You shouldn't have come," I said. "But I'm glad you're okay."

"I'm sorry. Your neighbor Mary came knocking on the back door. Vera answered; she thought she was a friend come to help, like you did. Mary asked where you were, and Vera told her you were off to help your brother at Sojourner. I had to warn you. I couldn't stay back. I didn't think they'd go after me. It's my fault. God, it's my fault."

I tugged at Lily's arm. "It was self-defense."

"That would never matter. You know that."

A tear traced down Lily's cheek; I wiped it away.

"It's not your fault. It's not anyone's fault. He came here to hurt everyone. To cause harm. We didn't start this. Darren and

Ben were the ones who left Harry there alone." I needed to believe this as much as I needed Lily to.

"Someone's here?" Lily said as a car pulled up.

I stepped closer. My mouth dropped open.

"Our father," Robert said. "I'll talk to him."

I followed Robert and he opened the door, his hands shaking.

"Let's go." Dad pointed his finger at me. Then he searched the room until his gaze landed on Lily. I swear his shoulders relaxed. "And your mother is terrified. You're coming with me too, young lady." Dad was firm, but his voice was warm.

In silence, Lily and I met him at the door.

As Robert began to close the door, my father put his hand out to stop him.

"What do you think you're doing? You're coming with me right now."

Robert and I looked at each other.

"I . . . It won't be safe. I'll stay here."

"I know. Alex called and told me everything," my dad said.

"E-Everything?" I stuttered.

"Well, someone had to explain what the hell was going on," my dad said. "The both of you are coming with me. We got a house filled with innocent people to protect."

"What if anyone sees me?" Robert said.

"I think our passing days are over."

My chest tightened. I didn't hesitate; we piled into the car.

When we entered the house, the blinds were closed. In the kitchen, my mother was sharing tea with Lily's mother. It was the first time I'd seen a genuine smile on my mother's face since the day we moved in. She had this high, open laugh, a hearty laugh. I watched my dad look at her with a starriness in his eyes. I hadn't realized that maybe my dad missed that about her. Maybe he was just as unhappy about the move as I was.

"Robert." Mom placed her tea down and ran to him. Her arms moved everywhere, touching Robert's face, then kissing my forehead and holding on to Robert like he would disappear if she let go of him.

CHAPTER 40

FOR TWO DAYS WE WAITED ROUND THE CLOCK, WITH BATS IN HAND, ready for the mob to arrive and force their way into our home. For Mary to tell the neighborhood that our house was full of the wrong kind of people. Lily and her family took over our third bedroom.

Robert paced with worry late into the night over not being there to protect Sojourner. He made calls on and off to his students as he promised them they were in a temporary situation. And at night, when everything was quiet, I could hear him talking to James, catching up on Eugene's and Harry's recoveries.

By late Monday morning, there had still been nothing about what was happening near Lily's house or in the community. But on the radio, there was a roar from a crowd that caught my ear.

"Turn it up," I said.

Rosa Parks fined for refusing to move from her seat
for a white woman.

As the story unfolded, our living room crowded with everyone. Hidden by shut blinds, we listened closely. For the first time, there was a sense of hope. There was something in the air that was different. It wasn't just the news rolling over the biggest story since Bobo's murder. Having Lily's family in our home, Robert there, my parents took off their mask.

That morning, the biggest story in the country was taking over. A massive boycott was brewing. I thought of our road trip to Virginia. I picked up the phone to call Eugene, who was now staying at James's place.

"How you guys doing?" I asked.

"I'm mostly better. They say Harry'll be fine. A cast, and fluids for recovery."

"Thank God. We'll be by soon to check on you, bring food." I paused as the speaker from the radio went on. "Eugene, listen."

I placed the receiver by the radio.

The radio announcer spoke:

Rosa Parks was arrested in Montgomery, Alabama, on December 1.

Dr. Martin Luther King Jr., a young minister, has taken over Montgomery after Rosa Parks refused to give up her seat on a city bus. Dr. King is now gathered here with nearly five thousand people at the Holt Street Baptist Church in Montgomery. This has now rallied a call throughout Montgomery, the first of its kind in the South.

Here is Dr. King.

We were mesmerized by Dr. King's voice. There was an urgency as he spoke about the love of democracy we hold. Citizenship in the fullness of its meaning. Chills went through our bodies. My faith grew as I thought about the work we were doing at Heritage and in exposing Mr. Vernon.

"In Alabama. I can't believe it." Mom leaned in closer to Dad.

Dad looked at Mom, his eyes watering. This was the kind of thing that would usually have brought my father irritation. The danger of it. He'd thought the way to our freedom was proving himself by being a good citizen. That his fighting in the war would give us equality. Robert's way had been to organize and fight at home. But now, Dad reached his hand over Robert's shoulder and gave a knowing glance.

When Dr. King's speech ended, the crowd joined in with chants and claps.

I picked up the phone to hear what Eugene thought. "Did you hear it? Dr. King? Our meeting in Virginia was about finding something to rally for. Do you think this is it?"

"This is . . . I don't even have the words." Eugene's voice broke off.

"I'll call you later. Take care of Harry."

"Always."

I hung up, then turned to Robert. "James is taking care of them good."

Dad glanced between me and Robert but didn't speak. His shoulders didn't tense up like so many times before. He seemed to take these words as comfort.

Dad turned the radio down, and we huddled in the living room.

"Our homes are segregated," I said. "It's supposed to be illegal, but it still happens here. Something happened to the people who lived here before us. We can't let Mr. Vernon and anyone else involved get away with that. That could've been us." I paused. "That can still be us."

"I know." Dad stood up and paced, running his fingers through his hair. "I'm not blind to it."

"Tell them, William," Mom said.

I swung my glance between my parents.

"Mr. Sampson was a friend in the war. His wife . . ." Dad paused.

"His wife was killed," I said.

Dad's eyes widened, surprised. "He couldn't deal with it. Knew it wasn't safe to stay. I'd planned to move, to . . . pass. So he sold the house to us. I promised I'd find out who was behind it. When I got the job at Concord Park, it was my way of helping, use passing to convince other white people it was okay to move into Concord Park. I'm ashamed for what I'm doing; it was my way of reconciling it."

"Wait, but how come you didn't tell me this?" I said. "Was me working at Vernon Realty your plan all along?"

"No, son, that was not the plan." My father's face reddened in embarrassment at our secrets unfolding before Lily's family.

"We were going to pass here. But it didn't mean I wasn't going to use my ability to help make progress. So there would be a better life for us, for you . . . for Robert."

My mind swirled, unable to think of the right questions to ask him. All this time? He hadn't completely lost himself. My father hadn't completely forgotten who we were.

"I was working toward finding out what happened, without drawing suspicion. I didn't get close."

"But I did." I told them about the letters between Vernon Realty and the National Association of Real Estate Boards. How Levitt & Sons developers were able to keep the Levittown community segregated. Dad's mouth dropped open.

"What were you going to do with it?" he asked.

I asked Mom to take out the card I'd left with her for safekeeping: Thurgood Marshall's card. "He could take on the FHA and NAREB."

Dad stayed silent, but he nodded. I glanced at Robert, a half smile on his face. We listened to the radio more about the responses, the building calls of people willing to go to Alabama to help.

CHAPTER 41

THE NEXT MORNING, DAD ROCKED ME AWAKE, THEN DID THE SAME TO Robert.

"We're packing up our things."

"What's happening?" I said.

"We're leaving. We're going back to Chicago. We'll get the files to Mr. Thurgood Marshall. It's only a matter of time before Mary tells her family, a friend at school . . ."

I looked at my brother, then at my mom.

Before, all I'd wanted to do was go back home. Back to Ray, my other friends, and family. Back to streets I could walk along and be myself. But now there was Lily. My throat closed tight at the thought of never seeing her again.

"We could stay and fight," I said. "We can help integrate, bring everyone from Sojourner here."

"We can't stay here," Dad said. "When they find out we were passing, that you got this evidence working for Mr. Vernon—"

"It would be worse for you than for anyone trying to integrate," Robert cut in.

"But we have to wait and see what happens. Make sure no one else gets hurt."

"We're all miserable," Dad said. "Your mother can't stay here any longer. She wants to go home."

"We could move to Concord Park." I couldn't believe I'd said that, after everything I'd felt about being away from Chicago.

Robert put his hand on my shoulder. "You can't switch worlds like that. Not here. If they found out Dad had fooled them, it would be dangerous." Robert looked at Dad.

"Robert, get your things—you can stay with us," Dad said.

"I can't go," Robert said.

I looked at Robert and understood. I might not have a choice, and everything inside Robert's eyes told me there was nothing more he'd rather do than have the family back. But things had changed. He'd built up Sojourner as his family. He couldn't leave them.

"Robert," Dad said, "I'm sorry for how I've been. But you're welcome home. Let's be a family. James can come too."

I looked from left to right between Dad and Robert. Robert was frozen, like he was replaying my dad's words in his mind before they sank in. Robert's eyes teared, and he gave Dad a hug. Then Robert pulled back, holding on to Dad's shoulders.

"I'll visit, Dad. I'll call. I promise. I want to be a family more than anything, but I can't. I'm all those boys got."

I wanted Robert to take Dad's offer and come back with us. But I knew it would be selfish. Robert was happy here; he'd made a life. Then I thought about Eugene. Harry. The rest of the kids at Sojourner. They would be left with no place to live. And I couldn't help thinking about Eugene. I had to be the scapegoat if Darren's body was ever found. And to do that safely, I could never come back to Pennsylvania. Eugene would need to be able to point out my name if it ever came to it.

We packed in a hurry. James was coming by to pick up Robert and take Lily's family to meet up with her father. Once I'd grabbed my things, I joined Lily in the extra room. Our first moment alone.

I watched her like I had the first day I caught her skipping school by the stump of the tree near the Capewoods. My throat ached at the thought of saying goodbye.

"If I could stay—" My voice cut short, twitching in pain.

"Come. Sit." Lily reached out her hand and held mine tight. I sat next to her. I could feel her heavy breaths.

"I would stay. But I can't. I have to go. Will you forget about me?"

"Calvin, stop." Lily kissed me. Tears reached the brim of my eyes and floated down as I felt her so close to me. My head was dizzy; a sob built at the back of my throat. I'd finally gotten what I wanted, but now everything had fallen apart and my heart was breaking.

"Will you write?" I asked.

"Will you?" Lily countered.

I looked into her eyes, knowing that I'd write every day, but I could already see my life floating away from her. What hurt most was that I knew that the life I was supposed to live had changed. I had been altered from the moment in the woods when a life was taken and I made the decision to cover it up. With the guilt of Darren's death, I couldn't blame her if she decided to be distant.

I shook those thoughts out of my head and focused on her, next to me. Right then, us giving in to desperate, urgent kisses. Kisses we could memorize, that would keep us through the times of distance. We made promises that she'd visit Chicago, that we'd choose our colleges together, but they were wishes that might never come true.

Mom called us when it was time to go. As we were leaving, I caught Mary Freemen frozen at her window. A chill ran down my spine.

"Ready?" Lily said.

I laced my fingers with hers. It was time to let this all be swept up into the past.

I escorted Lily to James, holding on to her until I was forced to let go. My throat ached saying goodbye as Lily piled in the back of his car with her sister and mom. She reached to the window, planting her palms on the glass. I leaned over and matched my fingers with hers.

"She'll be okay," James said. "I promise."

"If anything is wrong, you'll tell me."

"Nothing will go wrong," James said.

Robert joined us, gently touching James's arm. They shared a soft smile before Robert gripped my shoulders. "I'm proud of you."

I wanted to make one last plea to stay, but then I looked over at Mom.

"I'll call you," I said. "I won't let anything come between us."

"You moved the world to see me, brother. I don't doubt you."

"Christmas. Remember."

"We'll be there." Robert smiled at James before we all shared final goodbyes.

"We should go quickly," Dad said. "We don't know how long the silence will keep."

Robert stuck his hand out. Dad swatted it away and grabbed him in a hug, then pulled in James. "You watch out for each other."

"We will," Robert said, maneuvering to Mom for a kiss on the cheek.

Robert headed to his car with James and Lily's family. Dad called out, "I'm proud of you, son. You've always been braver than me. Take care of those boys."

Before Robert could answer, Dad headed to our car and Robert pulled away. Coming toward us was a car, rushing down the road.

"Get in quickly." Dad ushered Mom into the front seat. I jogged to the back seat of the car before realizing it was Ben blocking our exit.

I curled my fist, ready for a fight. Alex came out first, wide smile, running his hands through his hair. Then I looked to Ben, his face a beet red.

"We caught you," Alex said. "Ben's been watching over your house to make sure nothing happened. He saw you were all packing up, and he came to get me."

Alex rushed toward me and gave me a hug. It took a second before it all sank in. They were saying goodbye.

"You're going home?" Alex said.

"We're leaving." I wasn't yet ready to share where home would be. I glanced at Ben, who cautiously approached.

"I know you don't want to see me," Ben said. "But I wanted Alex to say goodbye."

I nodded, studying his face. So angry with him. So indebted in hope he'd keep our secret.

"I'm sorry," Ben said. "For everything." I studied the hand he stuck out, and eventually I shook it before he pulled me into a hug.

"How is Harry?" Alex asked.

"Better. He's still in the hospital but no longer in critical condition. He was lucky." I looked down, shoving my hands in my pockets.

"How's his brother?" Ben said.

"Stitches, but he'll be okay."

"Good," Ben said. "Tell him, tell Harry I meant it. I was coming for him. To help him. I'm not proud it took me that long, that I didn't tell anyone. I can't sleep thinking about how close it was and him out in the cold."

Ben began tearing up, his shoulders slumped.

"Will you call me?" Alex said. "I know you don't wanna say where you're going, but I wanna know you're okay."

"I'll call you," I said. Then I looked at Ben. "Can I trust this is over? You'll keep Darren a secret?"

"We talked about it," Alex said. "There was no other option, not one that wouldn't put you or Eugene unfairly in trouble."

"Darren went too far," Ben said.

I looked at Ben. He'd come around, but how much?

"You should know that Black folks in town feel they have a right to go to Heritage. There'll be lawyers."

They both nodded.

"We gotta go, son," Dad called, his eyes glancing over at Mary, now on the corner watching us.

I gave Alex a hug goodbye. Then he stepped out of the way for Ben.

"Get in here." I waved Ben over.

He chuckled before throwing his arms around me. "I'm sorry. For everything. For even what I said before about not wanting to be friends because you're Black."

"Make it right, then, Ben. When everything changes here, make it right."

They got in their car, and out the window Ben yelled, "Get on inside, Mary. This here is none of your business." Then they peeled away.

I was relieved Ben seemed to have changed for the better and our secret could stay buried.

Dad drove us down the road, winding past the mass-produced homes. Bland and delicate communities were worse than any nightmares. My chest ached for Lily, but I was filled with something else. A purpose. A reason to keep going. I'd be a changed man forever. I'd come here not knowing what I wanted, but now I knew what I would do. I was going back to Chicago. I could already see Ray's smile, wide and broad, as he waited on the steps of my aunt's house. I was waiting to see my friend, who now understood what it was like to lose someone.

We'd be bonded through the loss of Bobo and Charlotte. I'd finish school and go to college. Law school. I'd make something of myself—I'd be like Thurgood. I'd make sure that Charlotte's life meant something. Be a part of changing the world, making it the one that we wanted. And it was the drum of Martin, of Rosa, of Emmett, that would show me how.

CHAPTER 42

I STOOD ON THE CORNER OF THE MAIN ENTRANCE TO MOREHOUSE College for men. A fleet of cars was steadily moving in new students, Black families dressed to the nines, carrying small suitcases. I had arrived the night before in Dad's Chevrolet, which had been gifted to me. I wanted to be early, to give myself time to be comfortable with the idea of being away on my own. I wanted to be sure to know every corner within miles of what this new life would be like. Then I drove to the bus stop to meet my roommate. As each passenger climbed from the bus, sweat beads dripped down my forehead from heat and nerves.

With a wide smile and a suitcase in hand, Eugene descended the steps. I jogged over, tackling him in a broad hug as he flung his bag to the ground.

"Hold on, let me get my bearings. I've been on that bus for a day. I can barely walk."

"You look good, man," I said.

"What'd you expect?" He tapped his chest.

Even though we'd talked regularly, I had the last image of him stuck in my mind. The way he'd bent over after being stabbed, the blood trickling, sheer will pushing him forward to help his brother. I gripped his shoulders before giving him another hug while slapping his back.

"Come on. You're gonna love it here." I led him to the car, and we hopped in.

"I hope our room's okay," Eugene said.

"It's great." I chuckled.

"You didn't!"

"Hey, had to claim my bed by the window for when I wanna sneak out."

"You're gonna be worse than Harry, aren't you! I hope Robert and James know they're gonna have their hands full without me there to keep Harry out of trouble."

"*You* couldn't even keep Harry out of trouble." I elbowed him, turned the corner, and pointed to Morehouse.

"This is gonna be an amazing four years," Eugene said.

"Just wait till you see the girls at Spelman," I said.

"Thank you. I wouldn't be here if you and Robert hadn't convinced me. Can't believe they gave me a scholarship."

"You made news integrating twenty Black kids at Heritage."

"*We* did that."

I nodded. Even though we hadn't been able to stop Mr. Vernon or Levitt & Sons from their selling practice, I still smiled, proud having heard all the news about the fight for integration at Heritage. I pulled into the parking lot and exited the car before pointing to the entrance.

"Check in there. I'll catch up."

"Haven't been here five minutes and you're already ditching me."

I shook my head, jogging across the street to Spelman, swerving around lines of students moving in. I grabbed a map and made my way to the residence halls. Girls smiled at me, and I was on cloud nine, heart pounding, nervous as I headed to room 8 of a dormitory. I leaned on the door, lightly knocking.

The door opened, Lily on the other side.

"What took you so long?" she said. "My parents just—"

Before she could finish, I lifted her up and spun her until she cried out in laughter for me to stop. When her feet planted, our lips met, soft and urgent. She held my face, and we studied each other like it had been a thousand years since the last time we saw each other.

"I can't believe it's you," Lily said.

I kissed her again, then said, "Lily Baker, you have my whole heart." Our lips met again as we ignored yelps and claps from the girls on her floor.

ACKNOWLEDGMENTS

Publishing a book involves more than just writing the words; it takes a whole team. My deepest appreciation goes to my husband and two precious kids for all their support as I juggled homelife, work, and writing. Thank you to Mom for helping with the kids when we were traveling and to all my family and friends who continue to cheer me on.

Thank you to my agent, Jennifer March Soloway, for being an amazing champion of me and my work. To my editor, Caroline Abbey, for believing in my vision and helping me become sharper with each project. Thank you to Kathy Dunn for making sure the world knows about my work and doing it with grace and kindness. Thank you to the entire publishing team at Penguin Random House, including Barbara Marcus, Mallory Loehr, Lauren Stewart, Stephania Villar, Adrienne Waintraub, Katie Halata, Lisa McClatchy, Barbara Bakowski, Karen Sherman, and Cathy Bobak.

Thank you to Chuck Styles for illustrating another incredible cover for me and to Ray Shappell for the jacket design. All my books feel like art pieces, from the cover to the typography on each page.

Special thanks to the Oregon State University–Cascades MFA program: I am sincerely grateful to my thesis advisor,

T. Geronimo Johnson, the professor whose guidance and influence throughout the MFA program have had the most impact on me and my growth as a writer. Much appreciation to the entire program faculty, particularly Jennifer Reimer, Beth Alvarado, Christopher Boucher, and Raquel Gutiérrez, for their invaluable instruction, counsel, and mentorship and unwavering support. To Lauren Seiffert, the heart and glue of the program. To my amazing cohort mates, who read pieces of my work in workshop: Samantha Verini, Susan Hettinger, Tava Hoag, Chris Robb, and Luke Gonzalez. To my author community, which lifts me up and keeps me in friendship, especially Namina Forna and Kelly McWilliams.

Thank you to all my readers and to teachers, educators, book reviewers, influencers, and indie booksellers. Your enthusiasm and support by sharing my work means so much and truly makes all the difference in the world in getting my books to readers.

AUTHOR'S NOTE

The Jim Crow era, a dark chapter in American history, cast a long and painful shadow of racial discrimination. During this period, which endured for decades, Black Americans faced systemic racism and segregation. This era served as a catalyst for the Great Migration, a significant movement that spanned the decades from 1910 to 1970. It witnessed the mass exodus of Black individuals and families from the oppressive South to the more promising North, driven by aspirations for better opportunities and the pursuit of the American dream.

However, the Great Migration unfolded in parallel with another phenomenon—white flight. White residents began fleeing urban areas, seeking refuge in newly developed, predominantly white suburban communities. This shift was fueled by a combination of factors, including the housing crisis of the Great Depression, when widespread unemployment led to millions of foreclosures and evictions and stalled home building—challenges that President Franklin D. Roosevelt's New Deal housing policies attempted to address. Following World War II, the return of greater economic security and millions of veterans worsened the housing shortage.

Levitt & Sons played a pivotal role in suburban housing expansion, with Levittowns becoming iconic symbols of postwar suburban growth. However, this legacy is marked by a history of racial discrimination practices, including explicit exclusionary measures aimed at preventing non-white individuals from accessing homeownership opportunities—a condition that housing developers were required to include in order to receive federal government housing incentives.

Where one resides continues to have far-reaching implications, influencing access to quality education, employment prospects, and overall quality of life. Understanding this historical context is critical, as it brings to light the deeply rooted societal inequalities that persist today.

There is nothing unique about the discriminatory policy that characterized the development of Levittown communities in the mid-1900s. It is just one example of practices, legal and illegal, that have played a foundational role in shaping homeownership discrimination. The inclusion of the Trumbull Park community in Chicago was a way to highlight another example of all-white communities fighting against integration. Mentions of the Concord Park development recognized a community in the area that sought to create a different type of utopia, an inclusive community that encouraged integration. Our communities, whether evolving through colonialism, new housing developments, or gentrification, carry histories that affect future generations.

I hope this novel inspires you to learn more about these topics and to consider these questions: What would compel a family to consider passing? How does wealth in our homes, communities, and education systems impact our futures, often for generations? What else was occurring in the time period of this book that was significant? How does history still impact our lives today? What were the implications of traveling while Black, and how did the *Green Book* help Black Americans find safe travel and dining options during the Jim Crow era? What policies, practices, and disparities did the federal government, Federal Housing Authority, banking industry, and National Association of Realtors create?

If you want to further explore these topics, additional resources are available.

ADDITIONAL RESOURCES

Levittown History

"Crisis in Levittown, PA," produced by Dynamic Films, 1957. youtube.com/watch?v=xXQQ9o3R-Rc

Justice Network. "Levittown: Two Families, One Tycoon, and the Fight for Civil Rights in America's Legendary Suburb" by Neil J. Gillespie. nosue.org/civil-rights/integrating-levittown-1957

Levittown: Two Families, One Tycoon, and the Fight for Civil Rights in America's Legendary Suburb by David Kushner

Pennsylvania Magazine of History and Biography. "The 'Problem' of the Black Middle Class: Morris Milgram's Concord Park and Residential Integration in Philadelphia's Postwar Suburbs" by W. Benjamin Piggot. journals.psu.edu/pmhb/article/view/59058/58784

U.S. History Scene. "20th Century Levittown: The Imperfect Rise of the American Suburbs" by Crystal Galyean. ushistoryscene.com/article/Levittown

Homeownership and Redlining

The Color of Law: A Forgotten History of How Our Government Segregated America by Richard Rothstein

Evicted: Poverty and Profit in the American City by Matthew Desmond

Institute for Research on Poverty. Summary of the Robert J. Lampman Memorial Lecture "The Color of Law: A Forgotten History of How Our Government Segregated America," given by Richard Rothstein at the University of Wisconsin–Madison, May 2018. irp.wisc.edu/wp/wp-content/uploads/2019/03/Focus -34-4a.pdf

Race for Profit: How Banks and the Real Estate Industry Undermined Black Homeownership by Keeanga-Yamahtta Taylor

Social Justice Books: A Teaching for Change Project. "Gentrification and Housing." socialjusticebooks.org/booklists/ gentrification

Sundown Towns: A Hidden Dimension of American Racism by James W. Loewen

Trumbull Park by Frank London Brown

Passing and Identity

The Autobiography of an Ex-Colored Man by James Weldon Johnson

Boy, Snow, Bird by Helen Oyeyemi

Caucasia by Danzy Senna

Mirror Girls by Kelly McWilliams

Passing by Nella Larsen

The Vanishing Half by Brit Bennett

Traveling While Black

Opening the Road: Victor Hugo Green and His Green Book by
   Keila V. Dawson

Traveling Black: A Story of Race and Resistance by Mia Bay